Tag-teamed

When Cade's eyes flicked open, Brady reached down, grabbed him by his hair with one hand, and pressed a long skinning knife against Cade's throat with the other. "Now, Mr. Big Shot," he uttered in a drunken drawl, "I'm fixin' to slice you from ear to ear."

Fully alert by then, Cade immediately raised his arm from under the blanket and jammed his Colt .45 hard into the crotch of Brady's trousers. The big man grunted in shock. "Cut away, you son of a bitch," Cade growled. "I'll turn you into a gelding before you get halfway across."

Stunned, Brady staggered backward and sat down hard on the ground. Reaching for his pistol, he was stopped cold by a sharp rap against the back of his skull.

"Hardheaded bastard," Luke complained. "I hope he ain't bent my rifle barrel."

LUKE'S GOLD

Charles G. West

A SIGNET BOOK

SIGNET
Published by New American Library, a division of
Penguin Group (USA) Inc., 375 Hudson Street,
New York, New York 10014, USA
Penguin Group (Canada), 90 Eglinton Avenue East, Suite 700, Toronto,
Ontario M4P 2Y3, Canada (a division of Pearson Penguin Canada Inc.)
Penguin Books Ltd., 80 Strand, London WC2R 0RL, England
Penguin Ireland, 25 St. Stephen's Green, Dublin 2,
Ireland (a division of Penguin Books Ltd.)
Penguin Group (Australia), 250 Camberwell Road, Camberwell, Victoria 3124,
Australia (a division of Pearson Australia Group Pty. Ltd.)
Penguin Books India Pvt. Ltd., 11 Community Centre, Panchsheel Park,
New Delhi - 110 017, India
Penguin Group (NZ), 67 Apollo Drive, Rosedale, North Shore 0632,
New Zealand (a division of Pearson New Zealand Ltd.)
Penguin Books (South Africa) (Pty.) Ltd., 24 Sturdee Avenue,
Rosebank, Johannesburg 2196, South Africa

Penguin Books Ltd., Registered Offices:
80 Strand, London WC2R 0RL, England

First published by Signet, an imprint of New American Library,
a division of Penguin Group (USA) Inc.

First Printing, November 2008
10 9 8 7 6 5 4 3 2 1

For Ronda

Chapter 1

Lem Snider glared down in anger at the body sprawled on the ground before him. In a fit of rage, he kicked the corpse several times. "Goddamn dirt-poor bastard," he bellowed, cursing the pathetic remains of a gray-haired prospector who had had the misfortune of encountering the four men now searching every inch of his camp. "Tear this damn place apart. They must have somethin' hid around here somewhere, or they wouldn'ta been camped here so long."

He then turned his anger to level it at Henry Nix. "And hurry up, dammit. We got to get the hell outta here, thanks to you."

"Hell, Lem," Nix replied, "I couldn't help it if that other feller got away. If we'da come up on 'em from downstream, we'da seen their horses in the trees."

Snider was in no mood to hear excuses. His policy was to leave no witnesses. Nix had been the only one of the four to get a clean shot at the boy galloping away on one of the horses that had been tied below the camp, and he'd missed. To further infuriate Snider, Nix had pulled his bandanna down before he realized the boy was there. "We ain't got a lotta time before that boy gets into town, and he saw your face," Snider scolded.

"Well, he didn't have much time to see it," Nix said. "Hell, he was most likely too scared to remember my face."

They were interrupted by a shout from the stream. "Here it is!" Curly Jenkins exclaimed. "I found it! It's always hid under a rock somewhere." A big, simpleminded brute, Curly rolled a large stone over at the stream's edge. "Don't look like much of a poke, though," he said when he took the small hide pouch from under the stone. He immediately handed the pouch to Snider when Lem held out his hand.

Peering inside the sack, Snider snorted. "There ain't much here, but I reckon it's enough to split three ways." His comment caused raised eyebrows on all three of his companions.

"Whaddaya mean, three ways?" Bob Dawson wanted to know right away. If someone was going to lose his share, Dawson was damn certain it wasn't going to be him.

Lem Snider focused his gaze on Henry Nix, but said nothing. Feeling the stares now of three pairs of eyes, Henry glanced nervously from one man to another. "Now wait a minute," he blurted, "I don't know what you're thinkin', but I don't like the way you're lookin' at me."

"You don't get a split," Snider told him. "You got yourself spotted, and you ain't gonna take the rest of us to jail with you. That boy brings the sheriff back here, he's gonna identify you and the rest of us, too. I'm gonna be easy on you, and let you ride on outta here. Me and Curly and Bob will go our way, and you go yours. But you ain't gettin' no split of this little bit of dust, 'cause you ain't a member of my gang anymore."

"I'll be damned!" Nix blurted. "I worked just as much as anybody else for that dust. You ain't cuttin' me off." He looked quickly back and forth between Curly and Dawson, but saw no sympathy there.

Snider drew his pistol and leveled it at Nix. "You're runnin' outta time. Get on that horse and ride, or get shot down right where you stand."

Nix's heavy brows knitted as he scowled bitterly, the anger glistening in his eyes. For a moment, his hand hovered over his holster, but the gun barrel already staring at him discouraged a futile attempt. "All right," he finally said, "I'm goin', and no hard feelin's." He dropped a shovel he had picked up near the old man's body and walked toward his horse. As he walked past Snider, Snider stepped back, and when he did, Nix made a sudden lunge toward him, grabbing his gun hand and bowling him over. Down they went, rolling over and over on the ground, each man straining to get the upper hand.

Snider fought desperately to free his gun hand in order to finish Nix quickly, but Nix held Snider's arms locked in a bear hug. Snider responded by head-butting Nix. Nix was getting the worst of it, and retaliated by clamping his teeth down on Snider's right ear. Howling with pain, Snider jerked his head away, leaving the tip of his ear in Henry's mouth. Grinning malevolently, Nix spat the piece of cartilage in Snider's face, causing the injured man to explode in uncontrollable rage. Ripping his hand free, he smashed Nix's face with the barrel of his six-gun again and again until the battered man's resistance was reduced to a weak tremble throughout his body. Seeing that Nix was unconscious, Snider rested the barrel of his pistol on Henry's bloody forehead and pulled the trigger.

Snider rose slowly to his feet, breathing heavily from exertion. With his pistol still drawn, he looked in turn at each of the two witnesses, in his eyes the unspoken question they both understood. The first to respond was Curly, the simple hulk whose name derived from his hairless pate. "I'da helped you, Lem, but I was afeared if I'da tried to shoot him, I mighta hit you."

Bob Dawson simply shrugged his shoulders and muttered, "I figured you didn't need no help." When Snider continued to stare at him, he added, "He had it comin'."

Snider knew that between his two partners, the surly Dawson was the one to keep an eye on. Curly was mindless, and like a hound dog, just wanted someone to tell him what to do. The fact that Curly and Bob didn't like each other was a positive thing in Snider's mind, because it lessened the likelihood of their combining to gang up on him.

"Curly," Snider commanded, "turn over the rest of those rocks along the edge there. Make sure we don't leave anything." Turning to Dawson then, he said, "Let's get outta here before we have company." He reached down and ripped the front of Henry Nix's shirt. Then, using his knife to cut a section away, he used the square to dab his bloody ear. "We'll split up the dust after we put some distance behind us."

Riding out of the miner's camp, Snider led them toward the river. He was thinking about the little pouch of gold dust they had just taken. It wasn't much. He was thinking that it was time to leave this part of the country. They had left too many bodies in too many spent mining claims to make it healthy to hang around much longer. Each claim they had bushwhacked had failed to provide the big payoff he had been looking for, and his frustration was beginning to wear on him. He turned in the saddle to address the two following him. "It's time we looked for new pickin's. We'll head east toward Coulson."

"Well, at least there's a saloon and a whorehouse there," Bob Dawson muttered to himself.

Young Cade Hunter stood gazing down at the bay gelding lying still at his feet. His Colt .45 still in his hand, he shook his head in apology. "Damn, I'm sorry, Billy, but there wasn't any other choice." Just one month past his twentieth birthday, Cade could not remember a time when old Billy was not there. The horse was at least as old as he was, and was the last tie Cade had to his boyhood home. He looked again at the broken foreleg, snapped like a dried limb, the bone protruding awkwardly at an angle, the result of an unseen prairie dog hole. "You're just too damn old to heal that bone, even if I coulda put a splint on it," he tried to explain to the dead horse.

He found it difficult to believe that Billy was actually gone, his final breath taken by the hand of Cade himself. His mind was flooded with thoughts of his childhood, most of them recollections of stories his father had told him about the horse. He used to tell Cade that Billy was confused. Cade thought Billy was part dog, especially when as a toddler Cade wandered into the pasture and the horse took it upon himself to keep an eye on the boy. Cade's father said he could always find the youngster by looking out across the pasture to see where Billy was grazing.

John Hunter often told his son of the day he was repairing fences, and paused to see where Cade had wandered off to. As usual, he spotted Billy apart from the other horses, but the horse was acting strange. John stood and watched for a few minutes before deciding to ride over and investigate.

Little Cade had been playing near an outcropping of rocks at the lower end of the pasture. What had piqued John's interest was the way Billy appeared to be annoying the child, repeatedly circling him, and often nudging Cade, making him sit down on the ground. As John approached, he saw that little Cade was crying, frustrated with Billy's refusal to let him play in peace. Seeing the boy's father ride up, Billy stood still and waited. "What's got into you, Billy?" John said, and started to dismount. Before he took his foot out of the stirrup, his horse squealed and reared back a couple of steps. John then saw the cause of the horse's fright: a rattlesnake coiled on the rocks, rattles vibrating in angry warning. It was a story some folks found hard to believe, but John Hunter swore that the horse saved his son's life that day.

Cade shook his head sadly and holstered his pistol, telling himself that standing around lamenting the loss of the faithful old horse was nothing more than wasting time. Knowing it was going to take a little work to accomplish, he set about getting his saddle off Billy's carcass. Gentle and cooperative to the end, Billy had thoughtfully come to settle his body across the edge of a shallow gully after tumbling headfirst and throwing Cade clear of the saddle. As a result, the job of getting the cinches of the three-quarter-double-rigged saddle out from under him was a great deal easier. Even so, Cade had to find a stout limb to use as a pry bar before he managed to pull his saddle free of the body. Saddle, saddlebags, a Winchester '73, a Colt Peacemaker, and the rest of his tack, made up the bulk of his worldly possessions. There was also the few dollars he had left from the last cattle drive for Mr. Henry Travis down on the Cimarron. The money was tucked inside his extra shirt in his war bag. The war bag, which was no more than a two-bushel cotton grain sack, held his extra clothing and personal items. Every cowpuncher carried one. Now he found himself on foot in the middle of Colorado Territory. It wasn't a good fix to be in, and the possessions he stood staring at were not much to show for six years of working for various cattle ranches.

Since the age of fourteen, Cade Hunter had done a man's work. He found at an even earlier age that he had a gift for working with horses. It was a gift that stood him well with the ranchers he worked for. The only horse he'd actually owned was Billy, but he had his mind set on raising horses for himself. Deciding the time had come, he had started out for Montana Territory determined to make it one way or another. Intrigued by reports that there were bands of wild horses roaming the Montana plains, he wanted to see for himself if the tales were true.

The decisions to be made at this unforeseen moment, however, were more basic in nature, as they applied to his survival. He hadn't figured on Billy stepping in a prairie dog hole. A man on foot was no man at all in this wild country. He took a long hard look at his possessions before deciding just how much he could carry. As close as he could estimate, he should be no farther than eight or ten miles from the town of Pueblo. Although reluctant to leave anything behind, he knew he couldn't carry everything on his back for that distance, so he looked around for a place to hide his saddle and tack. Seeing a sharp rock protruding from the mouth of a narrow gully, he decided he could find that again easily enough. After making sure his gear couldn't be easily seen by any chance passerby, he drew his rifle from the saddle scabbard, slung his canteen over his shoulder, and set out along the trail to Pueblo.

After walking little more than a mile, he came upon a tiny stream. It was a welcome sight because there wasn't much water left in his canteen when he started his walk. The water looked clear enough, so he lay on his belly and sucked up a few mouthfuls to quench his thirst. Sitting back on his heels, he looked back the way he had come. At once, he spotted what looked to be a wagon approaching in the distance. With a renewed sense of optimism, he got to his feet and stared at the slowly moving object. As it closed the distance between them, he realized that it was a chuck wagon, which seemed odd since he had seen no sign of a herd of cattle. *Maybe it's a peddler or something,* he thought, *and just looks like a chuck wagon.*

As it drew near, however, he could see that it was, indeed, a chuck wagon. He stood waiting while the driver, a full-whiskered little man wearing a battered old hat with the front brim flattened back against the crown, pulled the wagon up to a stop before him.

"I seen your horse back yonder a piece," the driver said. "Figured I'd run across you sooner or later."

"Yep," Cade said, "I had to shoot him. He broke his leg in a prairie dog hole."

"I seen that right off." He looked Cade over for a moment or two. "I don't see no saddle or nothin'."

"I hid it back yonder near my horse."

The wagon driver studied the young man on foot for another long moment, making a judgment. "I can take you into Pueblo. Climb on and we'll go back and get your saddle."

"Much obliged," Cade said.

He waited while Cade climbed up beside him on the seat. "Warm day for walkin'," he commented. "My name's Stump Johnson." He offered his hand, and Cade shook it.

"Cade Hunter," he replied.

"You from around these parts?" Stump asked. "You headed for Pueblo?"

"I used to live near here. I'm just passin' through now," Cade said. "I was thinkin' about makin' my way up to Montana Territory, but I reckon I'm gonna have to find myself a horse now—maybe have to find a job to make enough money to buy one."

"That horse you were ridin' looked pretty long in the tooth to me. If he hadn'ta stepped in that prairie dog hole, he mighta died of old age before long."

"I reckon," Cade replied.

Stump spat a long stream of tobacco juice over the side of the wagon and wiped his whiskers with his sleeve. Then, taking an intense look at the young man beside him, he asked, "What kinda work are you lookin' for?"

"Well, I don't know anything but horses and cows. That's all I've ever done for the last six years. I worked the past couple of years for Mr. Henry Travis down in Texas."

"Henry Travis—is that a fact?"

"Yep. Do you know Mr. Travis?"

"No. I know of him," Stump replied. "He runs a big outfit." He took another look at Cade. "Six years, you say. You musta went to work right offa your ma's teat."

Cade smiled. It was the sort of remark he had grown accustomed to. "I'm older than I look," he said.

For about a mile or so after picking up Cade's possessions from the gully, they talked on, Stump doing most of it, generally in the form of questions about herding cattle. Cade's answers satisfied Stump that the young man seemed to know enough to talk a good game. "You say you was headin' out to Montana?" he suddenly asked. When Cade said that he was, Stump said, "Back there about four or five miles, on the other side of that line of hills, there's a herd of about eleven hundred longhorns, and they're headed for Milestown, Montana Territory. The obvious spark in the young man's eyes told Stump that Cade's attention was captured by his statement. "John Becker's the owner," Stump went on. "If you wanna take a chance on it, I could take you back with me, and maybe Mr. Becker will take you on. That would fit right in with you wantin' to get to Montana, wouldn't it?"

"It sure would," Cade replied.

"Course, if Mr. Becker don't offer you a job, then you're back out in the hills on foot again."

"I'll chance it," Cade quickly replied. It was a timely opportunity, and he was confident in his ability to sell himself to the owner.

"Good," Stump said. "We'll just ride on into town and I'll pick up some supplies. Then we'll ride on back to meet the herd."

John Becker was a big heavyset German with a barrel-like torso that was supported by two skinny legs. He reminded Cade of a great blackbird. With a skeptical eye, he eyed the young self-proclaimed cowhand who rode into his camp on the chuck wagon. "Stump tells me you're lookin' for a job," he said. When Cade replied that he was indeed hoping to join up, Becker simply nodded his head while he thought about it. Finally, after Cade felt he had been scrutinized from head to toe, Becker continued. "I need good men, men who know cattle, and you look a little young to have had much experience."

"I'm twenty years old," Cade responded, "and I ain't ever had a cow or a horse ask me my age."

"Is that so?" Becker grunted, and winked at Stump. "Well, I'll tell you what. Why don't you get your rope and cut out one of those horses in the remuda and throw your saddle on him. That red roan on the outside oughta be easy to rope."

Becker and Stump stood by the chuck wagon and watched Cade go about the task he had been given. "He ain't wastin' no time, is he?" Stump remarked as Cade shook out his rope and approached the roan. He stood there for only a moment before moving on past the horse in favor of a sorrel with white stockings.

"Uh-oh," Stump grunted. "That's a mistake."

The sorrel stood nervously watching the man walking slowly toward it, the rope hanging limp in his hands. It permitted Cade to approach to within ten feet before suddenly turning away, preparing to bolt. Cade's reactions were like lightning. In less than a couple seconds, he twirled his rope once over his head and threw it, catching the sorrel around the neck.

"Hot damn!" Stump exclaimed. "He's goin' for a ride now."

Much to his and Becker's surprise, however, the sorrel did not bolt and drag Cade across the valley as they had expected. Instead, the horse seemed hesitant as Cade hand-walked up the rope until he was close enough to stroke the sorrel's face and neck.

"Damn," Stump said, "what's got into that horse?"

Becker was impressed. "I believe that boy wasn't just braggin' when he said he was good with horses."

"I seen it right off," Stump said, and spat.

Becker stroked his chin thoughtfully while he watched Cade lead the horse back to the chuck wagon where he slipped a bridle on it, and then threw on his saddle. Becker had already seen enough to hire him, even before he gave him another test to demonstrate his ability. When Cade led the saddled horse over to him, Becker asked, "Why didn't you throw a rope on that roan?"

"He was tired," Cade answered. "That horse had already been worked hard today, so I picked this one instead since I didn't know what you wanted me to do with him." He put a foot in the stirrup and climbed in the saddle. Reaching down to stroke the sorrel's neck, he asked, "What's his name?"

"Red Pepper," Becker answered, still astonished by the horse's sudden transformation.

"Well, whaddaya want me and Red to do?"

Becker looked at Stump and grinned, shaking his head. Looking back at the young man astride the horse, he shrugged and said, "Oh, I don't know. Let me see you cut out four or five head of them cows over there and circle 'em back this way."

In a matter of minutes, Cade drove five longhorns past

the wagon, calling out as he rode by, "Whaddaya want me to do with 'em?"

"Nothin'," Becker called back. "Let 'em go. You're hired. We'll be startin' out to Montana in the mornin'."

Most of Becker's crew accepted the new hire with a simple nod and without many questions beyond where he had worked before, and where he hailed from. As with most drovers, they reserved their opinion of a man until he had ridden with the drive a few days. Of course, there was one exception to that general air of indifference. His name was Brady Waits, a big fellow, thick through the chest, with arms like hams. Every drive had its troublemaker. Brady played that role in Becker's outfit. It was inevitable that he would deem it amusing to test the new hand, especially one as young as Cade seemed to be.

Off to himself, apart from the circle of cowhands, Cade sat eating his supper of beef, beans, and coffee, content to have found the opportunity to work his way to Montana Territory. Concentrating on the plate of food, he suddenly sensed someone standing over him. Glancing up, he was confronted by the imposing bulk of Brady Waits, and he knew without being told that he was looking at the resident bully.

With a grin that was closely related to a sneer, the big man announced, "I'm Brady Waits. I'm the man that'll break your back for you if you get on the wrong side of me."

"That a fact?" Cade answered, unimpressed. "Cade Hunter." He stared at the beefy hand extended toward him for a long second before taking it.

His grin growing wider by the second, Brady clamped down hard on Cade's hand until Cade felt the bones rubbing together. "Cade Hunter, huh?" Brady snorted. "I think I'll call you Tater, 'cause you look like a tater to me. Whaddaya think of that?"

"I expect you'd best call me Cade," he replied calmly, "and I think you'd best let my hand go."

"What's the matter?" Brady chided. "Does your hand hurt?"

"I need it to eat with," Cade replied. Then, when Brady tried to increase the pressure, Cade, moving without haste, but very deliberately, took his knife and jabbed the back of Brady's hand. The brute yelped with pain and immediately released the hand.

"Damn you!" Brady roared. "I'm gonna break your goddamn neck!" In a rage, he reached for Cade, only to find himself staring at the business end of a Winchester rifle. Recoiling, Brady backed away a couple of steps. He thought about pulling his pistol, but the cold intensity he saw in the young man's eyes told him such a move could prove fatal. He was painfully aware, however, of the eyes of the other men upon him and the awkward position in which he had placed himself. Although a minor cut, the wound on his hand was freely dripping blood. That didn't help the situation any. He could feel the other men waiting for his response, but there was no course of action for him at the moment. "Damn you," he mumbled lamely, trying to save face.

"Why don't you leave him alone, Brady? The man just wants to eat his supper in peace." The comments came from a man who appeared to be a few years older than most of the other men. A tall raw-boned man sporting a modified handlebar mustache, Cade remembered his name to be Luke Tucker.

"I don't reckon I need any advice from you, old man," Brady immediately shot back. Looking back at the solemn face of Cade Hunter, he said, "There weren't no call to pull that gun on me."

"I expect there's a few of the fellers that wished he had pulled the trigger," Luke interjected, "so just count yourself lucky."

"All right, Mister," Brady said to Cade. "You got away with it this time, but I wouldn't count on it happenin' again. You're lucky I'm in a friendly mood, or things mighta been a whole lot different." He turned and walked away, the pain from the tiny cut on the back of his hand overshadowed by the sting of his humiliation.

After the bully had withdrawn to the other side of the chuck wagon, Cade resumed his supper. Luke Tucker picked up his plate and moved over to settle himself next to Cade. "Mind if I sit with you?" he asked as he sought a level spot to place his coffee cup.

"Suit yourself," Cade replied.

"I'm Luke Tucker. Don't let ol' Brady rile you too much. He's about the only son of a bitch in the whole outfit. He's mostly good at just talkin', but don't turn your back on him."

"Much obliged," Cade said, smiling. He offered his hand, saying, "Don't squeeze it too hard. That big bastard damn near broke it."

Later that evening when Becker returned from recovering some stragglers, he came over to talk to Cade. "Some of the boys told me about your little set-to with Brady. A fistfight is bound to happen once in a while, but I don't hold with anybody pullin' a gun, and they said you damn near shot him." When Cade made no reply, Becker asked, "Am I gonna have trouble with you on this drive?"

"No, sir," Cade answered. "I'm not lookin' for any trouble, but I will not be bullied—by him or anyone else."

Becker took a moment to study the determined young man before responding. "Fair enough," he replied.

*   *   *

John Becker was a reasonable employer. He tried to utilize the best skills of the men who worked for him. Being new, however, Cade was relegated to riding drag for the first week he was with the drive. It didn't take long for Becker to recognize the special rapport the young stranger had with horses and cattle alike. After that first week, he let Cade ride flank and swing.

Since he was the new man, Cade rode the least favored horses in the remuda—the rank and unruly mounts that the other men had little patience for. Every morning, the man riding nighthawk would bring the horses in where they were herded into a makeshift corral of ropes tied to the chuck wagon on one corner and the bed wagon on an opposite corner. With the horses corralled, the men roped their pick for the day's drive. The rest were released to the remuda until a change of mounts was necessary. Since Cade was the new man, he felt it only fair to let the other hands have first pick, so he waited till they had roped their mounts. Then he would pick from what was left, a practice that did not go unnoticed by his boss. Becker also noticed that those same horses seemed to perform differently for Cade.

Cade made it a point to stay clear of Brady Waits as best he could, and Brady never showed any sign of seeking retribution for the time Cade had bested him. The one friend that Cade seemed to have made was Luke Tucker. The other men were not unfriendly, but seemed to sense something different about the quiet young man who came riding into camp on the chuck wagon. Maybe it was his solemn demeanor, or maybe it was his strange bond with horses. Stump Johnson said it was because Cade could talk their language. "You watch the way them horses prick their ears up when he comes around," he said. "They know he knows what they're a'thinkin'. He's got the gift. I seen it right off." Luke couldn't disagree, although Stump very seldom knew what he was talking about. Luke decided that he liked the quiet young man from Colorado. He made it a point to approach Cade, and found him to be as friendly as anyone else, once you got by those eyes that seemed to look into yours like he could read your mind.

Cade had only been with the drive for a few days when the herd approached the South Platte River, and Brady Waits saw an opportunity to extract a measure of revenge for his first humiliating encounter. Cade was riding a particularly skittish horse the morning of the river crossing, a mottled gray named Loco. Everyone knew about the horse's jumpy disposition, but no one mentioned it to Cade. They figured he'd find out soon enough.

Harvey Farmer was riding point with Brady that day, and when he reached the riverbank, he dismounted while his horse drank. Walking down to the water's edge to wet his bandanna, he almost stepped on a snake coiled on a ledge under the rim of the bank. Jumping back, Harvey pulled his pistol, preparing to shoot the viper, but wisely decided to hold his fire because of the approaching herd of cattle. Mr. Becker would have his hide if he caused a stampede by shooting that pistol. As it was, the cattle would be hesitant enough to cross the river. Brady, having seen Harvey jump, rode over to find out what had startled him. Harvey pointed to the snake, and admitted that it had scared him, but after a second look, realized it was a harmless blacksnake.

Brady immediately saw it as an opportunity to have a little fun with the new man. "I'm gonna show you how to give that new feller a bath," he announced, and enlisted Harvey's help in catching the unsuspecting snake. Harvey made no objection to participating in the prank, even though hazing was not to his liking. He had no desire to get on the wrong side of Brady.

The blacksnake almost got away from them, but the two drovers, using their wide-brimmed hats, managed to shoo the reptile away from the water, where Brady was able to trap it in his rain slicker. "Now, by God," he roared with a devilish grin, "we'll see if that feller can stay on ol' Loco." With his surprise effectively captured within the slicker, he stood waiting for his victim.

It was no more than a quarter of an hour before the lead cattle arrived at the riverbank. Cade, riding swing, was one of the first to get there. He pulled up beside Brady and Harvey. "Right here's a good ford," Brady said, holding his slicker tightly in both hands. "Drive 'em on in the water." All the while his reluctant captive was getting more and more riled up.

The quaking slicker did not go unnoticed by Cade, and although puzzled by the grinning bull of a man holding it, he was not curious enough to question him. Instead, he prodded the horse with his heels and started down the bank. Brady walked down beside him, making sure the horse could see him. Just as Loco's front hooves entered the water, Brady gave out with a loud shout and flung the angry snake at the horse.

Predictably, the horse squealed in fright and pitched backward, almost throwing Cade. Then it went sideways and started bucking, but Cade proved to be a better bronc rider than Brady had figured. He stayed in the saddle while the terrified horse bucked and sidestepped away from the water. Cade finally managed to calm the nervous animal, and rode him around in a wide circle until he was under control again. He then turned the horse's head toward the river once more and slow-walked him back to the bank where Brady was chuckling contemptuously. "Well, you hung on," Brady jeered, "but you was 'bout shittin' your britches."

Cade made no reply beyond a wry smile. Guiding Loco

up beside Brady, he casually took his foot out of the stirrup, and before the smirking brute could react, planted it solidly into Brady's chest. Caught off balance, Brady stumbled backward and landed flat on his behind in the chilly water. Cade didn't bother to look back at the stunned bully, but continued across with the cattle. Sputtering furiously while trying to catch the breath that had left him when he hit the water, Brady hurled threats and obscenities at the broad back in the saddle.

Arriving in time to witness the incident, Luke Tucker speculated that the young newcomer was in for a whipping the likes of which he had never experienced before. And just as everybody who was in range of the dunking figured, Brady came after Cade with blood in his eye. Brady looked like a wet volcano fixing to blow. Cade never looked back, just continued moving the lead cattle up the opposite bank, but he knew Brady was coming after him. The big bully wasn't about to stand for a dunking like that. Forgetting his horse on the near bank, Brady sloshed his way across the shallow river, fuming and flailing the water along with the bawling cattle.

Scrambling up the bank, his sodden clothes dripping water, Brady charged after the man on horseback. Showing no more than a casual interest, Cade turned Loco around to face the irate bully. "Were you wantin' somethin'?" Cade asked in the soft voice that Luke would become familiar with as he came to know the quiet young man in the days that followed.

Momentarily flabbergasted by the apparent unconcern shown by Cade, Brady stopped in his tracks. "Why you . . ." he sputtered, his anger almost choking him. "I'm gonna jerk you offa that horse and give you a whuppin'," he roared, then charged toward Cade like a bull in season.

Cade appeared not to make a move. He just sat in the saddle, showing no emotion. Watching from his position on the bank, Luke noticed, however, that Cade had slowly reached down with one hand and loosened his rifle in its scabbard. When Brady got to Cade, the big man reached up to pull him out of the saddle. Spooked by the brute's attack, Loco bolted sideways. Cade pulled the rifle, and swinging it with both hands, laid the barrel across Brady's nose. Luke would swear later that the crack of Brady's nose was as loud as a gunshot. The force of the blow knocked Brady to the ground, and while he was staggering to his feet, Cade dismounted. When the stunned bully reached for his pistol, Cade swung the rifle again, this time cracking Brady right across his kneecaps. Brady howled with pain and sagged to his knees, only to howl again when his bruised knees hit the ground. He rolled over to lie on his side, still fumbling to draw his pistol.

"If you pull that pistol," Cade warned, matter-of-factly, "it'll be the last thing you ever do." There was something in the deadly tone of his voice that made Brady reconsider. He lay back, holding his injured knees, his mustache red with blood from his broken nose. There was nothing more said between them for three or four minutes as Cade remained standing over him, waiting for the bully to make up his mind.

It was hard to say if Brady would have attempted to take it further at that point because Mr. Becker arrived on the scene and put a stop to the altercation. "By God," he exclaimed as he pulled his horse to a stop before them, "you two end it right there! I don't give a damn if you kill each other, but it better damn sure wait till I deliver these cattle to Montana." He glared from one to the other, making sure they had heeded his words. "What's the trouble between you two?"

"It was just a little joke," Brady said. "And the son of a bitch broke my nose, and I think he cracked my kneecaps."

Becker looked then at Cade, waiting for his side of it. Cade shrugged. "He had no call to scare my horse," he finally said. "It's tomfoolery like that that makes a horse skittish."

Listening to the conversation from the seat of the chuck wagon, Stump Johnson leaned down to comment to one of the other spectators. "Brady had it comin'. I knew he was gonna get his ass kicked good if he kept after that boy. I seen it right off."

Week piled upon week as the drive continued up through Colorado into Wyoming Territory, past Cheyenne and on to Fort Laramie, crossing the Platte, and on northward to follow the Powder into Montana Territory. The days were long, and the work hard, but eventually the day came when the scouts came galloping back to the herd with reports that the Yellowstone was dead ahead.

Chapter 2

Luke Tucker picked up his saddle and walked it over to the circle of cowhands seated Indian-style in the shade of the cottonwoods next to the river. No one paid the old roper much attention, as the general talk floating back and forth over the group of men centered mostly upon prospects of cutting loose on the town of Miles City—as Milestown was now called—as soon as Mr. Becker arrived with the payroll. It had been a long drive, taking eleven hundred Texas longhorns from south of the Canadian River up the old Goodnight-Loving Trail all the way to Miles City, Montana Territory—and Luke could feel the toll of it in his bones. As he settled down beside Cade Hunter, he could imagine that he could actually hear his joints creaking with the effort.

Cade greeted him with a broad smile. "You look like you've got a little hitch in your get-along, Luke."

Luke chuckled. "I reckon." He leaned back against his saddle and stretched his legs out in front of him. "I ain't as young as some of you fellers," he said. They sat there a while, listening to the big talk between the gang of men, bragging about how much whiskey they were planning to down and how many women were in danger of hard rides. After a few minutes more, Luke said to Cade, "Reckon you're anxious to get into town, too, and spend all the money you made on the drive."

Cade smiled. "Well, it ain't really a helluva lot of money, is it?" he said. "I expect I'll have a drink or two, but I need most of my pay for new supplies and cartridges for my rifle."

Luke nodded approvingly. This was one of the reasons he liked the quiet young man. He had worked with a lot of young men over the years, but Cade Hunter was not the typical tumbleweed cowhand Luke had commonly ridden with. The man seemed almost reclusive at times, deep in thoughts he shared with no one. Some might think him shy, and think to take advantage. Brady Waits had made that mistake—not once, but twice. Luke had to smile when he recalled the incident at the South Platte crossing when Brady decided to seek a measure of revenge for the loss of face he'd suffered the day Cade signed on.

That was pretty much the end of it as Luke remembered, but no one else thought it a good idea to jape the new fellow. Brady had mumbled something to Cade as he had limped off to find a rag to stuff in his nose to stop the bleeding. Luke couldn't hear what he said, but figured it was probably a warning that it wasn't over. Cade didn't react to it one way or the other. During the month after that, the rest of the crew came to realize that Cade Hunter might be somewhat of a loner, but he was a solid, dependable man who never looked for trouble, and one who always pulled his share of the load. Of course, Brady Waits never warmed up to him, but Luke saw something in the young man that told him he was the partner he was looking for. He had a business proposition for Cade, and now, at the end of the drive, Luke decided he was going to approach him with it.

*   *   *

Cade watched as Becker counted out his wages and placed the money in his hand. When Becker had finished, he said, "You're a good man, Cade. I've never seen a man better with horses than you are. I'm gonna need a couple of men to drive horses back to Texas with me. As far as the rest of the men, I'm letting each man pick one horse for himself. I don't aim to turn anyone loose without a horse. After that, I'm selling most of the remuda here—only gonna keep the best of the stock to take back to Texas. So if you're of a mind to take it, I'm offering you the job."

The offer gave Cade something to think about. He had not planned to return to Texas right away. There was no one there waiting for his return, and he was still intent upon chasing wild horses in Montana. Becker's invitation came as a surprise, too, because Cade had assumed he would be paid off and cut loose like everybody else since he was the last man to hire on.

Overhearing the offer, Luke was more than an interested bystander, and he was somewhat relieved to hear Cade's response. "That's mighty generous of you to offer, Mr. Becker," Cade replied. "If you don't mind, I'd like to think it over for a bit."

Becker shrugged. "All right, but let me know by tomorrow morning, because if you don't want it, I'll pick one of the other men."

Luke let Becker walk away before he spoke. "That was pretty high praise coming from Mr. Becker," he said. "Most any of the other fellers woulda jumped on the chance to make wages all the way back to Texas."

"I s'pose," Cade replied. "I ain't turned it down yet."

"It kinda sounded to me like you wasn't all that anxious to get back down to Texas."

"Maybe." Cade shrugged.

"Whaddaya say we go get that drink you mentioned before," Luke suggested. "I've got a little somethin' I'm workin' on, somethin' you might be interested in."

A drink sounded like a good idea to Cade, so they left their saddles at the holding pens and walked into town. They weren't looking for anything beyond a drink, so they went into the first saloon they came to. Luke bought a bottle of whiskey and took it to a table in the back corner of the noisy room. When Cade reached into his pocket to pay for half of it, Luke wouldn't accept the money. "I'm gonna be the one doin' all the talkin'," he insisted, "so I'll pay for the whiskey." Cade was never one to do much talking, anyway, so it sounded like a good deal to him. He wasn't prepared for the story he was about to hear, however.

After one stiff drink to stir up the dust hanging on from the cattle drive, and another one to settle it down again, they leaned back in their chairs, and Luke began talking. "I ain't plannin' to head back to Texas, either," he said. "I'm headin' west outta here. Goin' to Virginia City, lookin' for gold."

His statement caused little more than one slightly raised eyebrow by Cade. "It's a trifle late for that, ain't it?" he asked. "Placer mining's pretty much played out in Alder Gulch from what I've heard."

A thin smile slowly formed on Luke's face. "Not the kind of gold I'll be lookin' for," he said. "The kind I'm lookin' for is in leather pouches, in mule packs." He went on to tell Cade his story. "Back durin' the war, I served in the Union Army—a fact I never done much talkin' about since I've been workin' cattle down in Texas the last few years." The statement surprised Cade. He had assumed Luke had worn the Confederate gray. It was news, indeed, to find that a Rebel minié ball he carried above his left knee was the reason he walked with a slight limp.

"Back in 'sixty-three, I was assigned to a contingent of troops under Captain James Liberty Fisk to protect emigrants travelin' from St. Paul to Alder Gulch. At the time, I couldn't understand the sense in using soldiers for escort duty for a bunch of emigrants when other units were being sent to fight the Rebs. But when we got to Alder Gulch, it wasn't hard for even a half-wit like me to figure it out. Virginia City was as much a Confederate town as Richmond, Virginia. It was plum full of Southern secessionists—but Montana wasn't a state, it was a territory, so it was controlled by the Union." He paused to pour himself another shot from the bottle, waiting for Cade to see the significance in the statement just made. Whether Cade did or not, he gave no indication, so Luke continued.

"You see, President Lincoln couldn't take a chance on all that gold comin' outta Virginia City gettin' sidetracked to the South. So they was encouragin' folks to move out there to water down Southern sympathies. Let me tell you, Virginia City was a wild ol' place durin' the war, as lawless a town as you've ever seen. It got so bad that a bunch of the men in town organized a vigilance committee to insure law and order, and brother, their justice was swift and final. The queersome part of it was that a lot of them outlaws they hung was loyal to the Union. Hell, they hung a deputy sheriff that everybody knew weren't no outlaw. The vigilantes claimed he was part of a secret society of road agents—run by Henry Plummer, the sheriff. All I know is there was a helluva lot of lynchin' in a short time back then, although it wasn't actually hangin'. Most of 'em was really just strangled to death. They'd throw a rope around their necks and choke 'em till they died—took about eight or ten minutes of pure hell for the victim. It was a helluva way to die.

"But protectin' emigrants weren't the only duty we had. We was also escortin' gold shipments back from there—and that's what I'm gettin' around to. In September of 'sixty-four, I was part of an escort detailed to guard a shipment outta Virginia City. There was a string of nine mules, loaded with dust, three civilians drivin' 'em, with a lieutenant and fifteen soldiers to guard 'em.

"We went down the Madison River a ways till we was a little north of the mountains. Then we cut across to strike the Gallatin, aimin' to follow it on up to the East Gallatin where there was a detachment of cavalry in camp—on the spot where Fort Ellis was built later on. That was as far as we were supposed to go before we turned the shipment over to them." He cocked his head to the side for emphasis. "Now, how that bunch of Rebs knew we were comin' that way, I'll never know. Somebody must have been in on that deal, but they was waitin' for us when we just caught sight of the river. There musta been fifty or sixty of 'em, and they had us right where they wanted us. We rode down a little gulch that led to the water, and all of a sudden all hell broke loose on both sides of us. We never had a chance. I think the lieutenant was the first one hit, and boy, they slaughtered all but four of us before we knew what was happenin'. Men, horses, mules—they were shootin' everythin' that moved.

"I was just lucky, I reckon. I was ridin' right behind Lieutenant Parker when he got hit—rifle ball hit him right side of the head—wasn't nothin' you could do for him. Me and Luther Adams slid off our horses and used 'em for cover while we tried to see what was goin' on. It didn't take but a second to figure we was done for if we stayed where we were. Two of the drivers were the only other men I saw standin', besides Luther and me, and they had the same idea we had. By then, there was only two mules still alive. Both our horses was already dead, so I took my knife and cut one of the mules loose, and me and Luther ran down the gulch leadin' the mule. I think them two civilians cut the other mule loose, but we didn't wait to see which way they ran. All we was thinkin' about was savin' our own necks.

"I swear, I don't know how them raiders never saw us runnin'. I guess they were too busy gettin' down to those dead mules in the gulch. But we were thankful for it. As soon as we hit the water, we headed downstream. The river wasn't deep there, but I thought we was gonna lose the mule a couple of times when we stepped in some holes.

"Back upstream, we could hear 'em shootin' at them other two fellers, and we knew they'd be comin' after us next, lookin' for that other mule. Me and Luther talked it over, and we decided we'd never make it leading that mule loaded down with gold. We could put that mule to better use, so we decided to unload the gold and ride that son of a bitch the hell outta there. Only trouble was, that was a helluva lotta gold dust in them packs. It wasn't natural to just run off and leave it. So we did the next best thing. There was a fish bed under the bank where the current had carved out around a rock. Quick as we could, we unloaded that gold up under the bank, and hoped nobody found it. Then we led the mule on downstream a little farther before comin' out of the river.

"We got on that mule, me in front, Luther behind me. If we'd got on the other way around, it'd be Luther here tellin' this story instead of me. One of them Rebs had rode down the other side of the river, and I reckon he only had time for two shots. The first one got Luther in the back, the second one got me in the leg."

Luke shook his head sadly and poured the last of the whiskey in his glass. "I'll never forget his last words before he slid off that mule, 'I'm done for, Johnny,' he said, and he was gone. I don't have no idea who Johnny was—somebody back home, I reckon." He paused to remember for a second, then tossed back his drink. "Anyway, that mule kicked up his heels when he felt his load lighten, and took off up through the hills. I've thought about it plenty since then. Maybe I shoulda stopped to help Luther, but, hell, he was dead. I know he was, and there weren't no sense in waitin' around to give that Reb time to reload, and me with a rifle ball in my leg already."

Cade sat there, fascinated, while Luke related his story while drinking the major portion of the whiskey. He'd thought he had come to know the older man quite well during the short time the two had become friends. Evidently, he decided now, there was a lot he didn't know. "Well, what happened after that?" he asked.

Luke shrugged. "I don't think they even bothered to come after me. When I was sure they weren't on my tail, I cut back to strike for that cavalry camp to tell 'em what happened. Now, it was my intention to tell Captain Willett that we had hid some of that gold, but it plumb slipped my mind. The captain said he was just waitin' there for the mule train, and he was goin' on back to Fort Lincoln. He ordered me to go back with his detachment, since I was wounded. I tried to tell him that I'd best get back to Virginia City, but he said he needed me more than they did."

Luke paused again, his eyes trying to blink away the effects he was beginning to feel from the alcohol. He cocked his head to give Cade a hard look, as if he wondered what his young friend was doing there. Remembering then, he said, "Well, they shipped me back east to the war, and I spent the rest of it trying to get them to transfer me back out to the territory."

"Why didn't you go back after the war?" Cade asked.

"I don't know. One thing led to another, and I figured somebody had probably found that gold by then, so I drifted on out to Texas 'cause I couldn't think of anything better." He gave Cade a big grin then. "But I started thinkin' 'bout that gold a lot after a few of these long cattle drives, and how much easier life would be if I had it. I'm already feelin' I ain't up to another one like the one we just finished. My bones are already creakin'. I'll tell you the truth, Cade. I've been workin' hard all my life, and nothin' I've ever tried made me enough money to have anything left over after buyin' grub and ammunition. When they first sent me back to Fort Lincoln, I couldn't think about nothin' but that gold just layin' there in a trout bed. It like to drove me crazy till I finally had to put it out of my mind. I was fixin' to desert the army, but they got us up in the middle of the night one night and marched us off to the war. I guess I still coulda slipped off somewhere along the line, but I don't know, I just didn't. After a while, the whole business with the gold just seemed like a dream, somethin' I figured wouldn't hardly happen to a nobody like me. After the war, a friend I served with talked me into goin' to Texas, said he had a cousin in the cattle business." He paused while he recalled the time. "Well, like I said, that just turned out to be nothin' but hard work and long hours." He stopped to gaze toward the distant horizon. "I'm tired, Cade, and I wanna die a wealthy man. I think I can find that trout bed under that rock, but I need a partner I can trust to go with me. That's why I'm tellin' you about it. Whaddaya say, Cade? You wanna help me find that gold?"

It was one helluva story and a lot to think about for Cade. He guessed it was a compliment that Luke picked him as a man he could trust with his secret. Cade couldn't help a fleeting question as to whether or not he could trust Luke. He decided at once that he could. "How come you don't go get it by yourself?" he asked. "Then you wouldn't have to split it with anyone."

"Oh, don't think I ain't thought about that," Luke responded. "But I ain't as young as I used to be, and I need a partner with a sharp eye and a steady hand with a rifle. There's Injuns roamin' that area around the Gallatin, and road agents and scoundrels of all kinds. I don't know to the dollar what that gold is worth, but it's more than one man needs—a man my age, anyway. I know that." He seemed almost stone sober for a moment as he looked Cade in the eye. "I sometimes find the need to drink strong spirits, and sometimes it can get the best of me. I need a partner I can trust to get me home again."

Looking at the nearly empty whiskey bottle, Cade had already figured that out for himself. Still, he didn't have to spend many additional minutes to make his decision. He sensed an honesty about the man, and there was bound to be a lot of prairie between saloons where they would be heading. Since he was of a mind to decline Mr. Becker's offer to return with him to Texas, there was no reason not to team up with Luke. "I'll tell you what," he said, "you've had a helluva lot to drink this evening. If you still want me to go with you in the mornin', we'll shake on it then. Fair enough?"

"Fair enough," Luke immediately responded, and started to get up from the table. "Damn!" he swore, and sat down again. "We're havin' an earthquake, or I've drunk enough whiskey to make the damn floor quiver."

Cade laughed. "Come on. I'll give you a hand, and you can try it again." He got Luke on his feet and steadied him as he walked him to the door. "I expect you'd best turn in early tonight," he said.

Luke was willing to give it a try, but he took no more than twelve paces before he started listing to his left, and Cade could see that Luke wasn't likely to make it back to the holding pens. It was only a matter of seconds before his legs realized that his brain was already asleep. Cade hurried around in front of him and lowered his shoulder to accept the load. Luke stumbled into him and collapsed gently across Cade's shoulder, where he was carried back to the cottonwoods by the river. Cade laid him on the ground as gently as he could and covered him with a blanket. Then, figuring he might as well turn in, too, he spread his blanket a few yards away from the already-snoring Luke. He took off his gun belt and removed his Colt Peacemaker from the holster. Using his saddle for a pillow, he laid down on one half of the blanket and folded the other half over him, his pistol in easy reach by his leg, and drifted off to sleep to the rhythmic sawing of imaginary logs from his partner.

Sleep came easily. It was quiet in the grove of trees since almost everyone else was just getting started drinking up all the whiskey in town. The majority would not stumble back to their blankets before sunup. Some wouldn't make it back at all. The lucky ones might still have a little of their hard-earned wages in pocket.

It was still a few hours before dawn when Brady Waits made his move. Inflamed by the whiskey he had consumed, and backed into a corner by boasts he had made to his drinking partners, he was determined to extract his revenge for his loss of face at the hands of Cade Hunter.

His brain dulled somewhat by the evening of drinking—although he had not reached the level of impairment attained by Luke—Cade's normal sense of danger failed to alert him. Consequently, he was not aware of the threat to his life until he was awakened from a sound sleep with Brady Waits standing straddle-legged over him. When Cade's eyes flickered open, Brady reached down and grabbed him by his hair with one hand and pressed his long skinning knife against Cade's throat with the other. "Now, Mr. Big Shot," he uttered in a drunken drawl, "I'm fixin' to slice you from ear to ear."

Fully alert by then, Cade immediately raised his arm from under the blanket and jammed his Colt .45 hard up into the crotch of Brady's trousers. The big man grunted with the sudden shock. "Cut away, you son of a bitch," Cade growled. "I'll turn you into a gelding before you get halfway across."

Stunned, Brady staggered backward and, tripping over Cade's leg, sat down hard on the ground. Reaching for his pistol, he was stopped cold by a sharp rap against the back of his skull, leaving him momentarily senseless. "Hard-headed bastard," Luke complained, "I hope he ain't bent my rifle barrel." With his foot, he rolled Cade's would-be assailant over on his side. "You all right, partner?" he asked Cade before prodding Brady with his rifle.

"Yeah, I'm dandy," Cade replied, getting to his feet, "but I've had about enough of Mr. Waits here, so I'm thinkin' I might as well shoot him and be done with it."

"I expect that would be doin' the world a favor at that," Luke replied. He wasn't certain whether or not Cade was japing the bully, but he played along anyway.

Still trying to clear his head, and gazing drunkenly at two guns pointed at him, Brady made an unashamed plea for mercy. "Ah, boys," he begged, "there ain't no use in that. I wasn't really gonna cut you. I was just foolin' with you, that's all. You don't wanna go shootin' somebody over a joke, do ya?"

"I'd just as soon," Luke said with a shrug.

"I don't like jokes," Cade said, his tone suddenly deadly serious. Looking Brady straight in the eye, he said, "Get up from there and get outta my sight. I don't plan on seein' you after today, but if I do, I swear I'll kill you." He stood back to give Brady room to get to his feet.

This was the third time the dull-witted brute had suffered humiliation at the hand of the soft-spoken man from Texas. It was a hard bite of gristle to swallow, and Cade could see that Brady was struggling with a decision—to yield or fight. Cade didn't care which way Brady decided. He just wanted to be done with the man.

Suddenly the air between the two men seemed to become still and vacant, like the dead atmosphere an instant before a lightning strike. Luke sensed it, and one glance into Cade's eyes told him that Brady Waits was a dead man. He decided he'd better step in before it was too late. "Brady, don't make the mistake that's gonna cost you your life," he said. "Get on outta here before you do somethin' stupid. We'll just call it a draw and go our separate ways." Without taking his eyes off the still-hesitating bully, he asked, "That's all right with you, ain't it, Cade?"

There was a long pause before Cade answered. "Yeah, I reckon."

Realizing that Luke had probably just done him a favor, Brady got to his feet. "Yeah, we'll call it a draw," he mumbled, picking up his hat and his knife. Then without looking either Luke or Cade in the eye, he walked away, feeling he had just stared death in the face.

They both waited until they were sure he was gone before lowering their weapons. "You always sleep with that Colt in your hand?" Luke asked.

"No," Cade replied. "I just figured this would probably be the time Brady would make good on his promise to get even for what I did to his nose."

"You had me goin' there for a minute," Luke confessed. "I thought you was fixin' to shoot him."

"I was," Cade said.

Luke thought about that for a moment. "Oh. . . . Well, it's mornin' and I'm sober as hell now, so I'll ask you again. How about goin' to Virginia City with me?"

Cade didn't answer right away. His mind had wandered elsewhere for a few seconds, thinking about how close he had just come to killing a man. It was not an idle boast to Luke that he would have shot Brady, but Cade felt relieved that his hand had not been called. His thoughts flashed back to a small boy struggling up between the adobe walls of two buildings, straining to hold on to his father's heavy rifle. For years, the shocked faces of two defenseless men often returned to haunt his dreams before they faded into the back recesses of his mind.

Realizing then that Luke was waiting for an answer to his question, Cade replied, "All right, partner," his face finally breaking into a smile, "let's go pick us a couple of Mr. Becker's horses, and get the hell away from here."

"Hod-damn!" Luke exclaimed. "Let's head for the high country!"

Becker had used one of the holding pens to separate the stock he planned to drive back to Texas. The rest of the remuda was left to graze on the bunchgrass near the river. It was early still, so none of the other men were there. Some of them would be lucky to make it back before noon after a full night of drinking and carousing. Of the eight horses Cade had used most often during the drive, he saw that most of them were left to graze. Luke had his eye on a bay mare named Sleepy that he said fit his gait better than any horse he had ever ridden, so they went after her. She wasn't particularly interested, but Cade finally threw a rope on her after a couple of tries. The rest of the horses had stood and watched the two men until Cade was successful in roping Sleepy. Then as if on a signal, they moved quickly off about a hundred yards. "Don't look like none of 'em wants any part of us," Luke joked as he slipped his bridle on Sleepy. Cade was about to agree when Luke spoke again. "Wait a minute. I believe we got us a volunteer," he said, pointing behind Cade.

Cade turned to see Loco plodding deliberately toward him from a grassy gully near the river. He expected the skittish gray gelding to trot off to join the other horses, but it continued to approach him until, finally, it halted before Cade and Luke.

"Would you look at that," Luke marveled. "It looks like he's pickin' you." He chuckled, amused by the notion that a horse every cowboy in the crew tried to avoid because of its skittish and unpredictable nature had actually taken to Cade. "Well, I'll be gone to hell," he exclaimed a moment later when the ornery gray horse took another step forward to nudge Cade in the chest with its muzzle. "That's the damnedest thing I've ever seen."

Cade was equally amazed by the gelding's unexpected behavior, but having worked with horses since he was barely able to sit in a saddle, he didn't question it. He believed that a horse could sense the worth of a man, and was gifted with a lot more intuition than his two-legged masters. Cade was convinced that Loco knew he wouldn't mistreat him. He gently stroked the horse's neck for a few moments. "You wanna go with me, boy?" he said as he slipped the bridle on. In answer, the gray willingly took the bit. Cade looked at Luke, who was wearing a silly grin on his face. Luke shook his head, still astonished, and the new partners led their horses back to the trees to get their saddles.

A little after sunup, Becker arrived after having rewarded himself the luxury of spending the night in the hotel. He was to meet with an officer from nearby Fort Keogh who was coming to look over the horses Becker wanted to sell. Spotting Cade and Luke all saddled up and ready to depart, he rode over to talk. He seemed genuinely disappointed that Cade had decided not to go back to Texas with him, but understood the pull of the Montana country on a young man's sense of adventure. "What have you got in mind?" Becker asked.

"Nothin' in particular," Luke was quick to answer for them. "We're just gonna see what's out there. Maybe do some huntin' in the mountains, prospect a little, whatever suits our fancy."

Becker nodded as if he understood. "I see you picked your horses already. You're probably gonna need a pack-horse as well."

"I expect so," Cade replied. "We were thinkin' about maybe buying one offa you."

Becker looked at the two for a long moment before deciding. "Ah, hell, just go ahead and pick one. I expect the soldiers will take whatever's left, and they always pay more than the horses are worth."

"Much obliged, Mr. Becker," Cade said. "And thanks again for offerin' me that job."

Becker nodded again. "Good luck to you, boys." With that he wheeled his horse, preparing to ride off toward the river where the rest of his crew were in the throes of early-morning hangovers. "If you don't find what you're lookin' for, come see me in Texas," he called back over his shoulder.

Chapter 3

"I declare, Mr. Thompson," Belle exclaimed while pretending to have lost her breath, "you are quite the lover." She rose from the bed and slipped into her robe. "I almost feel guilty for charging you." Then she laughed and said, "Almost." She brushed her hair back while she waited for him to get his pants and shoes on. "How long are you gonna be in town?"

"Just till morning," Thompson replied, "then I'll be on my way to Bozeman." This was not the first time he had paid for the services of a prostitute, so he was not so naive as to believe he had actually caused her to lose her breath. He had arrived that morning on the packet boat *Josephine* with his supply of samples and merchandise. It didn't take but a day to complete his business in Coulson.

"I'm sorry to hear you're leaving right away," Belle said. "I'd kinda hoped you'd come back to see me." When he only smiled in reply, while busily tying his shoelaces, she asked, "Are you staying in the hotel?"

"That's right."

"It's early yet," Belle suggested. "Maybe you might wanna drop back later for a little nightcap."

He looked up at her with a tired smile. "I'm afraid I'm

done for the night. I've got to get started early in the morning. It's a long ride to Bozeman."

"Oh, well," she said, "too bad—maybe next time you're through Coulson." She picked up his coat and held it till he was ready for it. "It must be exciting being a liquor salesman."

"It's like anything else, I guess—good times and bad times," he said as he hastily took his coat and grabbed the doorknob. On a sudden impulse of generosity, he paused at the door, pulled out his wallet, and peeled off a few more dollars. "This was one of the good times," he said.

Standing in the shadows of the cottonwood trees, Lem Snider watched the man emerge from Belle's tent and walk hurriedly toward town and the hotel. Judging from the man's clothes, Lem speculated that he was a lawyer or salesman. At any rate, he had enough interest in him to find out. He left the trees and headed toward the tent.

Entering the front portion of the tent, which was partitioned off from the rooms in the rear, Lem found Belle, having a drink with her partners, Lucille and Violet. He paused at the entrance to endow them with a sarcastic grin. "Well, ain't this a bouquet of faded flowers."

"You go to hell, Snider," Violet replied.

"Hell wouldn't have him," Belle said. "Are you coming to buy something?"

"I'm comin' for some information, but we might as well do some business while we're at it." He looked at Belle directly. "Who serviced the gent that just left?" When she answered that she did, Lem grabbed her by the arm and said, "Let's go in the back."

After they had completed the business that Belle specialized in, Snider asked her about the man she had pleasured before him. If Thompson had planned to be in town longer than one night, she would have been reluctant to share information with Snider. Since she saw no further opportunity for her, she was willing to sell what she knew about him.

"He's a whiskey salesman," she volunteered. "And he's leaving early in the morning on his way to Bozeman."

Snider's interest was sparked immediately. "A whiskey salesman, eh? Ain't that somethin'?"

"He's pretty well-heeled, too," Belle said. "His wallet was so thick, I thought it was a gun in his coat till he pulled it out to pay me."

Lem smiled as he pictured it. "Maybe me and the boys oughta make sure he gets started in the right direction in the mornin'."

"I figure that information is worth a little something extra," Belle reminded him.

"You'll get it," Snider said as he left the tent still buttoning up his trousers, "but first, we'll see how much it's worth."

"Don't you short me," she warned. "If something happens to Mr. Thompson, I might have to talk to the law."

He halted abruptly and turned to face her. "Now, Belle, you wouldn't ever wanna do somethin' that damn foolish. That's the kinda talk that gets whores' throats cut."

"That was quick," Lucille scoffed when Snider walked through the front room.

"It ain't how long," Snider said, "it's how good, and Belle ain't never had no better."

"Hah!" Violet snorted contemptuously. "I'll ask Belle about that." As he went out the front entrance, she called after him. "And tell that big dummy Curly it's gonna cost him more next time. I'd as soon mate with a bull elk."

Claude Thompson was at the stable behind the hotel before sunup the next morning, saddled and with his merchandise packed on a mule. His intention was to leave for Bozeman before daylight so as not to attract any attention. He had been warned by John Alderson, the owner of the hotel, that there had been some recent reports of road agents operating between Coulson and Bozeman. Thompson was not a timid man. He wore a .44 pistol and he was not averse to using it should the necessity occur. He was gratified to make his way out of town without seeing a sign of anyone out and about at that early hour.

Following the trail along the banks of the Yellowstone, he was well along his way by the time the sun made a showing behind him. As he guided his horse around a barren section of high bluffs, he spotted a lone rider on the trail ahead coming toward him. Always careful when encountering strangers, Thompson reached down and eased his .44 in the holster. He kept his eye on the approaching rider as the yards between them decreased to the point where he was able to make out the man's features. All he could really tell at that distance, however, was that the man had bushy whiskers that appeared to be a beard gone wild.

A sense of caution suddenly caused Thompson to look behind him. Caution turned to concern when he discovered two riders on the trail behind him, moving along at his pace. Concern now replaced by alarm, he looked around him, seeking some avenue of escape. There was none, for that stretch of river was treeless and slashed with narrow gullies that ran down to the water. *Maybe just coincidence,* he thought. *Might not be what it looks like.* He was not convinced. There was nothing he could do but keep riding and hope he was wrong.

"Mornin' to you, sir," Lem Snider called out as he drew up even with Thompson.

"Morning," Thompson replied curtly, and continued to ride past.

Snider wheeled his horse and trotted up beside Thompson again. "I just thought I'd better tell you there's a lot of road agents along this way. Maybe you oughta be on the lookout."

"Thank you for your concern," Thompson replied guardedly.

In the next instant, a rifle shot rang out. Thompson sat straight up for a second before keeling over to the side and dropping to the ground with a bullet in his back.

"Damn you, Dawson," Snider railed, "you coulda missed and hit me!"

Bob Dawson smirked as he and Curly caught up to them. Looking down at the body, he said, "Hell, I couldn'ta missed from that distance. I didn't see no reason to pussyfoot around with him."

"Yeah, well, next time wait till I give a signal before you go blastin' away." Eager to examine Thompson's wallet, Snider dismounted and rifled through the dead man's coat pockets until he found it. "Hot damn!" he exclaimed triumphantly. "It's just as fat as Belle said it was."

"Fellers, we've done hit the mother lode," Curly sang out as he searched through the packs on the mule. "Whiskey! Enough to drown in!"

The three outlaws rummaged through Thompson's possessions, scattering clothes and camping gear about in an effort to see everything the man carried. "We'll take the horse and the mule," Snider said. "Throw the saddle over the bank there."

"That's a fine-lookin' saddle," Dawson said. "I might wanna trade."

"Hell," Curly immediately responded, "what makes you think you get the saddle?"

"Shut up, both of you," Snider said. "We don't keep

things somebody might recognize, like saddles and boots. Throw it over the bank."

"What about the damn horse?" Dawson countered. "Somebody might recognize his horse, and we're keepin' that."

"It ain't got no brand on it. Who's to say we didn't find it runnin' wild? Look at the saddle. It's got his damn initials on it." *One of these days I'm gonna throw the both of you over the damn bank and be done with you,* he thought.

Following the Yellowstone River, it took Cade and Luke two and a half days to reach its confluence with the Big Horn. They camped at the site of Fort Pease, about seven miles below the Big Horn. There was nothing left of the fort but charred timbers. The army had abandoned it two years before, and the Indians had promptly set fire to it. To this point, there had been no sighting of Indians, nor did they expect any—at least not in any great numbers. Sitting Bull and about three hundred Sioux had reportedly fled to Canada in early May the year before, and Crazy Horse's band had supposedly surrendered. Still Cade and Luke kept a wary eye open for scattered groups of Sioux and Cheyenne. Their concern was not great, however, for they were fairly confident that, with two Winchester repeating rifles, they could hold their own against a sizable war party.

"At the pace we're goin'," Luke speculated, "we oughta make Fort Ellis in six or more days."

Cade, busily building a fire at that moment, only nodded in reply. This was new country to him, so whatever Luke said, he had no choice but to accept. He was not inclined to be concerned with it at any rate. He was happy to be riding west toward the high mountains, free of bawling cattle and the dusty trail they left behind them. He gave very little thought to the prospect of finding the lost packs of gold dust

Luke had hidden. He had never owned anything of value that did not come from hard work, so it was difficult to believe there would be riches waiting for him to simply come and fish them from the river. That's the way things had been for him since childhood.

Even as a small boy, he had always been good with horses, a trait passed down from his father. Cade had worshiped his father, and strove to walk in his footsteps from the time he stood on his own two feet. There was not a better man in Pueblo, Colorado Territory, than John Hunter, but that was not enough to save him from stopping a bank robber's bullet in an unsuccessful robbery of Pueblo's only bank. John Hunter had just withdrawn money from the bank to buy some supplies. It was not a large sum of money, but John refused to part with it when accosted by one of the robbers as they burst into the bank with guns drawn. Infuriated by the man's lack of fear, the outlaw shot him down with his revolver. The bank robbery was foiled when the sheriff and his deputy ambushed the pair of gunmen as they fled from the bank.

Lodged in the jail, the two outlaws awaited trial. That event was never to occur, however, for both men were shot through the bars of the one window in their second-floor cell by an unknown assailant. Due to the fact that the back wall of the jail was built adjacent to the rear wall of the sheriff's house, with barely two feet of space between the two, there was much speculation as to the possibility of a grown man being able to climb up in such a cramped space. Some argued that it would require a smaller person, maybe like Hunter's ten-year-old son to accomplish it. Others countered that it was hardly likely that Ada Hunter's grieving son had the nerve to do such a thing, even if he was capable of shinnying up between the two buildings, pulling up Hunter's nine-and-a-half-pound Henry rifle. At any rate, it was never determined for sure who the killer was. The boy never volunteered any information on the matter, and as far as his mother knew, he was asleep in his room that fateful night. Most folks, including the sheriff, figured the executions were deserved, and considered it a closed book.

Two years after his father's death, Cade's mother married again, this time to an attorney named Samuel Whitsel, and moved to his house in town. Young Cade never cared for the union. Samuel Whitsel was certainly taken by the widow Hunter, but he was not keen on the acquisition of a twelve-year-old son, especially one who many citizens of the town suspected of cold-blooded murder. Repulsed by the sight of his mother's doting upon the slick, nattily dressed lawyer, Cade avoided contact with his stepfather, spending the majority of his time out at the ranch with the horses. He stuck it out for two more years until Whitsel decided to sell the Hunter ranch and all the stock. When the horses left, so did Cade. The only possession left to him was old Billy and his saddle. The farewell to his mother was brief with little emotion, it being apparent to the fourteen-year-old boy that the parting made things easier for her new marriage. Nothing came easily to him after that, so it was just natural for him to expect that nothing ever would.

They started out again early the next morning, following the Yellowstone west. Luke commented that it seemed especially strange to him for the two of them to ride peacefully through country that used to be prime hunting grounds for the Sioux when he was last here. At that time, the only safety was in a cavalry patrol. They came upon more than a few cabins that had been built by settlers since the treaties with the Sioux had opened up the land along the river for settlement. By the time they reached the little town of Coulson, Luke was ready to stay over for an extra day—to rest, so he said. But Cade suspected that it was the saloon next to the general store that held the real attraction for his friend.

A man named Perry McAdow had bought some land on the Yellowstone the year before, and set up a sawmill along with the saloon and general store. It seemed to be a good location to receive the goods brought upriver by the steamboats. It looked to be a promising venture for Mr. McAdow, for now the little town boasted a hotel, a post office, and a telegraph office in addition to the saloons and general store. "Dang," Luke exclaimed upon seeing the progress, "if this keeps up, it'll be as big as Chicago."

It was late in the day when Cade and Luke rode into Coulson. "I don't know about you, partner, but that saloon there is a happy sight for this dusty throat."

Cade shrugged indifferently. "I guess I've got enough money left to spare for one drink," he said.

There were three horses tied up in front of the saloon when they dismounted and tied on alongside. The owners of the three animals were hovering around one end of the bar, nursing a bottle of whiskey. All three paused and gave the newcomers a thorough looking over. Cade merely glanced their way, while Luke ignored them altogether, his mind set on a drink. There being no tables in the saloon, they each propped a foot on a long wooden step that substituted for a brass rail, and waited while the bartender finished wiping a spot for them with a wet rag. "What'll it be, gents?"

"Have you got somethin' that'll burn the hair off the inside of my throat?" Luke asked good-naturedly.

"I reckon," the bartender replied, laughing. "You fellers are new around here, ain'tcha?"

"Just passin' through, friend," Luke answered, his eye never leaving the bartender's hands as the man produced two shot glasses from beneath the counter.

"Where you headed?"

"West," Luke answered briefly before tossing his drink down.

Cade noticed that the conversation between the three men at the end of the bar had stopped, and their attention seemed to be captured by Luke's banter with the barkeep. One of them in particular, a bushy-faced man with brooding dark eyes, continued to openly stare at them. Luke, oblivious to the scrutiny, continued his casual conversation with the bartender. Cade, however, being of a more cautious nature, moved around to the other side of Luke, where he could keep an eye on his friend and the three strangers beyond.

Bushy-face whispered a few remarks to his drinking partners, then moved up the bar to join Luke and Cade. "Couldn't help but notice you, friend," he said. "I'm thinkin' your name might be Tucker."

Surprised, Luke turned to face the man, looking him over. "Yes, sir," he replied, "I'm Luke Tucker. Do I know you?"

"Luke Tucker, that's right," Bushy-face replied, affecting a wide grin. "Corporal Tucker, right?" When Luke was obviously struggling to recall the man before him, Bushy-face said, "I'm Lem Snider from C Company. We served together under Lieutenant Parker."

"Oh, yeah," Luke finally replied, although without a great deal of enthusiasm it seemed to Cade, "Snider, I remember you. That was a long time ago. You wasn't much more than a kid back then." He gave him a long hard look. "I didn't recognize you right off with all that brush on your face."

"It has been a while," Snider allowed. Then with a fleeting glance at Cade, he asked, "Who's your friend?"

"This is Cade Hunter," Luke said. "He's my partner."

"Partner in what?" Snider wanted to know.

"Well, nothin' much right now, I reckon," Luke replied.

It was obvious to Cade that, for whatever reason, Luke was not enjoying this chance reunion with an old army comrade. He seemed guarded and unusually reserved for one who could talk a gopher out of his hole. As far as Cade was concerned, he didn't like the looks of Lem Snider. He had the gaze of a man who might be measuring you for a coffin, and there was something about him that didn't seem right. It took Cade a couple of minutes to figure it out, and then it struck him. The man's right ear was missing the very top part. Just a little piece was missing, like maybe someone had bitten it off in a fight.

"A lot of the boys back in C Company wondered what in hell happened to you," Snider said. "You were on that escort that lost the gold shipment over near the Gallatin. I rode on the patrol that was sent over to pick up the bodies." Snider shook his head slowly as if recalling the scene. "That was a shameful sight, all them dead boys layin' around in the sun." He glanced at Cade to see if he was listening. "Ever' last soul rubbed out, all except two. We found all the bodies but yours and Adams'. Then we found Adams' body across the river. We wondered what happened to you. Some got to thinkin' that maybe you was in on the ambush." He paused then and watched for Luke's reaction.

"Oh, they did, did they?" Luke responded. "Well, I got away, all right, with a rifle ball in my leg for my trouble. I made it on up to the East Gallatin where we was supposed to pass the shipment off to a cavalry unit. They ordered me on to Fort Lincoln with them. I wound up in Virginia by the time the war was over."

Snider didn't say anything for a few moments while he considered Luke's explanation, a hint of a smile on his face. "Well, that explains it, don't it?" he finally said, although without conviction. "And them Rebs got away with all that gold." He paused again, watching Luke's face closely. After a moment, he said, "You ain't said what you're doin' back in this part of the country again"—he shifted his gaze to Cade for a second—"you and your partner."

"Like I said," Luke replied, "we're just headin' west, lookin' for opportunity, I reckon. How 'bout yourself? What are you doin' back in these parts?"

Snider grinned. "Hell, I never left. Me and my partners are in business together." He turned to signal his friends. "Come on over, boys." The two picked up their glasses and the half-empty bottle, and moved up the bar to join them. "Luke Tucker, meet Bob Dawson and Curly Jenkins," Snider said. "I already forgot your partner's name," he added with a wide grin. Cade didn't bother to remind him. Dawson and Jenkins didn't say anything, just contented themselves to stand leering like two surly yard dogs.

"What kind of business are you in?" Luke asked Snider.

His question brought a sly grin to Snider's face. "Just business, any kind of business, sometimes cattle, sometimes gold." He paused and looked at his partners and winked. "Sometimes even hides," he said, causing a gruff snort of a chuckle from the man introduced as Curly, the remark obviously recalling some incident they found humorous. "Maybe you and your friend here would wanna join up with us," Snider suggested. "We could use some new ideas. Couldn't we, boys?"

Luke favored him with a wry smile. "Well now, Snider, that's mighty generous of you, but me and Cade ain't lookin' to go into business with anyone. We're just passin' through."

"Well, that's too bad," Snider said, suspicion written all over his wooly face. "It was mighty good to see one of the boys from the old company, though." He offered his hand to Luke. "Your partner don't talk a helluva lot, does he?"

"Nope," Luke replied. He tossed his drink back, and turned toward the door. "Come on, Cade, we'd best be goin'."

Outside Luke hurried Cade to their horses. "Partner, it woulda been better to run into the devil himself than to run up on Lem Snider. He mighta acted like we was old friends, but I never had any use for the low-down son of a bitch back then, and I sure as God don't have any use for him now. He'd steal the pennies off a dead man's eyes."

"I figured as much," Cade said, untying Loco's reins.

Luke frowned up at the early-evening sky. "Damn, it's gettin' a little late to start out now."

"The horses need rest, anyway," Cade reminded him. "We can go up the river a piece to camp."

Stepping up in the saddle, Cade turned Loco's head up-river and led Luke and the packhorse west along the bank. The dark figure of Lem Snider stood just inside the saloon tent flap, watching them depart. Bob Dawson walked over to stand behind him. "You thinkin' what I'm thinkin'?" Bob asked. "They're both totin' fine-lookin' Winchesters. Didn't look like there was much on that packhorse, though."

Lem continued to watch the two riders moving along the riverbank a long moment before answering. "No, I ain't thinkin' what you're thinkin'. I'm thinkin' there might be a helluva lot more than three horses and a couple of rifles for the takin'." He turned to explain to his partner. "Luke was mighty tight-lipped about where the two of them was headin'. I got a feelin' them two are up to somethin' they don't wanna talk about. I didn't see no picks or shovels or whatnot on that packhorse—nothin' a man would likely be totin' if he was plannin' on doin' some prospectin'. Maybe all that shipment of gold didn't get to the Rebs. He said him and Luther Adams hightailed it together, and we found Luther's body on the other side of the river with a bullet in his back. Maybe Luke knows where some of that gold's hid. They're up to somethin', and I aim to find out what it is."

*   *   *

Luke and Cade made their camp in a stand of cotton-woods that flanked the wide river. The water was fairly deep here despite the fact that it was late summer. The spot they selected for their camp lay opposite a wide gravel bar that divided the briskly flowing water into two channels. From the edge of the bank where they built a fire, the prairie swept away to the north, a moving sea of lusty grass as the evening breeze skipped across the land. It was a peaceful place to make camp, and Cade hobbled the horses, then left them to graze while Luke sliced some strips from a slab of bacon. It was just beginning to get dark when their guest arrived.

"Now, who the hell is this?" Luke uttered when a horse pulling a buckboard suddenly appeared among the trees.

Cade set his coffee cup down by the fire and reached for his rifle. Looking back toward the trail beyond the trees, he saw that the buckboard was alone. As it approached their camp, he was surprised to see a woman holding the reins. Still cautious, however, he got to his feet and moved away from the firelight. Luke got up as well, but remained by the fire, staring at their visitor. "Well, I'll be . . ." he mumbled under his breath when he discovered that the caller was a woman.

"Evening, gents," the woman called out cheerfully upon pulling her horse to a stop before the fire. "My name's Belle. I heard there was a couple of fine-looking gentlemen pass-ing through our little town, and I thought it would be a shame if I didn't at least give you a little word of welcome."

"Why, yes ma'am, Miss Belle," Luke was quick to re-spond. He unconsciously reached up to twist the ends of his handlebar mustache. "Step down and light a spell. We can offer you some coffee. That's about all we got right now." He moved quickly to offer his hand to assist her. One glance at the buxom woman left little doubt of the kind of welcome she specialized in.

"I've got a better idea," she said with a giggle. "Me and two other ladies run a little social club between the sawmill and the ferry. Why don't you and your friend there come on back with me, and we'll have a little drink of whiskey—and anything else you boys might have a hankering for."

"Well now," Luke replied, his face alight with the thoughts stampeding through his brain, "that sounds like a right friendly idea." Unable to take his eyes off Belle, he asked, "Whaddaya say, Cade? We could stand a little female company right now, couldn't we?"

Cade, silent to that moment, was not sure he and Luke were seeing the same woman. Evidently not as desperate for female companionship as his partner, he was not intrigued by the obvious assets of Belle Whatever-Her-Name-Was. In fact, he was inclined to believe that inside the billowy gingham frock there might lie a generous landscape that could frighten a man. He had no prior experience with prostitutes, and there was nothing about the aging puffy face behind the rouge and lip paint that tempted him to gain that experience at this particular moment. She looked to be a few years older than Luke, and Luke claimed to be forty.

"Whaddaya say, partner?" Luke asked again when Cade failed to respond right away.

"You go ahead," Cade finally replied. "I'll stay here and watch the camp."

Luke immediately showed his disappointment. "Don't you wanna get . . ." He hesitated as if he might offend the lady.

"I'll guarantee you a good time," Belle offered in hopes of changing Cade's mind. "Since you boys are just passing through, I might consider knocking a little off the price if both of you come along."

"Much obliged," Cade said, "but if you just make sure Luke has a good time, that'll do."

For the short time the two had been partners, Luke had already learned that his young friend was not easily swayed when he had made up his mind. And Luke picked up the note of finality in Cade's tone. *Well,* he thought, *it's his loss. No reason I can't have a little fun.* Breaking out a wide grin for Belle, he said, "Come on, honey. I'll throw a saddle on ol' Sleepy, and we'll go have a party."

Cade emptied the dregs of the coffeepot into his cup and stood watching while Luke hurriedly saddled his horse. He wasted no thoughts on judgment, although he could think of a good many better uses for the money Luke was bound to part with before the night was over. Their morning departure might be postponed for a day as a result, but Cade was in no particular hurry, anyway. Better that Luke get his itch scratched now that he had developed it, Cade supposed. *But it's gonna take more than that old whore to give me the itch.* He continued to watch until the image of Luke faded into the evening shadows, following along behind Miss Belle's buckboard. Then he threw the last few swallows of coffee on the ground and went down to the river to rinse the cup.

It was sometime in the wee hours of the morning when Loco's welcoming whinny awakened him. Alert at once, Cade rolled out of his blanket and picked up his rifle only to find it was just Luke coming back, and Loco's welcome had been for Sleepy. He rose up on one elbow to watch his progress, and from the look of it, it was apparent that Luke was lucky just to have stayed on the horse. Sprawled forward in the saddle, he was holding on with both arms wrapped around the horse's neck. The horse, with no direction from her master, walked up to the campfire and stopped.

Cade got to his feet. "You all right?"

"Cade?" Luke asked, not sure where he was. "I'm drunk as a cross-eyed hog."

"Damned if you ain't," Cade agreed. "Here, I'll help you down. Let go."

"I can't, Cade. Ever' time I let go of her neck, the damn horse starts spinnin' around."

Cade shook his head. "Well, she's standin' still right now," he said. "Let's get you offa there quick before she starts spinnin' again." Then without giving Luke time to think about it, Cade reached up and dragged him from the saddle, catching him on his shoulder like a sack of corn.

"Oh, Lord," Luke groaned. "Lemme down—my insides is comin' out!"

Not wanting to get Luke's evening consumption of alcohol down his back, Cade immediately granted his request. Kneeling quickly, he rolled Luke off his shoulder onto the ground. Luke immediately struggled up on all fours only moments before the retching began. Once it started, it seemed there was no end to it. Cade could do little more than feel sorry for him as Luke heaved over and over again, crawling from one fresh spot to another, until there was nothing left to lose. Still his stomach convulsed until tears started streaming from his eyes. He was as sick as Cade had ever seen any man.

When it was finally over, and the evil spirit was done with him, Luke flopped to the ground like a limp rag, totally spent. Cade let him lie where he dropped, covered him with his blanket, then unsaddled his horse. That done, he looked up at the sky where there was now a thin streak of light peeking over the horizon to the east. *Might as well stay up,* he thought. After taking another look at Luke, who was sleeping peacefully by then, he built up the fire before going down to the water's edge to fill the coffeepot. *He's damn sure going to need some coffee when he wakes up—if he wakes up.*

It was a couple of hours past sunup when Cade came

back from watering the horses and saw the body under Luke's blanket stirring. He paused at Luke's feet to watch the rebirth as Luke cautiously pulled the blanket from over his head and peeked timidly out at the daylight. "I reckon you're the second man I ever heard of that was raised from the dead," Cade commented. "What was that other fellow's name? Lazarus or somethin'?"

Cautiously aware of a head more fragile than a bird's egg, Luke slowly rolled over and managed to sit up. "Damn," he swore, "for a while there I thought I was gonna get sick last night." Cade merely shook his head, amazed. "Is that coffee I smell?" Luke asked then. Cade poured him a cup and handed it to him. Luke, his hand shaking slightly, reached for it gratefully. "Boy, that's what I needed," he said, drinking the hot liquid in quick sips. Gradually, he began feeling as if he might live, and with the second cup he was ready to talk again. "Cade, boy, you shoulda gone with me. I ain't never had such a good time in all my life—Belle and Lucille, and I don't remember the other'n's name—I mean, they was all fine. And whiskey! They had some of the smoothest whiskey you've ever drunk—and plenty of it. But that Belle, I'd marry her if she'd have me." He sank back on his elbows as he let his mind relive an evening that he judged to be the best of his life. "Damn," he uttered reverently, "you shoulda gone with me."

Cade could only shake his head. It was astonishing to him that a man staring at the gates of death such a short time before could look back on the adventure as a pleasant experience. That was Luke—his mind only retained the good times. "I expect you'd better eat somethin'," he said. "I know for a fact there ain't nothin' in your stomach but a little bit of coffee. You can rest up a bit, and we'll get movin' again when you're ready."

"Hell, I'm ready now," Luke insisted. "We coulda set out at first light. I was ready."

"Yeah, I could tell," Cade commented sarcastically.

"You owe me for two bottles of whiskey on top of that fifty dollars," Belle stated emphatically. "If you'da told me that man could drink that much whiskey and still damn near wear out the three of us, I'da charged you more."

"Our deal was for fifty dollars," Lem Snider replied. "There wasn't nothin' said about no extra for whiskey." He counted out the money, and she quickly took it from his hand. "So, what did you find out?" he pressed.

"Two bottles of whiskey," she insisted. "If we hadn't got him drunk, we wouldn't have got him talking."

"All right, dammit. I'll pay for one of them bottles, but the other'n's on you. Now tell me what he's up to, or I might take my money back and whip your flabby ass for wastin' my time."

"Well," Belle smirked, "he asked me to marry him three or four times. And about the time Lucille said she couldn't take any more—and that was not too long before daylight—he got to telling me about how he could take care of me in style. All he would say was he was on his way to do some business, and that he'd be a rich man when he came back."

"I knew it! That son of a bitch!" Lem exclaimed. "He's got some of that gold shipment hid somewhere. That son of a bitch!" His mind already calculating the possible value of the gold one mule could carry, he pressed for more information. "Where did he say he was goin'?"

Belle shrugged. "He wouldn't say exactly where he was heading, just that it wasn't that far from here. He did say one time that all the gold wasn't in Virginia City or Bannack, either."

"I reckon not," Snider remarked, a sly smile of gratification gracing his dark features. *It can be found somewhere between here and Virginia City, somewhere close to the Gallatin River, I'm bettin'.* The question of why Luke waited for so many years before coming back to claim the gold dust never entered his mind.

Belle moved up close to him, and taking his arm in both her hands, affected her most coquettish expression. She pressed her face against his shoulder and purred, "You ain't gonna forget ol' Belle if you make a big strike, are you, honey?"

"Huh," he snorted, "who said anythin' about makin' a big score?"

"I know you, Lem Snider," Belle insisted. "You'd play cards with the devil himself as long as you could deal. Hell, me and the girls would like to get outta this little town. I'm just sayin' don't forget them that helped you, that's all."

Snider suddenly broke out a laugh. "Why, Belle, honey, how could I ever forget you?"

Chapter 4

Two days out from Coulson, near a bend in the river, Luke and Cade sighted a herd of antelope some five or six hundred yards distant. The bluffs along that stretch of the river were broken with a multitude of gullies, making it a convenient place for the animals to move down to the water's edge.

"I don't know about you," Luke commented, "but I've got a godawful hankerin' for some fresh meat. That looks like a natural waterin' hole at that bend. Whaddaya say we pull back to that gully we just passed and make camp? It's gettin' on toward evenin', anyway. I ain't real sure, but if my memory serves me, we can't be more'n a half a day or so from Big Timber. We might not run up on another herd of antelope before we strike the Boulder River. Maybe we can slip on up there to their waterin' hole in the mornin' before they come back to drink."

The plan suited Cade. He, too, was a little tired of salt pork. Of course there was the possibility that the herd would not return to the same bend to drink, but pronghorns were like everybody else—they had their habits. Both men had hunted antelope enough to know that this was the only chance they'd have to get close enough for a shot at the swift animals. They were already lucky not to have been spotted by the herd before they backed their horses out of sight. The pronghorns' eyesight was unmatched, and they could easily outrun the fastest horse without breaking a sweat.

Since they determined they were downwind of the antelope, they decided there was little risk in building a small fire to boil some coffee. Every so often, Luke would walk up to the edge of the gully to check on the antelope. As the evening approached, the herd gradually moved farther and farther away, casually grazing until Luke commented, "They're dang near out of sight." He came back down to the fire and settled himself. "If we've got any luck at all, we'll be eatin' antelope tomorrow night for supper."

"I just hope they come back to the same spot to drink," Cade said. He got up and emptied the last swallow of coffee from his cup. "I expect they've moved far enough now. Let's move up closer and find us a spot to wait for 'em."

The bend in the river where the antelope had come down to drink was almost devoid of trees, except for a few willows close to the edge. Some berry bushes struggled to live on a sandy spit that jutted out from the river's bank after a drop of about twelve feet. The many hoofprints down the gullies that ran from the bluffs bore evidence of the herd's recent visit.

"There sure ain't much trees or brush to hide in," Luke said, looking around him.

A few yards from him, also looking around the bluffs, Cade said, "I expect we could leave the horses in that stand of cottonwoods up ahead before daylight, and we'll have to hunker down in one of these gullies and wait."

"I reckon," Luke replied, unable to think of any better plan. "Might as well go ahead and move 'em up, and we can just go ahead and settle in a gully for the night." Cade agreed, so they moved their camp up to the bend and made themselves comfortable in a deep gully.

Both men were up before sunrise, watching for the return of the herd of antelope. As the darkness began fading to gray with no sign of the swift animals, they were about to decide their gamble a poor bet. "Uh-oh," Luke whispered. "There they are."

Gradually emerging in the fading darkness like slowly materializing ghosts, the antelope moved toward the water. Closest to the gully in which Cade and Luke had hidden, a buck corralled his harem of seven does, keeping a wary eye out for any challenges from other bucks. "Come on down for a drink," Luke whispered, "and we'll take a couple of them ladies offa your hands." In a few moments, the buck did as Luke had requested, and led his does down from the bluffs.

"Which one you thinkin' about?" Cade asked, making sure they didn't both shoot the same one.

"That'un right behind him," Luke answered.

"All right, I'll take the one behind her." They had already decided to take two antelope so they could have fresh meat and dry the rest to take with them. Two shots rang out, almost at the same time, and the herd of antelope scattered, leaving the two does crumpled to the ground in their wake.

"Hoo-boy!" Luke exclaimed. "I can already taste that fresh meat." He scrambled up out of the gully after Cade, who was standing on the lip watching the fleeing herd. "I'll build a fire, so we can cook up some of that meat while we're butcherin'."

"What the hell was that shootin'?" Lem Snider demanded, running up to the top of a low ridge where Curly Jenkins was keeping watch.

"I don't know," the confused man answered, trying to

blink the sleep from his eyes. "I don't see nothin'. Heard two shots, but I don't see nothin' over toward that gully where they camped. Them shots sounded like they came from somewhere upriver from there."

Snider knelt at the crest of the ridge, staring hard to see through the early-morning light. After a few minutes, he declared, "Hell, they're not there anymore." He turned then to Curly. "Gawdammit, Curly, you're supposed to be watchin' 'em."

"I've *been* watchin' 'em," Curly insisted.

"Well, they're gone. If you've lost 'em . . ." Snider started to threaten, but paused when he caught sight of the antelope scattering from the bluffs approximately a half mile beyond the gully where he had last seen the two men they tracked. The faint trace of a smile appeared on his face. "Hell, they're huntin'. That's what them shots were. They've moved their camp farther up the river."

"They musta moved out before daylight," Curly said, "else I'da seen 'em."

"Hell, you were most likely asleep," Snider snarled, no longer angry now that he knew the two had not given him the slip. "Let's get movin'. I wanna get close enough to keep an eye on 'em."

Back at the base of the ridge, Bob Dawson was just in the process of freshening the fire in preparation for making some breakfast. He looked up in surprise when both of his partners came down the slope. He jerked his hand away just in time to keep from getting struck by Snider's foot as Lem kicked dirt on his fresh flame. "What the hell's wrong with you?" Dawson demanded.

"We're movin'," Snider, ordered. "Let's get saddled up."

"What was the shootin'?" Dawson wanted to know. Snider told him that he was pretty sure Tucker and his friend had just shot at some antelope. Dawson considered that for a moment. "Well then, they most likely ain't goin' nowhere for a while if they're gonna be skinnin' and butcherin' an antelope. So what's the hurry? I'm hungry, and I say let's fix somethin' to eat first."

One of these days I'm gonna have to settle with you, Snider thought. Of his two partners, Bob Dawson was the more contrary, and the one more likely to argue. A dark, humorless man, Dawson's face was dry and leathery, etched with deep frown lines. Unlike Curly, Bob figured he had as much to say about things as Snider. Curly, on the other hand, was not very bright and he knew it, accepting Snider's domination without question. He wore a battered Montana Peak hat to protect his shiny, hairless dome from the sun. His prominent feature in an otherwise blank face was an abundance of hair protruding from each nostril. The two men served a purpose for Snider, and as soon as their value to him diminished, he would be quick to discard them.

"Dammit," Snider said, "it don't matter what you say, Bob, we're movin' up closer." When Dawson looked like he was about to get his back up, Snider softened his tone a bit. "We don't know for sure that they killed any game. I'm just tellin' you that's what it looks like. Now, we need to get closer so we can see for sure what they're up to. You can fix somethin' to eat then."

Dawson fixed his partner with a wary eye, and was about to retort when Curly interrupted. "I wish we had some of that fresh antelope to eat. Why don't we see if we can get a shot at one of them antelopes, Lem?"

Both Dawson and Snider cast disparaging gazes at their bald companion. Dawson explained, "Think about it, dummy. If we shot at an antelope, they'd likely hear the shots."

Curly considered that for a moment before his face lit up

with understanding. "Right. I didn't think about that." He nodded his head several times as he digested his enlightenment. Then another thought entered his head. "But, hell, we heard *their* shots."

Snider looked at Dawson and slowly shook his head, the near argument over authority between them temporarily forgotten. To Curly, he suggested, "Why don't you think on that while you saddle your horse? We need to get ourselves up where we can see Tucker and that other feller."

Curly looked from one face to the other. "I said somethin' dumb again, didn't I?"

"You sure as hell did," Snider snorted. "Now get a saddle on that horse."

"You big damn dummy," Bob Dawson remarked as he passed Curly to fetch his saddle.

"How'd you like it if I slit your throat one night?" Curly threatened and drew the long skinning knife from his belt.

Quick as a flash, Dawson whipped out his pistol and stuck the muzzle hard against Curly's forehead. "How'd you like it if I blow your brains out?"

"We're wastin' time," Snider complained, impatient with the badgering that was common between the two. If he didn't think he needed their guns, he'd have already shot both of them. As it was, however, he figured that after they killed Tucker and his partner, then he'd goad one of them into shooting the other, and he would finish whoever was left standing. If what he suspected was right, there should be plenty in those gold pouches for three men, but why split it when it was his idea to follow Tucker? He figured he had a right to the gold. He was there at the time it was lost, and had ridden in the detachment sent to retrieve the bodies. Ever since leaving the army, he had looked for that one big score. Feeling that this was finally it, there was no reason in his mind to share it with two no-accounts like Bob and Curly. He had killed men for a whole lot less.

After moving the horses up to the point where they had last seen Cade and Luke's first camp, Snider left the other two to make a small fire, and proceeded on foot. He had an idea where Luke and Cade might have set up their second camp, so he cautiously made his way along the riverbank, using the gullies and sparse patches of willows as cover. After walking a few hundred yards farther, he came upon the still warm ashes of a campfire, and knew that he had to be getting pretty close. Seeing a stand of cottonwoods near the river, he headed for them, using them for cover as he made his way along the banks. About to leave the trees to cross an open area, he glanced down to discover fresh horse droppings, telling him that they had left their horses here while they stalked the antelope. A slow grin crept across his whiskered face as he thought about how surprised Luke Tucker was going to be when he found out he'd been followed. Moving to the edge of the trees, he pulled up when he caught sight of the hunters down close to the water's edge. *Just like I figured,* he thought. Each man was busy butchering a carcass. Snider settled back on one knee and watched for a while as Cade and Luke carved up the two antelope. The aroma of roasting meat drifted by his nostrils as he watched Cade cutting up strips of meat to dry over the fire. Satisfied that his prey would not be leaving any time soon, Snider backed carefully away and retraced his path.

When he rejoined his partners, he found them sitting next to a small fire waiting for a coffeepot to boil. "We ain't goin' nowhere today," he said. "They're fixin' to dry some of that meat. They'll be doin' that all day."

"Why don't we just go on up there and jump 'em where they stand?" Dawson demanded. "Then, by God, I bet I get that hidin' place out of 'em. I know how to pry a man's tongue loose so he'll be tellin' things he didn't even know he knew."

"Now, see," Snider replied, "that's the reason I'm runnin' this show. If we did it your way, they could tell you anything. We wouldn't have no way of knowin' it was the truth or not. They'd just send us off on a wild-goose chase." He glared hard at one and then the other to make sure they knew that he was calling the shots. "We'll wait 'em out, and let 'em lead us to that gold, just like we've been doin'."

"I reckon you're right," Dawson gruffly admitted. He knew he was wrong, but he was getting restless and anxious to take some kind of action, even if it was wrong. He stewed over it in his mind for a few moments before suggesting, "Hell, we ain't a half a day's ride shy of Big Timber. Why don't we circle around 'em and get on their trail again when they come through town? I could use a drink."

"Me, too," Curly piped up.

Snider favored his partners with a look of disgust. "All right, you two go ahead and do that if you want to," he said. "I'm stayin' right here where I can keep an eye on 'em. Maybe I'll see you again, and maybe I won't. There ain't no tellin' where they'll head from here." He knew it was just talk. Dawson just had to have something to complain about.

"You look like you've done that before," Luke commented as he watched Cade hang thin strips of flesh on a limb he had suspended over the fire.

"Well, I ain't," Cade replied. "I just know that Indians smoke meat to keep, so I figured I'd try it."

"How long do you have to let it dry?"

"I don't have any idea. Till all the water's out of it, I guess. I figured I'd leave it till dark at least. What do you think?"

"I don't know, either," Luke said. "That's probably long enough. Hell, if it spoils, we'll just throw it away."

They filled their bellies with fresh roasted meat, then turned in for a contented night's sleep, with no suspicions of the danger barely a quarter of a mile away. On their way again early the next morning, they made Big Timber before the sun climbed directly overhead. With only a brief stop in the little settlement between the Yellowstone and the Boulder to rest the horses and ask about Indian activity in the area, they decided to ride on until nightfall. Informed that the only Indians in substantial numbers were Crow, they anticipated no trouble from that quarter.

A little before dusk, they came upon a peaceful meadow where a healthy stream emptied into the Yellowstone. There was no discussion necessary. Both men knew this was the place to camp. After the horses were taken care of, Cade walked a few yards up to the top of a little rise in the prairie, and stood gazing around him in every direction. He felt as if he had seen the place before in spite of the fact that this was the first time he had set foot in this part of the country. It was the vision of Montana he had seen in his dreams.

From where he stood, the tall, sweet grass of the prairie ebbed and flowed with the gentle evening breezes, giving the impression of a green, living sea, tipped here and there with obscure plumes of white, like ocean foam. The vast sea of grass swept away to the north to touch the base of a distant rugged mountain range of silvery peaks standing against the deep evening sky. Luke told him they were the Crazy Mountains. Behind him, to the south of the Yellowstone, rose the mighty heights of the Absarokas, the home, Luke said, of most any kind of game a man could imagine. *Why, then,* Cade asked himself, *would anyone want to wander farther?* This was the place to breed his horses. He could feel the pull of the country on his soul.

He turned to find Luke gazing at him quizzically. "What's ailin' you?" Luke asked. "I called your name three times. You look like you got buck fever or somethin'."

"Nothin'," Cade replied, "I was just thinkin', I guess."

"Well, maybe you oughtn't to do it if it freezes your brain like that," Luke said with a chuckle. "Whaddaya say we have us a little supper?"

Once again, the two partners filled their bellies with the fresh meat and washed it down with hot coffee. "I'm gonna bust if I take another bite," Luke finally admitted and leaned back against the side of the gully. He relaxed there a while, content with his world. After a few minutes of reflecting, he asked, "What you gonna do with your share of that gold, Cade?"

Cade shrugged. "I don't know—set myself up in the horse-wranglin' business I reckon. I ain't thought much about it." His answer was truthful. He had not spent any time speculating on the prospects of being wealthy. There were still too many *if*s to interfere with their plans. He told himself he'd wait until he had it in his hands.

"Well, I've thought about it," Luke said. "I just might set myself up in a hotel somewhere, one that's got a big porch with rockin' chairs—maybe find me a woman like Belle back there in Coulson to keep me warm at night. Prop my feet up on the porch rail in the daytime, and on the bed board at night."

Cade laughed. "Hell, you're too young for that. You'd get tired of that in six months' time. Then you could come help me raise horses." *And you'd be welcome,* he thought as he watched the lanky cowpuncher chuckling over his remark. Cade realized at that moment that Luke was a good friend. He had never really had a close friend before, and the idea gave him a feeling of peace, a feeling that he was not strictly a loner as he had been all his life up to now. It was a good feeling.

Unable to go any farther without the risk of being seen by the two they trailed, Lem Snider knelt at the top of a grassy rise, a pair of field glasses in his hand. After a while, he rose and descended the rise. "They're making camp, so I reckon we can, too."

"I wish to hell we had stopped back there in Big Timber long enough to find somethin' to eat besides this damn moldy bacon," Bob Dawson complained.

"We couldn't take a chance on losin' 'em," Snider said.

"Ain't much chance of losin' 'em," Dawson replied. "They're just followin' the river west. We coulda caught up with 'em anytime we wanted to." Snider didn't bother to grace the comment with a reply.

"I reckon they'll be fillin' their bellies with some more of that fresh pronghorn," Curly said, rubbing his stomach. "I can almost smell it from here."

"Don't surprise me none," Dawson scoffed, "you're part coyote. Too bad you got a coyote nose, and none of the brain."

Curly frowned, his eyes in an angry squint while he tried to think of a reply. "I got enough brains to skin a two-legged coyote," he said, and drew his long skinning knife. Waving it back and forth, switching it from hand to hand, he said, "Lem, tell him how I skinned that Injun woman down on the Big Horn." When Snider didn't bother to answer, Curly made a gesture like he was slitting his throat. "I could carve you up real pretty, Dawson."

"I just might shove that damn knife up your ass," Dawson retorted.

Curly's frown faded into a malicious grin, and he gestured with his fingers. "Come on, then."

Dawson drew his six-shooter, and leveled it at Curly, but once again Snider stepped between them. "Damn you two. Bob, put that damn gun away. You want them to know we're right behind 'em?" When neither man made a move to back down, he railed, "Dammit, we're in for a big payday if you two can just leave each other alone. After we find that gold, you can kill each other. Matter of fact, I hope to hell you do."

Finally, Curly put his knife away and Dawson holstered his pistol, although they continued to glare menacingly at each other. "Fry up some of that bacon," Snider said, making an effort to hide his disgust for his partners. "After dark, we can sneak up a little closer to keep an eye on that pair. Curly, you take the first watch. Bob, you take the second. I'll finish up the night."

"Hell," Dawson grumbled, "I'll bet they ain't even goin' after no damn gold—probably just headin' west like they said—and us followin' along behind 'em like hound dogs. How many years ago was that again?"

"You can turn around anytime you want," Snider said, weary of the squabbling. "Ain't nobody says you gotta go with me."

Curly, already with his knife out again to slice off some strips of bacon, looked at Dawson and grinned. He stuck his tongue out and touched the tip of the razor-sharp skinning knife to the underside of it. "I got lookout first," he taunted. "Maybe you'd best sleep with one eye open tonight."

"You big dummy," Dawson jeered.

Lem Snider poured himself a cup of coffee and sat down across the fire from his two companions. Waiting for the black liquid to cool a little in the metal cup, he considered the two men he had taken as partners—thinking that maybe he should have let them go ahead and settle the bad blood between them. He had no intention of sharing that gold with the sorry likes of Curly Jenkins and Bob Dawson. He had struggled too long and hard to find the big payoff he needed.

"You want some of this, Lem?" Curly held the frying pan up from the fire.

Snider shook his head. He was hungry. He had been hungry for as long as he could remember, but not for food. He never ate much, a fact that astonished his two partners, and his hard, lean body bore evidence of this. Living primarily off coffee and whiskey, with an occasional slab of meat to keep the sides of his belly from rubbing together, he seemed to get his nourishment from the black deeds he was good at.

After the war broke out, he had joined the Union Army simply because he was in Nebraska at the time. He felt no sympathy, or loyalty, to either North or South. Little more than a kid at the time, he joined because he was down on his luck, and he figured there would be opportunities to collect on the spoils of war as the army marched through the South. Much to his disappointment, he was posted to a frontier fort, and detailed to escort duty for emigrants. There was some fighting, mostly with Indians. His first murder, however, was a sergeant in his own company who had made the mistake of fighting with him over a whore in Virginia City. During a minor skirmish with a band of Sioux, the sergeant was hit with a rifle ball in the back. There had been more murders after his army days, resulting in very few financial gains, but murder was a necessary part of his occupation. Looking across the fire at Curly and Bob, that fact struck him even more so.

Tossing down the rest of his coffee, he said, "It's gettin' dark. Curly, you'd best get up there and start watchin' them fellers. We don't want them to decide to move off some-where in the night."

Though reluctant to move from the fire, Curly got to his feet and picked up his rifle. As he passed Dawson, he leaned down and whispered, "One eye, best keep one eye open."

"I've got a good mind to put a bullet in that simple brain of yours right now," Dawson retorted. He could hear Curly chuckling to himself as he walked away.

Chapter 5

Another day's ride found Cade and Luke at the point where the Yellowstone turned south. Saying good-bye to the river, they continued west toward the Bozeman Pass. Luke tried to hide it, but Cade could readily see that his friend was getting a little anxious as the end of their journey approached, for he urged Cade to continue on past their usual time to camp. Darkness was already descending when finally Luke selected a campsite. He was ready to go again early the next morning. They arrived in the town of Bozeman the next afternoon, and made one more camp near the banks of the Gallatin River.

"There's sure a helluva lot more folks in this town than the last time I saw it," Luke had commented when they had reached the edge of the settlement. "I expect we'd just as well circle on around it." Cade was surprised that Luke showed no interest in finding a saloon, preferring to stay in camp. He decided that Luke must be so close to realizing his treasure that he feared any distraction that might somehow hinder his reaching the gold.

Luke was up well before sunrise the next morning, and Cade wondered if he had slept much at all during the night. While Cade stirred up the coals and rekindled the fire, Luke strode back and forth along the riverbank, mumbling to himself. Finally, Cade asked, "What's eatin' at you? You're as nervous as a cat."

"I don't know," Luke answered. "Well, I reckon I do know. What if that gold ain't there no more? I mean, we came a long way to go fishin' if it ain't."

"I reckon you'll just have to help me round up some horses for breed stock instead of sitting around somewhere with your feet propped up," Cade said. "If you're thinkin' you mighta put me out some by ridin' all this way with you, hell, I was comin' out here, anyway. I found what I want, so if the gold ain't there, at least I ain't lost nothin'." He recalled to mind the picture of the lush grass prairie that stretched from the Yellowstone to the Crazy Mountains near Big Timber.

"I reckon you're right," Luke said. "Hell, let's get saddled and head on up the river. There's a lot of things different around here, but the river's still the same. I oughta be able to find that rock where I left them sacks."

As Luke had feared, his memory had faded considerably after thirteen years. Right away he began to doubt his recollection of how far upriver he and Luther Adams had been when they unloaded the gold from the mule. At the time, his mind was beset by many distractions, as the two of them had been desperately trying to save their necks. Things had changed. He didn't remember that the river forked around a little island here, or took a sharp bend there. The trees were taller and the brush thicker than he remembered. There was nothing he could do but push on, following the river, hoping to see something that jogged his memory. It was past midday when Luke, about to admit that he was whipped, suddenly pulled up short.

"We've gone too far!" he exclaimed excitedly. He waited for Cade to pull up beside him. Pointing to the other side of the river, he said, "That's the gulch we got ambushed in! That's the gulch we rode down into the water." He looked back toward the way they had just come. "We got to go back. I got to figure how far we drifted downstream before we came out."

With renewed optimism, Luke wheeled Sleepy around and started a thorough scout along the bank of the river. Cade followed, leading the packhorse. At last, he began to catch some of Luke's excitement. If luck was with them, he might be able to buy his breed stock instead of trying to catch wild horses. There were a number of places along the shore where rocks of various sizes protruded out into the water. Unable to tell for sure from the bank, Luke waded out into the water and continued downstream while Cade led the horses.

Wading in water waist-deep, Luke worked his way along the bank. A couple of rocks looked promising, but turned out to be nothing, causing Luke to wonder if one of them might have been the place, but the gold was gone. He continued wading along the edge of the river, moving another fifty yards before he came to it. The rock was smaller than he had remembered. Cade couldn't even see it from the shore. Luke ducked under water, and in a few seconds, came back up. "Glory be!" he shouted. "It's still here! Goddang it, I knew it would be! I knew it!"

Hardly able to believe that they had really found it, Cade tied the horses in the trees, removed his gun belt and hung it on his saddle horn. Unable to keep from grinning when he saw the expression of sheer joy on Luke's face, he waded into the water to help him retrieve the gold. Luke's gold, sixteen leather pouches, originally bound for the Union Army, undisturbed after so many years, were now carefully transported to dry ground. Once all sixteen of the heavy pouches were accounted for and resting on the grass above the rock,

Luke opened one of them to make sure everything was all right. "Sixteen sacks of gold, Cade!" he said. "And half of 'em is yours."

No sooner had he uttered the words when they heard the horses snort and blow. Cade knew at once that they had company. His first reaction was to retrieve his weapons, but before he could take the first step toward his horse, the .44 rifle slug slammed into his chest, knocking him backward into the water. He never heard the shot that hit him, and remembered nothing of the next few minutes after he hit the water.

Caught completely by surprise, and with no chance to get to his weapons, Luke could do nothing but cry out with rage when he saw the three intruders leaving the cover of the trees. "You murderin' sons of bitches!" he roared.

With his rifle leveled at Luke, Lem Snider sneered, "Now, Luke, that ain't no way to talk to an old army buddy." He moved to position himself between Luke and the horses. "I knew you were up to somethin' when we talked a few days ago. You coulda cut me in on this deal. I got just as much right to that gold as you, and if you had, why, hell, we woulda gone partners on it. But you was too greedy to share with an old friend."

"You can go to hell," Luke growled, knowing that his life could now be measured in seconds. "You never was a friend of mine."

Snider chuckled softly, amused by Luke's attitude. With his rifle steadily trained on him, he spoke aside to Curly. "Take a look in the river to make sure that other one's dead." Back to Luke, he warned, "Uh-uh," when Luke started to take a step toward the horses.

"What are you waitin' for?" Luke demanded. "Why don't you go ahead and finish your dirty business, you murderin' thief? You weren't worth the powder it'd take to blow you to hell back in the army, and it looks like you're still the back-shootin' son of a bitch you were then."

A malicious grin slowly formed on Snider's bushy face as he watched Luke's defiant reaction. He paused a second to hear Curly report that Cade looked dead to him, his body floating downstream with the current. "Well, I reckon you're itchin' to join your partner," he said to Luke. "I'll take good care of the gold for you." He squeezed the trigger, cutting Luke down with a slug in his gut. Taking his time, he ejected the spent shell and fired again, this time aiming a little higher, the bullet catching Luke in the neck. Luke dropped to the ground, dead.

Watching with childish excitement, Curly giggled nervously, and in a moment of uncontrolled fever, pumped two more slugs into the dead man. Bob Dawson, silently watching up to that moment, was less concerned with wasting ammunition by shooting a corpse. His interest focused upon the sixteen pouches lined up on the riverbank. "Look at that," he murmured, talking to himself as he counted the sacks of gold. "That's more gold than I've ever seen at one time."

"Well, get you a good look," Snider snarled, and swung his rifle around. The rifle bucked, sending a slug into Dawson's back as he bent over the pouches. Staggering, trying to keep from falling, Dawson tried to bring his rifle around, only to be met with two more shots ripping into his chest. Snider immediately turned to confront a stunned Curly Jenkins. Too confused to react, Curly was struck dumb for a few seconds while waiting for his inferior brain to tell him what to do. Snider smiled at him and said, "We didn't need that double-crossin' snake, did we? That gold will be easier to split between the two of us. Right?"

It took a moment more, but Curly finally believed he understood what had just happened. He didn't like Dawson, anyway, and it appeared to him now that Snider didn't, either. Smiling, he slowly nodded his head and answered, "Right." Things couldn't be better, although he would have preferred to be the one to have sent Dawson to hell.

"Let's have a look at them sacks," Snider said. After untying each pouch to make sure there was gold dust in every one, he told Curly to load them on the packhorse. When that was done, he took inventory of the minor spoils he had acquired in the form of horses, guns, and supplies. "Untie them other horses and bring 'em over here," he instructed Curly.

Excited as a child at Christmastime, Curly hurried to do his bidding, fairly giggling to himself at the thought of the immense riches he had come by. When he approached the two horses tied in the trees, they both stamped nervously and tried to back away. Curly untied Luke's horse, but when he untied Loco, the mottled gray gelding jerked free of his grasp and bolted off through a dense stand of evergreens. "Come back here!" Curly yelled, but the horse would have no part of the clumsy man.

"Dammit, Curly!" Snider swore when he turned to see the horse galloping through the trees. Thinking the guns and the saddle more valuable than the scruffy-looking gelding, he raised his rifle and fired at the fleeing horse, his shot whistling harmlessly through the branches. "Too late," he complained. "I couldn't get a clear shot." He lowered his rifle. "We can look for him later." Then he remembered that he was now a wealthy man, and a smile crept across his face. "To hell with that damn horse. I got more guns than I need."

"You reckon we oughta do anythin' with these bodies?" Curly asked when he had finished stripping Dawson and Luke of anything he thought useful.

"What for?" Snider replied. "Hell, just let 'em lay. Put all that stuff on them other horses." He stood and watched while Curly, uncomplaining, loaded up the weapons.

Finished, Curly grinned and said, "I reckon we can have us some of that antelope meat I been smellin' for two days." He turned to face his partner, his grin fading to a look of confusion when he saw the rifle leveled at him. His simple mind still failing to understand, he asked, "You want me to—" The question was never completed as Snider's rifle bucked again, leaving a dark hole in Curly's forehead.

Levi Crabtree knelt motionless as he watched from the screen provided by the lower boughs of a massive fir. The object that had captured his attention was bobbing gently against a small boulder in the middle of the river, and he could now confirm that it was a body. He had heard the shots fired a short distance upstream from where he now crouched, and his first impulse was to gather up his traps and seek the cover of the fir trees that stood by the bank of the river.

Watching what he now knew was a body bumping repeatedly against the boulder, he could not be sure if the victim was alive or dead. If he were to guess, he would say the man was dead. His instincts of self-preservation told him to remain still, and the river would carry the corpse away. The party responsible for the killing might show up at any minute looking for the body. His natural curiosity won the battle, however, and when the current finally swept the body around the boulder, Levi decided to take a closer look. Besides, he reasoned, there may be something of value on it.

Speculating that he had ample time to wade out to intercept the corpse before the current floated it past him, he scanned the riverbanks carefully before leaving his hiding place. He owed his longevity in the mountains to the fact that nobody knew he was there, and already he was beginning to wonder if it had been a mistake to venture this far from the safety of the high peaks. With the body almost to him now, he pushed out into the water, being careful not to lose his footing on the slippery rocks of the riverbed. With one hand, he reached out and snagged the body by the collar, and quickly pulled it back to the bank and the cover of the firs.

He's dead, all right, Levi thought at first glance. *Young fellow, shot through the chest, blood still seeping through the hole in his shirt. The thought struck him as strange. He's dead, but his heart's still pumping.* He dragged the man out of the water and up under the limbs of the fir. He looked at the face, drained of color except for a blue shading around the eyes and mouth.

A cursory glance at the body told Levi that there was nothing of value to be salvaged—no weapon or ammunition, not even a knife. He decided to leave the corpse under the limbs of the fir tree and start back up the mountain, but he hesitated, still intrigued by the continuous bleeding from the wound. As he stared at the young face, wondering what circumstances caused him to wind up floating down the river, he suddenly recoiled. Had the body just twitched, or was it his imagination? In the next moment, the body stiffened in spasm, then relaxed, and river water gushed from its mouth.

Astonished, Levi didn't know what to do, but he determined to do something. For lack of a better idea, he turned the body over on its stomach and began pounding on its back, hoping to force more water out.

Alive or dead, he wasn't certain. He didn't even know what had happened. Everything had suddenly gone black. When his mind began to function again, he had found himself facedown in the water, and he seemed to be drifting. He remembered that his first impulse was to hold his breath, and when he tried to turn his face out of the water, he couldn't move. The only thing he could think to do was to continue to hold his breath. That was his last clear thought before blacking out again.

He awoke with a cough and with someone or something pounding his back. As water spewed from his mouth and nose, he realized that he was on solid ground. The pounding stopped and he was rolled over on his back. He stared up at a dark form hovering over him. His eyes slowly began to focus; the murky features gradually became more clearly defined, and he found himself gazing into the clear blue eyes of a stranger. The face that stared back at him was thin, almost gaunt, with a dark beard liberally streaked with gray.

Not a word was exchanged for a long moment while each man stared at the other with confused curiosity. Suddenly aware of the throbbing in his chest, Cade struggled to sit upright, but fell back when the movement caused a fiery stab of pain to shoot through his body. His mind shifted back to those last moments by the riverbank when he heard Loco warning him that someone was approaching. "Luke!" he uttered, not sure if his partner was nearby.

"Don't know who Luke is, young feller," Levi said. "I just fished you outta the river." He was still amazed that the corpse he had pulled from the current was speaking to him.

"What happened? Where's Luke?"

"Can't help you there, friend," Levi said, "but what happened is you've been shot." He studied Cade for a few moments as if trying to make up his mind. "I reckon since you've come back to life, we oughta do somethin' about that hole in your chest before you die again." In his mind, Levi was damning his luck for deciding to venture down out of the mountains on this day. If he hadn't been there, this fellow would have simply floated on down the river, and stayed dead like fate intended. On the other hand, his conscience worried him with the possibility that it was fate that sent him down from the mountains today. One thing that Levi felt certain about was that the young man was dead when he pulled him up on the bank. *Dead as last week's horse turds,* he thought, *unless he's got gills, and I don't see any.* He had never had any dealings with somebody who came back from the dead, and he wasn't sure if he was comfortable with the situation.

"Luke, my partner," Cade forced weakly. "We musta got jumped by somebody." He feared Luke had met with the same fate as he.

His decision made, Levi pulled a bandanna from around his neck and stuffed it inside Cade's soggy shirt to control the bleeding. He'd do the best he could for the unfortunate soul, not knowing if he was helping an innocent victim or an outlaw. "My name's Levi," he said. "I don't know nothin' about your partner. I heard the shots, four or five of 'em, so I expect you're right. You musta got jumped by somebody."

Details came rushing back to Cade's mind of the moments just before he was shot—the sixteen pouches on the bank, Loco's warning that other horses were approaching. They had been attacked, all right, but by whom, and what had been Luke's fate? "My name's Cade Hunter," he told Levi, "and I need to get back to my partner. If you can help me get on my feet, I've got to find out what happened to Luke."

"You plan on walkin'?" Levi asked, more than a little skeptical. "I ain't got no horse. I mean, I got one, but he ain't between my legs right now."

"If I have to, I'll walk," Cade insisted.

"I'll help you if I can," Levi said, "but you don't look like you'll get very far, and we'd best be on the lookout for whoever shot you. Them shots I heard sounded mighty close. How do we know they ain't lookin' for you?"

"Maybe they think I'm dead, like you did, else they'd most likely have already been down here lookin' for me."

"I expect you could be right," Levi allowed. "Them shots sounded mighty close, though." He reached down to give Cade a hand. "We'll give 'er a try."

After a painful struggle, Cade was able to get to his feet. He tried to walk with Levi's help, but they both saw right away that he wasn't going to be able to make it, even for a short distance. They finally ended up with Cade riding piggyback, but even that was too much for Levi with a rifle and traps to carry as well. After hiding his traps to be picked up later, Levi was able to carry Cade to the site of the assault, but only after stopping to rest twice. Each stop made it more difficult for Levi to load Cade up on his back again, and by the time he reached the clearing by the riverbank, he was staggering under his burden, and Cade was almost too weak to sit up.

"Glory be," Levi murmured when he saw the scene left behind by Lem Snider. Not one, but three bodies lay on the grassy bank above the rock. "They're all dead," he said between gasps for air. He instinctively looked around him, fearful that the men responsible might even then be watching them.

The prospect that Luke was dead had already struck Cade, but he had held out hope that maybe there was a chance that, like him, Luke had somehow survived the attack. Now his first assumption after finding three bodies was that Luke had taken two of their assailants with him. When Levi had lowered Cade to the ground beside the first body, he recognized the man as one of the three that Luke had sought to avoid back in Coulson. He looked beyond to the body of Curly Jenkins. A short distance from the other two, Cade recognized Luke's body. The one missing was Lem Snider. Cade remembered the name. He had heard Luke repeat it enough, and it was easy to speculate on what had taken place here. "Lem Snider"—he repeated the name to make sure he never forgot it. He could logically tell himself that there was nothing he could have done to prevent Luke's death. But he could not escape a feeling that he had let Luke down. The best he could do now was to make a silent vow to his late partner that he would not rest until he found the man who murdered him. He turned to Levi then. "I can't leave him out here like this."

Levi frowned, not sure what this stranger expected of him. He had already carried him almost half a mile on his back. After a moment, he said, "Well, I ain't got nothin' to dig a grave with." He paused, then, "Let alone three graves." He gestured toward the bodies. "Hell, the buzzards will take care of 'em."

"I don't care about the other two," Cade said. "I just don't want the buzzards to get Luke's body." Luke was the only real friend he'd ever had. He couldn't abandon him to be a banquet for carrion.

You're wanting a helluva lot for a helpless man with a bullet in your chest, Levi thought. Still, he had to admit that, in his place, he would feel the same for a friend. To Cade, he said, "Tell you what, I'll fetch some rocks from the river to keep the buzzards off of him. That's about the best I can do."

"I appreciate it," Cade replied. "I'm sorry to put you out so much. I wouldn't blame you if you'd just gone on about your business and left me to the buzzards, too." Levi nodded thoughtfully, admitting to himself that he had given it some consideration.

Not really sure if he was going to live or die, Cade could only lie against a tree trunk and watch while Levi brought rocks up from the edge of the water and entombed Luke's body. The pain in his chest was increasing as he lay there, and he was fighting a desire to close his eyes, but he was determined to see Luke properly protected. As he watched Levi laboring with the burial, he remembered Luke telling him that the prospect of finding the gold had taken hold of his mind, and he didn't want to end up a poor man. The thought occurred to him that Luke had, in ironic fashion, had his wish fulfilled. He had died a rich man even though his wealth had been brief.

Satisfied that the body was safe from predators, Levi pushed his hat back and scratched his head while he thought about a more serious problem. "The worrisome thing now is what to do with you. You can't walk, and I sure as hell can't carry you up in them mountains to my place. If somebody'd told me I was gonna have to tote a man up to my place, I'da rode my horse." He looked at Cade, studying the problem in his head. "I reckon I could leave you here while I go get my horse. You think you'd be all right?" He knew if he was going to doctor the man properly, he would need the healing skills of his wife, a full-blood Blackfoot woman. *This was one time when I wish I'd stayed the hell away from the river,* he thought. *No beaver, no muskrat—just a fellow with a hole in his chest, and me with no way to carry him home.*

Though his Samaritan was trying not to show it, Cade sensed that Levi was regretting fishing him from the river. "Friend, you've already done a helluva lot for me. I don't reckon I've got much choice but to stay here." He could feel his voice growing weaker as he spoke. "If I'm still alive when you get back, then that's the way it's supposed to be. If I'm dead, no hard feelin's."

Levi started to reply when suddenly he was startled by a sound behind him. He immediately dropped to one knee and grabbed his rifle, fearful that the murderer had returned. "Well, I'll be . . ." he began, then gaped in disbelief as a horse slowly approached from the trees, saddled with a rifle in the sling and a gun belt hung on the saddle horn.

Equally astonished, Cade rose up on his elbow to find

that Loco had returned to find his master. "That's my horse," he rasped weakly.

Levi stepped aside, and watched dumbfounded as the piebald gelding walked slowly up to stand over the man lying on the ground, and nudged Cade's belly with its muzzle. "Well, I reckon that takes care of our problem, don't it?" He looked at Cade and grinned.

With Levi's help, Cade managed to get up in the saddle, but got less than a hundred yards before realizing he couldn't make it. In actuality, it was Levi who decided when he saw fresh blood seeping through the crusted hole in Cade's shirt and him starting to list to one side. Levi caught him just before he fell off the horse. With a small hand ax that he carried on his belt, Levi was able to fashion a travois to carry the wounded man. It was a patchwork contraption held together with rope from Cade's saddle and some vines from the trees. Loco didn't like it at first, but with Cade's calming voice to settle him down, the horse finally accepted the strange attachment. "It'll be a heap longer goin' up than the way I came down this mornin'," Levi said. "With the horse and travois, we'll have to wind around a lot before we get to my place, but it's doable."

The trip up the mountain seemed endless to the wounded man as the makeshift transport bumped along over roots and small stones, each jolt bringing a sharp pain shooting through his chest. The trail wound back and forth across the mountain with turns sometimes so steep that it was all Cade could do to keep from rolling off. Before he was halfway up, he began to wish that he had just told Levi to leave him to die by the river.

Chapter 6

Willow paused to listen, her bone-scraping tool held motionless over the elk hide she was working. Levi's bay mare whinnied again, causing the Indian woman to look in her direction. She noted the horse's ears flickering nervously as if another horse might be approaching the cabin. With no further hesitation, Willow dropped her scraper and hurried to get the rifle that was propped by the door. Taking the rifle, she positioned herself inside the cabin door and waited. In a few moments' time, she was surprised to see Levi come riding up astride a mottled gray horse, pulling a travois.

It had been a long, rough ride up from the valley of the Gallatin. Cade's chest felt as if it were being ripped apart as the travois poles bumped and jarred over the rocky trail that wound up the side of one mountain, across a narrow saddle to a second mountain, and around to the eastern side of that one—weaving through thick stands of pine and spruce and patches of juniper. Cade thought it would never end. Mercifully, he passed out before they finally arrived at Levi's home.

For the second time in one day, Cade awakened to find a strange face bending over him. At first, he didn't remember where he was, but the dark brown eyes that gazed down into his softened as he stared back, and the full lips parted to grace him with a warm smile. "He awake now," the woman announced to her husband. "I am Willow," she said to Cade. "You have bad wound, but you are strong. You will be well, but you must rest your body."

Levi walked over to examine the patient. "You was out for a while, Cade, but I knew Willow could fix you up. She's put me back together more'n a few times. The slug's still in there, but Willow don't think it hit your lungs or your heart. She thinks you got a broke rib or two, though. We'll get you back on your feet again, but it'll take a little time." He didn't mention that he had told Willow about finding him face-down in the river, and that he was convinced Cade was dead when he pulled him out. From the look of the patient when he finally got him to the cabin, Levi was halfway convinced that Cade had gone back to being dead.

"I'm much obliged to both of you," Cade said. "I don't know how I can repay you for what you've done."

"Never you mind about that," Levi said. "There's game aplenty in these mountains, and we got room in the cabin, so you ain't puttin' us out none. You just get yourself healed up." Still not quite sure it was the smart thing to do, bringing a stranger to recover in his mountain hideaway, Levi decided he might as well make Cade feel welcome. On the surface, Cade seemed to be a decent enough young man, although Levi couldn't help but wonder what kind of mischief he was involved in that resulted in getting himself killed. All he knew at this point was that someone had bushwhacked Cade and his partner. As to why, Cade had not offered to explain.

The days that followed had a tendency to slide by in a daze of fitful patches of sleep and half consciousness that left Cade weak and at times disoriented. It seemed that every time he awakened, it was to see Willow's eyes searching his.

She assured him that he was getting better, but he was not convinced until the fourth day, when he felt like eating.

"I expect it's time I tried to see if I can get up from this bed," he told Willow as she changed the poultice she applied daily to his wound. She quickly took his arm to help him when he struggled to sit upright. He immediately leaned back against the log wall when the effort caused him to feel a little dizzy.

"Not strong yet," Willow said. "Need food." She left him, and returned in a few minutes with some dried meat. "Bear meat," she said, holding it out to him. "Make you strong."

"I kilt that bear last spring, no more'n fifty yards from the cabin," Levi said, entering the cabin just then. "He was a big'un. Made a nice robe, too."

After a short while, the feeling of dizziness left him, and he was able to eat the meat Willow offered. His ability to take food seemed to encourage both his hosts, and Willow nodded to Levi, smiling.

"Danged if I don't believe you're gonna make it," Levi said. "I told you my woman would pull you through." He cocked his head to one side to state, "It didn't look too promisin' there for a while, though." He paused for a moment when his wife handed Cade a cup of coffee. "Hope you like the coffee . . . it's your'un." He paused again. "I found it in your saddlebags," he confessed sheepishly. "Like I said, for a while there, it was less than even money whether you'd make it or not."

Cade grinned. "You're welcome to it. I already owe you and Willow more than I can repay."

"We ain't had no coffee for quite a spell, have we, Willow? I just about forgot how it tastes. Matter of fact, I reckon you're the first white man I've seed since I built this cabin. Curiosity is my biggest weakness, I guess. It's got me in trouble more times than not, but if it weren't for curiosity,

I'da never pulled you outta the river. Anyway, I had to take a look in your saddlebags when you looked like you was goin' under." That thought caused him to recall another. "That's a mighty spooky horse you're ridin'. I thought I was gonna have to shoot him before I could unsaddle him."

Cade laughed. "Yeah, Loco's a little particular about strangers."

Feeling stronger by the minute, Cade sipped the hot coffee while he took a closer look at his benefactors, having been too sick before to care. "How long have you been up here in the mountains?" he asked, his curiosity aroused. "This high up, it must get pretty rough in the winter."

"It does at that," Levi answered. "I lost track. Maybe Willow knows better, but I reckon it's been two or three years now." He glanced at Willow for confirmation.

"Two winters," she confirmed.

"Seems longer sometimes," Levi uttered softly, "but it's better'n livin' down below."

Cade looked around him then, observing for really the first time the small cabin he was recuperating in. Levi had done a commendable job of construction. The log walls were tight and chinked with sod, the stone fireplace looked neat and sturdy, probably capable of putting out plenty of heat in cold weather. There was a rifle propped in one corner, an early model Henry by the look of it. Next to the rifle, an unstrung bow and quiver rested against the fireplace.

Noticing Cade's eye settle upon the bow, Levi elaborated. "A man better learn to hunt with a bow if he lives up here. Cartridges is too scarce to waste . . . and a bow don't make no noise."

"That's a handy skill to have," Cade said, "especially if you don't want anybody to find you." Levi raised an eyebrow, but did not respond at once, causing Cade to believe he might have struck a sensitive area. There might be a reason for Levi to avoid visitors. "It's unusual for a man to live in hard country like this unless he's pannin' gold or somethin'. It ain't none of my business why you're way the hell up here, but I would appreciate knowin' if there's a need for me to keep my rifle close."

Levi exchanged a brief glance with Willow before turning back to Cade. He hesitated a few moments before answering. Then, deciding that his story was safe with Cade, he explained. "Curiosity got me again," he said with a grin. "I was havin' me a little drink in the saloon down in Bozeman a couple of years back when these four fellers came in and set down at a table. They got to drinkin' pretty heavy and started talkin' louder and louder. I couldn't help but hear what they was talkin' about. They was goin' on about a little Blackfoot woman they had in the wagon. They bought her from a band of Crows that had captured her, and they was gettin' lickered up to have a go-round with her, arguing about who oughta be first.

"Well, I slipped on outside to have a little peek in their wagon, and there she was, tied hand and foot, with a gag in her mouth. She looked at me with those big ol' eyes, scared and shakin' like a lamb at the slaughter . . . and I was done for." He glanced again at Willow, who smiled warmly at him. "Yessir, I felt so sorry for her, and what was waitin' for her when them fellers got enough whiskey in 'em. I said, 'Levi, you ain't never done a smart thing in your whole life, and you're about to make another dumb move.'

"Well, I cut her loose. That was all I was gonna do, but she looked so lost and scared. She didn't know which way to run. I couldn't leave her to make it on her own, so I told her to climb up behind me on my horse, and we hightailed it outta there. We didn't get away clean, though. One of them fellers came out to the wagon just in time to see me gallopin' off with their woman. He jumped on his horse and came after us, hollerin' and shootin'. Hell, I shot back. I wasn't even aimin'—couldn't, bouncin' around on a gallopin' horse. Don't you know I hit him—killed him deader'n hell from the looks of him when he came off his horse.

"Come to find out the four of 'em was brothers; Willow told me that. So now I got three of 'em comin' after me for stealin' their woman and killin' their brother."

"So you ended up here in the mountains," Cade surmised.

"Yeah, after a few days of runnin' and hidin'. I gave her the choice of tryin' to go back to find her own people, but she decided to stay with me. So we decided to go back up in the mountains and build us a cabin. It's worked out pretty good so far. At least she ain't tried to run off after two or three years." He glanced over to receive an affectionate smile from Willow. "And I s'pose them three brothers have give up by now, but I don't know for sure, and there ain't no use being careless. The hard part is not being able to go down to Bozeman to get supplies like coffee, flour and beans, and cartridges. The only place I can get a little flour once in a while is by tradin' hides at a tradin' post on the far side of the mountain. That's the reason I was down in the valley where I found you. I was lookin' to trap beaver and maybe catch a few fish to eat."

"I reckon I cut your fishin' short," Cade said.

"You did at that," Levi said with a chuckle, "and you were the only thing I caught all day." Then he asked, "Who were them fellers that jumped you and kilt your partner?"

Cade told him the whole story of the gold dust his late friend, Luke, had hidden in the river and their journey from Miles City to retrieve it.

"Damn!" Levi exclaimed, thinking about the little grassy clearing by the river. "I most likely fished or trapped right over that gold three or four times durin' the last couple of years." His mind reeled with thoughts of what it would have meant to him to discover its existence. "Sixteen pouches," he repeated, shaking his head in wonder. "No wonder them fellers was after you." He inhaled sharply and grimaced. "And now this feller Snider's run off with all of it." He knew the answer to his next question before he asked it. "So now you'll be goin' after this feller?"

"Just as soon as I can stay on my horse," Cade replied calmly.

"It ain't gonna be easy," Levi said. "By the time you're strong enough to ride, it's gonna be a mighty cold trail."

"I s'pose," Cade agreed. The odds were not in his favor. Lem Snider could have gone in any direction. There would be little chance that any sign of his trail would be left by the time Cade had healed enough to go after him. He was going to need a lot of luck, but there was no question about whether to hunt him or just decide it was wasted effort, rationalizing that the gold was never his in the first place. The truth be told, Cade's motivation sprang less from the possession of the treasure, and more from the determination to seek vengeance for Luke's murder. He had never really had a close friend before Luke. It stuck in his craw that a murdering skunk like Lem Snider could get away with killing a good man like Luke Tucker. There was also the little matter of the bullet Snider had left in Cade's chest.

With the passage of each day, Cade gradually regained his strength, thanks to a strong constitution and the excellent care of Willow. She was a fine-looking woman, and seemed always to wear a smile upon her face. Levi was extremely proud of her and the fact that she had chosen to remain with him when freed from the four brothers who had bought her. The Blackfoot were a handsome people, and Levi, a homely man, felt himself especially honored to have such a woman as his wife.

Levi spent much of his day tracking the game that popu-
lated the rugged mountains surrounding his cabin. As he had
first boasted, there was game aplenty, but his existence there
had naturally pushed the deer and other game farther and
farther away. So there were many days when his hunting resulted in limited success. He admitted to Cade that he and
Willow had talked about leaving their mountain retreat
and heading north along the Musselshell toward Canada to
find Willow's people. He was afraid of getting old and being
unable to provide for the two of them where they now were.
In spite of Levi's stated preference to live apart from other
people, Cade could sense the loneliness his host denied
when finally it was time for him to leave.

"I'm much obliged to you folks for takin' such good care
of me," Cade said as he tucked the dried venison Willow had
wrapped for him in his saddlebag. He checked his rifle to
make sure it was seated in the saddle scabbard, then turned
back to extend a hand to Levi. "If I can ever repay you, I
will."

"Be careful," Willow said, smiling. "Don't get no more
shot."

Cade laughed and replied, "I'll try not to. You take care
of Levi. He's a good man." He stepped up in the saddle.

Levi stepped up close beside his stirrup. "I can't help my
curiosity, Cade, and maybe it ain't none of my business, or
maybe it's a secret you can't tell, but I gotta ask you somethin'. When I pulled you outta that river, you was dead. I
mean, you had to be, but you came back. You got a little
peek at what it's like on the other side, didn't you? Could
you tell? I mean, were you there long enough to see other
dead folks?"

Astonished by the question, Cade took a moment to answer. "Hell, Levi, I wasn't dead, I just passed out, I reckon,
but I sure as hell wasn't dead, or I wouldn't be here right

now, would I?" Loco began to stamp nervously, eager to be on the move again. Cade held the gray gelding back a couple of seconds while he smiled and tapped his forehead in farewell, and then he was off, following the shorter trail down, now that Loco was unencumbered with the travois. He had intended to leave that morning, but it was already midday by the time he finally got started.

Levi stood with his arm around his wife's shoulders, watching until Cade dropped below the rocky shelf and disappeared in the trees. "He seen the other side," he assured Willow. "He just ain't supposed to tell anybody about it."

Chapter 7

Dorsey Braxton pulled up at the edge of the trees that bordered the Gallatin River, surprised by the scene he had come upon at the riverbank. "Look what I found," he called back to his two brothers, who were following behind him. Being the eldest, Dorsey usually led. He and his brothers had spent more than two years, off and on, combing the mountains between the Absarokas and Virginia City, looking for the man who shot their younger brother. Their lack of success in finding the man and the Blackfoot woman did nothing to discourage Dorsey's lust for vengeance, and he kept coming back to the valley of the Gallatin. He was convinced that this was the most likely country Levi Crabtree would have picked to hide in.

"Damn," Cobb Braxton uttered when he pulled even with his brother and saw the remains of two bodies. "Looks like somebody had a little piece of bad luck. The buzzards didn't leave nothin' but rags and bones."

Gentry Braxton guided his horse around his two brothers and dismounted to take a closer look at the pile of rocks that was Luke Tucker's grave. "Reckon what's so special 'bout this one?" He started pulling rocks away until he had made a hole big enough to see what they guarded. "Another dead one," he announced. "The buzzards didn't get to this one, but the worms are doin' a pretty good job."

"Anything on him worth takin'?" Cobb asked.

"Hell, I don't know. I can't see that much. If you wanna see him, you dig him out. He's smellin' too rank to suit me."

"Does it look like that bastard we're after?" Cobb asked.

"How the hell do I know? I ain't ever seen the son of a bitch. Franklin's the only one that saw him." The youngest of the four brothers might have gotten a good look at Levi Crabtree moments before Levi shot him, but Franklin was dead when they got to him.

"How long you reckon he's been dead?" Dorsey asked. Something else had caught his eye at the edge of the clearing.

"Hard to tell," Gentry replied. "Two weeks, maybe."

"About the same as these marks cut in the dirt, if I had to guess," Dorsey said. The hoofprints were barely discernable, but there were two reasonably sharp marks left by what surely must have been a travois. "Somebody hauled somethin' or somebody away from here. Wonder what it was?"

Cobb and Gentry came over to take a look for themselves. "I don't know," Gentry answered his brother after studying the two deep marks left in the sandy soil, "but it sure looks like there was a shoot-out here over somethin'."

"I'm thinkin' we oughta find out if we can see where these tracks lead," Dorsey decided.

Since there was no better suggestion from either of his brothers, they set out along the trail left by the two poles of the travois. After this much time, it was no easy trail to follow, but there were enough areas of soft dirt here and there to leave occasional imprints to tell them they were still on the trail. Leading away from the river, the riders paused when they lost the tracks in a wide field of shell rock at the base of the mountain.

"This don't make sense," Cobb snorted. "Ain't no horse gonna pull a travois up that mountain."

"Look around, dammit," Dorsey snapped. "They sure as hell went somewhere." He had a feeling about the bodies they had happened upon. Maybe it had nothing to do with the man who killed Franklin. On the other hand, it fit right in with the picture of a man hiding out in these mountains, bushwhacking some innocent souls, and scurrying off up to his secret camp with the plunder.

After a frustrating thirty minutes of searching the rocky outcropping, they were rewarded when Gentry discovered a pair of ruts leading through a thick forest of firs that led to a meandering game trail just wide enough to accommodate a horse pulling a travois. "By God, he did go up that mountain," Dorsey pronounced solemnly. "I aim to see where this leads to." His mind was beginning to work on the possibility that the rider of the horse pulling the travois and the man he'd hunted for more than two years might be one and the same. He could envision a scene where this squaw-stealer had bushwhacked the men whose bodies they had just left and hauled off the spoils on a travois. There were two unanswered questions. What happened to the victims' horses—and why the one rocky grave? Maybe, he thought, he would find the answers at the end of the trail they were now following.

Late afternoon found the three brothers high up in the mountains with still no sign of human existence. "It's gonna be gettin' dark before long," Cobb complained, "and we ain't seen nothin'." The trail had led almost to the top of the mountain and now started down.

"Dammit," Dorsey snapped, "somebody hauled a travois up here. He's gotta be goin' somewhere."

"Hell, maybe it ain't even a travois," Cobb commented. "There ain't enough tracks to tell for sure."

"Yeah, Dorsey," Gentry chided, "maybe it's a deer with a peg leg." His remark caused him and Cobb to chuckle.

Their elder brother chose not to appreciate the humor in the suggestion. He was about to say so, when he suddenly paused and sniffed the air. "I smell smoke," he said. All three looked around them, searching for a telltale column of smoke.

"There!" Gentry exclaimed, pointing to a thin ribbon of smoke on the mountain next to them.

"We're on the wrong damn mountain," Cobb complained.

Not ready to admit he had led them up a false trail, Dorsey frowned and peered through the maze of juniper ahead. "I ain't ready to turn around yet. Them tracks was left by a travois, and they lead to somethin'."

"Maybe," Cobb muttered begrudgingly. He was not so sure. He looked at Gentry, who shared his lack of faith in the tracks, and shook his head. They were accustomed to following their older brother's lead, however, so there was no vocal objection from either.

Half an hour later, when rounding the base of a rocky cliff, Dorsey was vindicated. A narrow hogback joined the two mountains, and the trail led across it. "I knew it, dammit," Dorsey crowed. "It's a good thing you two half-wits have me to tell you what to do."

Levi walked from the edge of the clearing carrying an armload of wood for the fire Willow had built between the cabin and the lean-to where he kept his horse. She often cooked outside during the summer months. It was cool up this high, but cooking inside sometimes made the cabin too warm. He dropped his armload down next to the fire and started to add a couple of pieces onto the flame. "What's the matter, girl?" he said, pausing to listen. The bay mare had heard something. He strained to listen, thinking it might be a mountain lion or a bear. It wouldn't be the first time a mountain lion ventured this close to the cabin. Glancing back toward the door, he saw Willow coming out with the meat to cook. "Honey," he called back to her, "fetch my rifle when you come. We might have a visitor."

Lying on their bellies, concealed by a thick stand of pines, the three stalkers watched the man tending the fire beside the cabin. "Whaddaya think, Dorsey?" Gentry whispered. He waited for a few moments. When his brother failed to answer, he said, "There ain't no real way of knowin' if he's the one we're after or not."

Dorsey was about to agree, but he was of a mind to bushwhack the man kneeling by the fire anyway, although he doubted there was much to gain in the way of plunder. Just as he started to speak, Willow emerged from the cabin carrying a rifle and some meat. "Now there is," he said, responding to Gentry's comment. "Lookee yonder!"

"That's her!" Cobb blurted in a hoarse whisper.

"Keep your voice down!" Dorsey scolded, a sly grin forming behind his whiskers. It was her, all right. There was no doubt in his mind. He was not a patient man, but he had patiently searched for over two years for the man who killed his youngest brother. The Indian woman was of no real concern to him, but she was his property, bought and paid for, and he had been equally determined to find her. He would probably cut her throat once he and his brothers were through with her. Ignoring Cobb and Gentry's anxious expressions, he took time to enjoy the moment he had been looking forward to for so long. "All right," he finally whispered. "Be careful, and don't hit the woman. We ain't done with her yet." He pulled his rifle up and aimed it.

*   *   *

"What is it?" Willow asked, bringing the rifle.

"I don't know," Levi said, "maybe nothin', but somethin's makin' Bess nervous." He turned to take the weapon from her when the late-evening air was suddenly shattered by the crack of a rifle. In the process of rising from one knee, Levi was struck in the shoulder, the shot spinning him around to drop at Willow's feet. She screamed and dropped down beside him. "Git in the cabin!" Levi gasped desperately as she tried to help him up. A couple more shots snapped close beside them to strike the cabin wall with a solid *thunk-thunk*. With Willow trying to support him, Levi crawled to the cabin door under a hail of angry lead. Splinters of wood were sent flying as they just made it inside the door and Willow slammed it shut and barred it. Levi took only a moment to examine his wound before crawling over to the window. Dorsey's bullet had caught him in the left shoulder. The shoulder felt numb at that moment, and he motioned Willow away when she started to tend to it. "It ain't that bad," he said. "I can still shoot. Stay low to the floor and get me that box of cartridges." She immediately went to fetch them.

"There are not many left," she said, her voice trembling with fright.

It was a fact that Levi already knew, but he sought to reassure her. "They may be enough. We can make it pretty hot for them to try to break in here. They might decide it ain't worth the trouble." He eased his head up to a corner of the window, trying to see where their assailants were hidden. With no way of knowing for sure who was attacking them, he could only speculate. He felt sure they were not Indians. The Indians on the other side of the canyon were Crow, and friendly. Simple logic told him that it was not a party that just happened upon his cabin on this remote mountaintop. It made more sense that it was someone who had come specifically to find him—and he feared who that someone might be. A few minutes later, his fears were confirmed.

"Hey, you in the cabin there," Dorsey Braxton's deep voice boomed out. "You know what we come for. You might as well come on outta there, and maybe we'll let you go. We just come for the woman."

"You go to hell," Levi replied. It wasn't very likely he'd be excused for killing their brother. He told Willow to crawl over beside the fireplace where the stones might better shield her. "Keep an eye on that back window in case they sneak around behind," he said. She nodded and did as he instructed, pausing under the window long enough to reach up and close the shutters.

Outside, Cobb and Gentry moved a little farther away from Dorsey in case the man inside had pinpointed their older brother's location by the sound of his voice. "Too damn bad you missed him with that first shot," Cobb complained. "Hell, he was settin' right there waitin' for it."

"He moved, dammit," Dorsey blurted, "just when I pulled the trigger. I didn't see any better shootin' from you two." All three had been overly cautious trying to target the wounded man as he struggled to seek cover—none wanting to hit the woman and spoil the sport they planned to enjoy with her.

Dorsey called out again. "Mister, you ain't got much sense. We've got you cornered. You ain't got no place to go." The cook fire caught his eye then. "There's a nice little fire goin' out here. We just might decide to burn you outta there."

"Why don't you just do that?" Levi called back. "I got a clear shot at that fire and the first one that tries to get across the yard from them trees you're hidin' behind is a dead man." He ducked quickly away from the window seconds before a volley of shots ripped into the shutter and the frame.

The siege continued until it was almost dark, with sporadic shots from the three in the pines, borne mostly out of frustration. "It's gonna be dark before long," Dorsey said, his eyes studying the tiny cabin. "One of us can get around behind that cabin while the other two keep that bastard pinned down."

"There might not be a window in the back," Gentry said.

"We could smoke him out," Cobb suggested. "When it gets dark, I could climb up on the roof and stop that chimney up with somethin'—smoke 'em out."

Dorsey didn't bother to comment. Gentry did. "You ain't got brains God give a tumble-turd," he said. "Do you see any smoke comin' outta that chimney? Whaddaya think they built a fire outside for?"

Cobb had to think about it for a moment before coming up with an angry retort. "Well, if you're so smart, why don't you think of somethin'?"

"How 'bout you walk up to the door and knock, and when he opens it to see who it is, I'll shoot the son of a bitch."

"Shut up, both of you." Dorsey had tired of the senseless drivel between the two. His frustration with the situation was wearing upon his nerves. Over two years in tracking down the man who shot his brother, and it had come down to a standoff. "We're gonna rush that son of a bitch as soon as it gets a little darker. Gentry, you go ahead and work your way on up the slope, and get around behind that shack. See if there's a window in back. Then get back here and let me know." Gentry nodded and backed away from the edge of the trees.

Smiling to himself, Gentry Braxton made his way up through the thick forest of pines, climbing for several dozen yards before sidling along the slope to descend toward the cabin again. If there was a window in the back of the cabin, and he could get a clear shot, he didn't plan to wait for Dorsey and Cobb. The death of his brother, Franklin, didn't sorrow him as much as it did Dorsey. He was more interested in the Blackfoot woman. She was a right handsome woman, and from the glimpse he got of her a couple of hours ago, it looked like she hadn't changed.

Darkness had already found the thick forest by the time Gentry slid down a steep mound that landed him in a little patch of fir trees. From there he could see the rear of Levi's cabin and a single window in the back. The shutters had been closed, but he figured he might be able to squeeze a gun barrel through the strap hinges on the side. *It's gonna be you and me, little missy,* he thought as he made his way carefully up to the rear log wall.

As he had figured, the shutters, though drawn and latched from the inside, were hung using leather straps as hinges. Working as quietly as he could, he took his knife and cut enough of the leather away on one side until he had a hole big enough to see into the cabin. There she was! Huddled over next to the fireplace, a gentle creature, small and timid, like a rabbit cornered by a coyote. Gentry felt the lust filling his veins, even stronger than his excitement over killing the man who had stolen her. Moving slightly, he could see most of that man crouched by the front window. The hole he had cut in the strap was big enough to stick a gun barrel through, but would not allow him to aim his rifle at Levi. Stumped for a second, he then realized he could cut through both leather hinges and jerk the whole shutter away. With a wide grin upon his face, he immediately set to work with his knife.

Back in the pine trees facing the front of the cabin, Dorsey began to wonder why Gentry was taking so long to report back. "Maybe you oughta get around behind that cabin and see what the hell he's doin' back there. Dammit, I told him to come back here as soon as he found out if there's a window or not." With a quick nod, Cobb backed away from the tree that hid him, and followed the route his brother had taken up the slope.

Having already cut through the bottom strap, Gentry was working furiously away at the top. Timing was going to be important he told himself, so he propped his rifle against the wall next to his leg. He had heard no shots for perhaps ten minutes or so, telling him that Dorsey and Cobb had tired of plinking away at the solid log wall. *They'll shit*, he thought. *By the time they figure out what happened, I'll already have that little squaw bedded down.* He pictured Cobb's look of jealous anger, and smiled.

The top hinge was hanging by a thread now and Gentry prepared for the sudden move. Finally, his knife cut through. The wooden shutter was held in place by nothing more than the tightness of the fit and a latch on the inside. Easing his rifle up with one hand, he placed the other on the edge of the shutter between the severed straps. When he thought he was ready, he suddenly gave the shutter a hard jerk and flung it aside. With a triumphant roar, he quickly brought his rifle up to sight on the startled man at the front window. Before he could pull the trigger, he was staggered by the impact of the arrow that slammed into his throat. His eyes, blown wide-open by the shock, stared in horror at the Indian woman who had just released the bowstring. Too stunned to do anything but drop his rifle and clutch his throat with both hands, he stumbled backward and fell on his back.

Startled as Gentry had been, Levi reacted quickly. Scrambling to his feet, he ran to the back window to discover his would-be assailant struggling to get up from the ground, the arrow protruding all the way through his neck. Gurgling with each panic-stricken breath he attempted, he managed to get to his knees before Levi sent him on his way to hell with one rifle slug through his brain.

Levi looked at Willow, his face reflecting the devastation of his life if he had lost her. She tried to give him a brave look in return as she drew another arrow from the quiver by the fireplace. Thanks to her quickness, there was one less assailant to deal with, but Levi now had to be concerned with an open window behind him while he watched the front. Guessing his concern, Willow notched her arrow, and giving him a reassuring nod, moved closer to the open window.

Halfway down the hill, Cobb Braxton was stopped in his tracks by the sound of the rifle shot from the back of the cabin. Pausing to listen, he wasn't sure whether it sounded like Gentry's rifle or not. He heard no additional shots, so he clamored on down the slope, stopping again about twenty yards from the back corner of the cabin. Although darkness had set in, he could clearly make out the form slumped under the back window. It could be no one but Gentry. The first reaction in Cobb's simple brain was disbelief. It had never entered his mind that anyone but the man in the cabin, and eventually the woman, would die. The sight of Gentry lying dead upon the ground brought confusion and then anger. "You're a dead man, Mister!" he suddenly roared out. "I'm gonna cut you up in little pieces." Unaccustomed to making decisions on his own, however, he knew that first he had to get back to tell Dorsey. He turned then to confront a shadowy figure standing in the trees above him. Surprised, he stopped and called out. "Dorsey?"

"Yeah, Dorsey," Cade Hunter uttered through clenched teeth and pumped two rounds into Cobb's belly. Cade remained where he stood for a minute or two, making sure Cobb was dead before moving off through the forest to take care of the last of the stalkers.

What the hell's goin' on? Dorsey Braxton wondered. Cobb seemed to have been gone for a long time when Dorsey heard the shots on the other side of the cabin. The gunfire worried him. Something was wrong. What had his brothers run into? As a precaution, he decided to change his position and drop back closer to the horses. He suddenly felt a clammy uncertainty about the new quiet that settled around the small cabin after the last two shots. After a few minutes more, he called out. "Cobb? Gentry?" He waited, but there was no answer. With a strong certainty now that something had gone wrong, he decided he'd better move again, this time even closer to the horses.

Inside the darkened cabin, there was an equal amount of uncertainty. Mystified by the last two shots that came from off the back corner of the house, Levi decided to back away from the front window. He motioned for Willow to follow him, and then crawled over to station himself in the middle of the side wall. With his wife behind him, he sat next to the wall where he could watch both front and back windows. There was nothing to do then but wait.

Dorsey shifted his body slowly, making a concerted effort not to cause a sound. Something had happened to his brothers. He was certain of that now. It had been too long without hearing from at least one of them. The leaden quiet of the mountain weighed heavily upon his senses. It was as if all life had ceased, and the longer he knelt there in the dark, the more uneasy he became. He called out to his brothers again and waited for their response. As before, there was only silence, and his mind started working on the possibility that he was alone. The man by the fire with Willow—he had shot him—he was certain of that. There had to be someone else or something prowling these dark woods.

Finally, his sense of self-preservation caused him to wonder whether it was wise to hang around to find out. Maybe he'd better get while the getting was good. Something unnatural was at work here. Once that thought took hold of him, he decided not to linger. He wasn't sure what had hap-

pened to Cobb and Gentry, but he told himself he wasn't
fool enough to wait to find out. His decision made, he gave
no more thought to the fate of his two brothers, but sprang
up from the thicket he had chosen to hide in, and ran for his
horse. The animal sensed his panic and sidestepped away
from him, causing Dorsey to have to grab for the reins and
lunge for the saddle. Getting one foot in the stirrup, he
swung his other leg over, but instead of finding the other
stirrup, he felt two powerful hands around his ankle. In one
continuous move, Cade grabbed Dorsey's leg and pulled the
hapless man off the horse. Dorsey grunted with the pain that
knocked the wind from his lungs when he collided with the
ground. Terrified as if attacked by a demon, he managed to
pull his pistol from his belt. Gasping for breath, he fired
blindly around him, his assailant unseen in the dark. His
shots scattered harmlessly through the trees, except for one.
His horse screamed in pain when the bullet struck it, and it
bolted, revealing the man who had been standing behind it.
Seeing his target at last, Dorsey pulled the trigger, only to
hear the damning click of an empty chamber. Cade unhur-
riedly raised his Winchester and dispatched the last of the
Braxtons to join his brothers and whatever awaited them on
the other side.

Left in a state of total confusion, Levi automatically
shifted his attention from the rear window back to the front
when he heard the burst of gunshots from that direction.
Clueless about what was going on outside the darkened
cabin, he was at a loss as to what actions he could take to
protect Willow and himself. The shots he had heard were not
directed at them. None had hit the cabin walls. With no options available to him but one, he sat against the wall with
Willow pressed close to him, waiting, his rifle aimed at the
door. There was no more shooting, and in a few minutes he
heard the call.

"Levi, are you all right in there?"

Levi sat up straight. "Cade? Is that you?" He could not mistake the familiar voice.

"Yeah," Cade called back. "It's me. I'm comin' in."

Still mystified over what had just happened, Levi went to the door and lifted the bar. Even though he recognized Cade's voice, he stood to one side of the door with his rifle ready to fire. "Come on in, then," he said. In a few moments he released a sigh of relief when the door swung open and it was indeed Cade Hunter. "Boy, am I glad to see you," he exclaimed. "Have they gone?"

"Well, yeah, they're gone, and they ain't comin' back from where they've gone," Cade replied. Then noticing the bloody shoulder, he said, "Damn, looks like you stopped a bullet. You better get that fixed up."

Willow hurried to light a lantern. "I fix that now," she said, and pulled Levi toward a chair at the table.

Impatient to hear what had gone on outside the cabin, Levi pressed Cade for details. He sat quietly and submitted to Willow's doctoring while Cade related the events that led up to the elimination of the other two Braxton brothers. "I don't know how long we coulda held 'em off," Levi admitted. "I didn't have many cartridges left." He paused to think about it. "But where'd you come from? You were long gone."

"I took the short trail down, and they musta come up the way you hauled me up on the travois. I was already down the mountain when I heard the shootin'. I wish I coulda got here sooner, but that's a steep climb back up, and I had to walk and lead my horse most of the way."

"Well, friend," Levi exclaimed. "I'm mighty grateful you showed up when you did. You sure as hell saved our bacon, didn't he, Willow?"

The Blackfoot woman looked up from Levi's wound and smiled at Cade. "We owe you much," she said.

Cade nodded and said, "I just lost one friend. I couldn't afford to lose two more."

There was not much they could do about cleaning up after the attack until daylight. Levi went out with Cade while he brought his and two of the Braxtons' horses in. One of the horses was missing, the one that Dorsey shot. "I'll try to find him in the mornin'," Cade said as they stood over Dorsey's body with a lantern. "Reckon I'll take care of him and the others in the mornin', too."

"He don't look like he's goin' anywhere," Levi said.

"Are these the men you and Willow were runnin' from?" Cade asked.

"Yep," Levi replied. "They're the ones."

"Well, I reckon you and Willow don't have to run any-more."

"Reckon not." The thought just then struck him that this was a fact. There was no longer a need for him and his wife to hide out in the mountains, fearful that someone might find them. "I reckon not," he repeated, now with a different tone. A sudden feeling of freedom came upon him as he realized the significance of the night's conflict. "Hell, let's leave the bastards where they lay tonight. Maybe the wolves'll eat 'em. Let's go build up the fire and fix us somethin' to eat. Me and Willow was about to cook some supper when they hit us."

All had not escaped harm, however. When they led the three horses back to the lean-to that Levi used as a stable, it was to find his horse lying dead, a victim of the barrage laid down by the three brothers. The horse had been shot several times in the head and neck, evidence of a deliberate execution of the animal. The loss of the horse lent a sad note to Levi's feeling of celebration over his new freedom. But

Cade remembered that out in the forest somewhere there was still a horse with a bullet wound. He would have to wait till morning to find out if it was dead or alive.

There was work to be done when morning came to the little cabin high up in the mountains. Utilizing the two Braxton horses as a team, Cade dragged Levi's horse to a cliff on the opposite side of the mountain that dropped two hundred feet to a ridge below. Dumping the carcass at the rim of the cliff, it was almost as much work to force it over the edge as it was to haul it up there. Finally, after chopping down a small tree to use as a lever, he was able to move enough of the carcass over the edge that it fell on its own. Later, Cade returned to drop three bodies to the rocky ridge below to join Levi's horse. The last to go over was Gentry Braxton's body with Willow's arrow still protruding awkwardly out of his throat. His grim chore finished, Cade stood on the brink of the cliff looking down at the previous night's carnage. Two of those men below him on the rocks had met their death at his hand. Just as there was no satisfaction in that fact, there was also no sorrow. Like the killing of mad dogs or preying wolves, it was a cold act of necessity. There was passion in his heart for only one killing, Lem Snider, and he reminded himself that it was time now to get on with it.

Dorsey Braxton's horse wandered back early that morning looking none the worse for its wound. The pistol bullet had struck the animal high in the left withers, where it had lodged deep in the muscle. There had been a minimal amount of blood from the hole in the horse's hide, so Levi said he would watch it, and if it festered, he'd try to remove the bullet. All told, the Braxton brothers left Levi and Willow quite a bit better supplied, with an extra horse, saddles, tack, guns, and ammunition. There was even a sack of coffee beans in one of the saddlebags. Cade satisfied his need for a packhorse with one of the horses. He decided to take the one with a bullet in him instead of leaving it with Levi. In truth, Cade had to admit that Loco picked the horse, as it had originally picked Cade. Lucky, as Cade decided to call the sorrel gelding, was the only horse of the three that Loco had not tried to take a nip out of.

"If I can ever help you," Levi started as Cade tied down the pack he had fashioned on Lucky's back.

"Don't mention it," Cade interrupted. "You and Willow took real good care of me. I owed you, and I'm glad I was able to repay you in some fashion." He turned to give Willow a smile. "Take care of him, Willow." She nodded, smiling. Turning back to Levi, he asked, "You gonna stay up here on this mountain?"

"I don't know," Levi answered. "For a while yet, I guess. Since there ain't no reason not to, we might decide to go down below where the winters ain't so rough—maybe someday head north to find Willow's folks. She don't complain none about it, but I know she'd like to see her people again." He looked at his wife and grinned. "I don't know if that would be a smart thing for me to do, though. The Blackfoot ain't really partial to white men."

"That's somethin' to think about all right," Cade said, and stepped up in the saddle.

"Good luck to you, Cade," Levi said. He and Willow watched until the rider and horses disappeared below the ridge. "You know what I think?" he said to his wife. "I think the Good Lord was lookin' to answer our prayers when he sent Cade Hunter floatin' down that river to come back from the dead and help us."

Willow looked up into Levi's homely face and smiled, nodding her agreement. She had heard of stranger tales at the feet of her grandfather when she was a small girl.

Chapter 8

Trying to follow tracks that had long since grown cold, Cade gave up after a while and followed the river back toward Bozeman. With nothing to go on, he decided he had no choice but to cover every town he could find, hoping to strike a trail. It was a reasonable conclusion that Snider had not tried to follow the river south through wild rocky passes that led deeper into the rugged mountains. Snider had to assume that everyone who knew about the gold was dead, so he was most likely heading for places where he could spend his fortune.

It was just at nightfall when he rode into Bozeman. He decided the first place to get information was the small stable at the edge of town, so he pointed Loco toward the open end of the building.

"I was just fixin' to go get me some supper," the owner of the stable said when Cade rode up. "If you're wantin' to leave your horses, you can unsaddle 'em and turn 'em out in the corral. I'll take care of 'em when I get back."

"I wasn't plannin' on leavin' 'em," Cade said. "I was hopin' you might have seen a man I'm lookin' for."

"Oh . . ." the owner replied, obviously disappointed that Cade wasn't a customer. "Who you lookin' for?"

"A fellow named Lem Snider—kinda tall, bushy whiskers, got a piece of his ear—" That's as far as he got before the stable owner interrupted.

"Oh, Lem Snider, yeah I know him. He comes through town every now and then. I bought a couple of horses offa him a week or two ago."

"Is he still around?" Cade asked.

"I ain't seen him. I doubt it, though. He seemed in kind of a hurry. Go ask Tim Hardy in the saloon yonder. That was where you'd most likely find Lem Snider and his friends if you were lookin' for him—which most folks weren't." He hesitated for a moment, watching Cade's reaction. When there was none, he squinted his eyes in an effort to scrutinize Lucky more closely. "That horse has got a bullet hole in him."

"Yep," Cade replied.

"He don't seem to mind it much, does he?"

"Nope." Cade turned to look up the dusty street in the direction the man had indicated. "Much obliged," he said, and pointed Loco toward the saloon.

"Yeah, he was in here a week or so ago," Tim Hardy said in answer to Cade's inquiry. "You a friend of his?"

"Nope, I'm just lookin' for him," Cade replied.

"Well, like I said, he was in here—didn't have his usual riffraff with him this time." The bartender eyed the young stranger up and down, wondering what business he had with Lem Snider. "He walked in like he'd just robbed a bank or somethin'," Hardy went on. "Bought drinks for everybody in the saloon." He smiled and grunted when recalling it. "Damned if I've ever seen him do that before. I wouldn't be surprised if he did rob a bank." He cocked a curious eye at Cade then. "That ain't why you're lookin' for him, is it?"

"No, I've got some lead that belongs to him," Cade answered, thinking of the bullet still lodged in his chest. He saw no reason to mention Luke's murder and the stolen gold dust.

"Well, he didn't stay around long—left the next day, I think."

"Did he say where he was goin'?"

"No."

"Well, much obliged," Cade said and started for the door.

"I don't know why you wanna find Lem Snider, but you be careful, young feller. That man's as liable to shoot you in the back as say good mornin'."

Cade acknowledged the warning with a simple wave of his hand as he walked out the door. Outside, he stopped to study the night sky for a few minutes. It was going to be a cool evening. When the sun came up in the morning, he could go east, back toward Coulson where he and Luke had run into Snider, or he could ride west. Where would a man like Snider likely gravitate? Away from law and order, Cade speculated, and decided to gamble on west. With that settled, he stepped up in the saddle and headed back to the river to make camp for the night.

A full day's ride brought him to Three Forks, where three rivers converged to make up the headwaters of the Missouri. There at a trading post, a man named Lewis remembered someone of Snider's description stopping there to buy some supplies. He didn't recall the name, but Cade felt sure it was Snider. It was enough to encourage him that he had lucked onto the right trail. Snider was definitely riding west. With no further sign of the man, Cade was forced to gamble again. He could have followed the Madison River south to Virginia City, or gone north along the Gallatin to connect with the Missouri River. From what Luke had told him about Lem Snider, Cade guessed he was the kind of man who would head for the most wide-open town he could find.

Cade's first thought was Virginia City, even though its hey-
day was long past. Lewis had told him that the hot spot now
was Butte, a day and a half's ride from Three Forks. Left
with choices between Butte and Virginia City, Cade decided
on Butte.

Lewis had not exaggerated when he said that Butte was a
bustling town. First starting as a gold mining camp in 1864,
it continued to attract miners with the discovery of silver,
which contributed to the town's influx of people in the sev-
enties. The most recent addition to Butte's wealth was the
appearance of copper. According to a bartender named Zeke
in the first saloon Cade visited, some folks thought copper
might be the gold of the future. Cade had little interest in
prospecting for the treasure lying underneath Butte's soil.
His thoughts were on finding one man, Lem Snider. The bartender could not recall hearing of a man by that name, nor
seeing a man of his description. There were many other saloons, stores, and stables in the town in which to inquire. All
brought the same results. No one knew anything about Lem
Snider, and Cade had to finally conclude that Snider had not
come this way. After three days spent in Butte, Cade was
ready to leave, after having seen enough of the rowdy boom-
town and searching out every corner he could find.

Frustrated, but still maintaining his patience, he sat by his
campfire a few miles west of town trying to decide what to
do. Butte was the kind of place that should attract the likes
of Lem Snider. His last stop in Butte had been to pay a return visit to Zeke at the first saloon. The bartender seemed
to know more about what was going on in the town than any
of the others. Zeke suggested that he should try Helena, a
town that four men from Georgia had struck gold in about
the same time it was found in Butte. Cade thanked him and
determined to set out for Helena the next day.

*   *   *

Half a day out of Butte, Cade was in the process of checking his cinch after having stopped to rest the horses. Standing by a wide stream that meandered along the eastern side of a narrow valley, he was startled when suddenly a horse emerged from the thick firs that bordered the creek. Splashing through the water at a lope, it had scarcely passed by the surprised man when it was followed by two more. Their hooves spraying water almost to the toes of his boots as he stood there astonished, they loped off after the first horse. A few seconds later, another horse appeared, this one with a rider. A small fellow, Cade thought at first, but as the rider approached, he saw that it was a boy of ten or twelve.

Cade sized up the situation in a second, and concluded that the youngster wasn't making much headway in turning the horses around, as it appeared he was desperately trying to do. Without giving it another thought, Cade jumped in the saddle and gave Loco his heels. Angling across the stream, Loco hit the opposite bank at a gallop. An experienced cow pony, the horse knew exactly what was required of him, and soon headed off the three fleeing horses. Cade slowed the lead horse and turned it, pulling all three back to a walk. By the time the boy caught up to them, the three horses were standing peacefully with Cade's horses.

There was a strained look of uncertainty on the youngster's face as he rode up to confront the stranger who had suddenly appeared to take control of the horses. "Those are my pa's horses," he managed with as much authority as he could summon.

Cade smiled at him. "And fine-lookin' horses they are, too. It just looked like they were gettin' a little ahead of you, so I thought I'd give you a hand."

Openly relieved that there was to be no dispute over ownership of the horses, the boy said, "Thanks, Mister. I've been chasin' 'em for half a mile, I bet."

Cade looked around him. "Where'd you come from?" he asked, for there was no sign of anyone else behind the boy.

"Yonder side of that ridge," he replied, pointing toward the western wall of the valley. "We was drivin' 'em down a draw on the other side, and these three slipped over the top."

"You're drivin' a herd of horses on the far side of that ridge?"

"Yes, sir, me and my pa and my brother."

"How many head are you drivin'?" Cade asked.

"Sixty. And I'd best be gettin' these three back before Pa wonders what happened to me."

Cade slowly shook his head, amazed. "How old are you, son?"

"Ten," he answered, sitting up as tall in the saddle as he could.

"Ten," Cade repeated, smiling. "What's your name?"

"Ben."

Cade couldn't help but chuckle. "Well, Ben," he said, "maybe you'd best get these horses back to your pa. Come on, I'll help you drive 'em back." Knowing horses as well as he did, Cade figured the boy probably caused the animals to stray by chasing after them, possibly getting between them and the herd. If left alone, a horse will naturally try to return to the herd. A horse is a scary animal, and when frightened, his instincts tell him to run. He feels safest when he's close in the herd.

Hank Persons pulled his horse to a stop when he saw the three strays coming up from a treeless ravine to rejoin the herd. Starting up again, he immediately reined back hard when he saw his son followed by another rider leading a packhorse. At once concerned, he dropped his hand to rest on the rifle strapped to his saddle. He hailed his elder son riding the other side of the herd. "Johnny! Keep 'em movin' on down the valley." He then rode out to meet Ben and the stranger.

"How do," Hank said guardedly as he came up to face them, glancing from Cade to Ben, and back to Cade again, trying to get a measure of the stranger.

"Howdy," Cade returned.

"He turned them strays around and helped me bring 'em back, Pa," Ben reported.

"Your son didn't need much help. I just mostly followed him back," Cade said. He looked over the herd, noting another youngster on the far side of the slowly moving horses. "You look like you got your hands full, just you and the two boys."

"I reckon we can handle it," Hank said, still wondering if the stranger had any funny business on his mind, like rustling a herd of horses. Shifting his gaze back and forth along the tree line, he searched the edge of the valley half expecting other riders to appear.

"Well," Cade said, "I'll be movin' along. I just wanted to make sure the boy got back all right." He turned Loco's head toward the opposite side of the valley and touched the horse lightly with his heels. "Good day to you," he called back over his shoulder.

The stranger had ridden no more than a dozen yards when Hank made a quick decision. "Hold on, there, Mister," he called out and rode up to catch Cade. "I ain't bein' very neighborly, am I?" He reached over and extended his hand. "My name's Hank Persons, and I wanna thank you for givin' my boy a hand."

Cade smiled and shook his hand. "Cade Hunter—no thanks necessary. Like I said, I mostly just followed him back."

"We're fixin' to stop for some chuck pretty soon. There's a stream at the north end of this valley. You're welcome to join us for a little coffee and beans if you ain't in a hurry to get someplace." Hank told himself he might be making a big mistake. *Lord knows I've sure misjudged some folks before.* But he thought Cade Hunter looked like a decent man. And the truth be told, he had lied when he said he and his sons could handle the horses. He wasn't sure of that at all.

Cade hesitated, then decided. "Sure, why not? I just ate somethin' when I stopped back there to water my horses, but I could use another cup of coffee. Much obliged."

At the end of the valley, Cade helped herd the horses down to the stream to drink. When they were drinking and grazing peacefully, the small family of wranglers gathered to start some coffee to boil. "Well, you already know Ben," Hank said. "This here's my older boy, Johnny."

Cade shook hands with each boy, noting that Johnny couldn't be more than twelve or thirteen. It was a considerable undertaking for a man and two boys that age to drive a herd that size anywhere at all, and he expressed as much to Hank.

"Well, I had a hired hand to help me," Hank confessed, "but he run off with my wife a week ago Tuesday, and left me a little shorthanded." When Cade blinked hard in surprise, Hank continued. "I wouldn'ta minded so much if they'd just waited till I got these horses delivered to Coyote Creek." At a loss for what to say, Cade glanced at the two young boys busily fixing the noon meal. Noticing his concern, Hank said, "They know what it's all about. It don't bother them none."

It was an awkward moment for Cade, but Hank didn't seem overly concerned about it. He pulled a coffeepot from one of the boys' saddlebags and knelt down by the stream to fill it. Cade studied the lean features of his host while he waited for the pot to fill. Hank Persons wore a forlorn expression that Cade at first thought was for the loss of his wife. After talking to the man for a while, however, he decided that forlorn was Hank's natural state. As thin as he was, Cade figured his wife had not been much of a cook.

As if reading Cade's thoughts, Hank blurted, "Ted Randell, that was my hired hand's name. He was pretty good with horses." He shook his head while he thought about it. "Left me and the boys in a bind." He laughed then. "Wait till he finds out what a she-cat he run off with." Cade didn't know whether to laugh or not, so he just nodded. Hank went on. "I noticed when we brung 'em down to water you looked like you ain't no stranger to workin' with horses."

"I've done a bit," Cade replied.

"Where you headin'?"

"I thought I'd go up to Helena," Cade answered, "look around, maybe run into somebody I know there."

"Don't seem like you're in much of a hurry to get there."

Cade shrugged. "Maybe not, just so I get there sometime, I reckon."

"How'd you like to earn a few dollars doin' a little wranglin'?" Hank's sad features took on an even more serious expression as he looked Cade in the eye. "I'll tell you what's the truth, Cade. I could sure as God use some help. I ain't got but two days' drive from here to Coyote Creek where I'm supposed to deliver these horses to Mr. Carlton Kramer's foreman, but I'm afeared it might be a little too much for my young'uns to move 'em through the mountain passes between here and the prairie. Make it a lot easier if I had one more experienced man to help out." He paused, waiting for Cade's reply. "Whaddaya say, Cade?"

Cade took a moment to weigh his priorities. He had a mission to complete, and he wanted that to be over and done with, but Hank did need some help. "I suppose I could lend a hand," he finally said. "Although it looks to me like that boss-mare over there has a pretty tight control on the herd." He motioned toward a white mare standing a few yards away from the other horses. Cade had picked her out as soon as they had reached the stream and the other horses waited to drink until after she'd had her fill. Looking at her now as she grazed peacefully on the other side of the stream, Cade knew without looking that the other horses were relaxed and peaceful as well. "Seems to me if you can get her to go where you want, the rest of 'em will go with her."

Hank glanced over at the mare when Cade gestured. "What you said right there is why I want you to go with us," he stated.

Cade grinned. "Well, what the hell," he said, "if Ben don't mind, then I reckon I'll come along." He reached over and tipped the boy's hat over his eyes.

Both boys laughed, and Ben pushed his hat up and replied, "I reckon I don't mind, Pa." Hank extended his hand and he and Cade shook on it.

While they were drinking their coffee, Cade asked, "Who is Mr. Carlton Kramer?"

"If you was from around here, you'd know who Mr. Kramer was," Hank replied. "He's got a butcher shop in every minin' town and gold camp in the territory." Hank flashed a quick grin when Cade looked concerned and glanced at the horses grazing peacefully. "He needs horses to tend the cattle he raises for the butcher shops. I expect he's the biggest cattle rancher in the territory, too."

Cade laughed. "For a minute there . . ."

For the next couple of days, Cade found peace again doing what he loved best: working with horses. Lem Snider was not forgotten, but the bushwhacking murderer was pushed to the back of Cade's mind as he helped Hank and his sons deliver the herd to Coyote Creek. It was late morning when they drove the horses through a narrow pass that led to a wide expanse of bunchgrass prairie. A creek ran along the base of the hills they had just left. On the other side of the creek, Cade saw a small shack and a series of rough corrals. Hank had explained that Kramer used the place to train the wild horses he bought to herd his cattle out on the free range. A couple of men rode out to meet them as they herded the horses toward the creek. One sat ramrod straight in the saddle, and he rode with his elbows sticking out like wings. He looked to be older than Hank, with gray sideburns. The man beside him appeared to be Indian.

The white man greeted them. "Howdy, Hank. We figured you oughta be showin' up any day now." He looked over at Cade and the boys. "See you got a new man. Where's Randell?"

"He lit out for parts unknown," Hank replied. "Reckon he got the itch to wander." He didn't bother to mention the baggage his hired hand had taken with him. "This here's Cade Hunter." Cade nodded.

"I'm Jack Walker," the foreman said. Tilting his head toward the rider next to him, he added, "This here's Jim Big Tree." Walker looked Cade over before asking, "That a '73 Winchester you carrying there?" He didn't wait for Cade to answer. "I hope you know how to use it. You might need it." Looking back at Hank, he explained, "We've been havin' a little trouble with Injuns. There's been a couple of raidin' parties hit us durin' the past two weeks. Jim says they're Blackfoot. We didn't have no horses the last time they hit, so they just snooped around and left. Time before that, they run off fifteen head, so if they've still got scouts watchin' us, we might get a visit from 'em again." He gazed at Cade. "So I hope you're handy with that Winchester, young feller."

"I expect I'm a fair shot," Cade answered, "but I wasn't

plannin' on stayin'. I was just helpin' Hank and the boys drive their horses this far, and then I'm on my way to Helena."

When Walker's expression showed a trace of disappointment, Hank spoke up. "That's right, Jack, Cade just said he'd help us as far as Coyote Creek." He glanced at Cade then. "I owe you some pay, too."

Cade shrugged. "You don't owe me anything. I'm glad I could help."

"I'da had to pay Ted Randell," Hank countered.

"All the same, we'll call it even," Cade said.

Jack Walker listened to the exchange between the two, thinking that with the threat of Blackfoot raiding parties about, he'd feel a hell of a lot more comfortable if they'd all stay around for a while. "Listen, fellers," he said, "Mr. Kramer is sendin' a crew over here from Deer Lodge to break these horses. I expect they'll show up any day now, but in the meantime, me and Jim are gonna have our hands full holdin' on to 'em if we get hit by Injuns again. I can guarantee you wages—the boys, too—if you'll stick around till they show up."

"Hell," Hank replied at once, "me and my boys will stay. We ain't in no hurry to get back." He glanced over at Johnny and grinned. "Hell, we don't have to get back a'tall, do we?"

Cade thought about it for a minute, then shrugged. "I reckon I can stay and help out."

"I appreciate it," Walker said. "If it's the same bunch that comes back, there ain't but about twelve of 'em, and they know there was only Jim Big Tree and me to take care of the horses. By God, we can give 'em more'n they bargained for if they make a try for these horses." He paused, then asked Hank, "Those boys know how to use a rifle, I reckon?"

"Ever since they was old enough to lift one," Hank answered.

Walker suggested that they should pair off and guard the herd after nightfall. "Might not have to do it but one or two nights. The crew from Deer Lodge oughta be here by then." He looked at the two young sons of Hank and said, "We can split the boys up—maybe one with me and the little feller with you, Hank."

Ben spoke up. "I wanna go with Cade. We've already worked together."

"Well, I don't know," Jack said, looking at the boy's father, thinking that he might want his younger where he could personally keep an eye on him. "Whaddaya say, Hank?"

Hank shrugged. It was already obvious to him that Ben had taken a shine to the young man from Colorado. "Is that all right with you, Cade?" he asked.

"Why, sure," Cade replied at once. "Me and Ben make a good team." The boy beamed, and walked over to stand next to Cade.

Walker smiled as well. "All right, whaddaya say Cade and Ben take the first watch? Hank, you got any preference?" When Hank volunteered to take the second watch with Johnny, Jack said, "Me and Jim'll take over till sunup, then."

With that settled, they moved the herd farther out in the prairie to keep the grass from being overgrazed near the camp. When the sun started sinking low on the horizon, Jack and Jim Big Tree rode back to start supper, leaving the others to bring the horses back close to camp. "Come on, Ben," Cade said, "we'll show 'em how to move those horses where we want 'em."

"I expect you'll need some help," Hank said.

"Nah, we don't need any help, do we, Ben?"

"Nope," Ben replied confidently and pulled his horse up beside Loco while Hank and Ben's brother held back to watch. When Ben was close to Cade, he leaned forward in the stirrups and quietly asked, "How you wanna do it?"

"Let's do it the easy way," Cade said as he started Loco forward with Ben keeping pace beside him. Holding Loco to an easy walk, he headed toward the white mare grazing near a blue roan stallion that was obviously the leader of the greatest part of the herd. Ben, knowing the roan to be the leader, started for him. Cade held him back. "Never mind about ol' stud there," Cade said. "You go on up and turn that white mare. She's the boss-mare. The others will follow her, even the stallions." He held his horse back while Ben approached the mare. "Let her know you're the boss," Cade called after him.

A curious audience of Hank and Johnny watched in openmouthed surprise as little Ben rode brazenly up to the mare and effectively turned her toward the camp. As soon as she lifted her head and loped away, she was followed by the rest of the horses, the blue roan stallion right behind her with a group of bachelor stallions bringing up the rear. "Look at that," Hank chuckled.

"He's already too big for his britches," Johnny mumbled.

When the horses were back in close to the camp, everybody helped drive them into the two largest corrals. That taken care of, all hands took a little time to eat supper. As the sun gradually sank behind the mountains behind them, Cade and Ben prepared to take their turn as nighthawks. "Ben, you keep your eyes open," Hank couldn't resist cautioning his younger son.

"Pa," Ben complained, embarrassed, "you don't have to tell me that."

Cade was careful not to show the smile the ten-year-old's remark caused. Ben was a rambunctious kid, eager to fill a man's role. Cade understood that. It was reminiscent of an-

other kid he remembered: young Cade Hunter. That youngster had taken on the role of executioner of the men who
killed his father. It was something Cade tried not to think
about too often. Looking now at young Ben Persons, he
hoped the child would never know the burden of living with
something like that on his conscience. Realizing he had permitted his mind to wander to unpleasant places, he shrugged
and blinked away the dark memories. "Come on, partner,"
he said to Ben. "We'd better get on the job."

According to what Jack Walker had told them, the
Blackfoot raiding party had come down from the mountains
to the north, probably following the river. Walker had figured that, if it was the same bunch of Indians, they would be
discouraged by the sight of more men in the camp, and
might decide it was not worth the risk. Cade was inclined to
agree, but he felt the responsibility of taking care of Ben. So
he stationed Ben at the back corner of the upper corral, the
one closest to the shack. He didn't tell Ben that they had decided to give him and Cade the first watch out of concern for
the boy's safety. Jim Big Tree and Walker figured if they
were raided, it would most likely come in the hours before
dawn, just as before.

As hard dark set in, the two lookouts took a wide tour
around the corrals to make sure everything was peaceful.
Then Cade sent Ben back to his post with instructions to fire
his rifle in the air if he saw anyone approaching the corral.
"And everybody'll come a'runnin'. You see that stand of
pines over there?" he said, pointing toward a spot near the
base of the hills north of the camp. "That's where I'll be, so
make sure you don't shoot me if you see me comin'." Seeing
a questioning look on the boy's face, he was quick to assure
him. "I'll be comin' over to check on you every half hour or
so. If you need me, just whistle like a whip-poor-will three
times. You can do that, can't you?" He demonstrated, and

Ben immediately imitated his whistle. "Right," Cade said. "You do it better'n I do."

"We have been away from our village a long time. I think it is time we returned home." Running Fox tore another strip of meat from the portion of deer haunch roasting over the fire. It was the same conclusion that his friend Bear Track had come to. The Blackfoot raiding party had been away for more than two weeks, and their village was a long way from this valley where so many white men now lived. Starting out with twelve warriors, they had been successful in running off fifteen horses from the white man's camp at the edge of the hills. Half of their raiding party returned with the stolen horses, but Bloody Feathers, Running Fox, and four others elected to stay and plan for a second raid on the camp. When they scouted the camp a week later, there were no horses in the pens the white men had erected, only a couple of horses the two men rode—and these were kept too close to the hut to chance stealing.

Running Fox had been in favor of going home when their second attempt brought no results, but the others, especially his wife's brother, Bloody Feathers, argued that there was no honor in returning to the village with nothing to show for their lengthy absence. Consequently, they had spent the past seven days scouting the valleys beyond these mountains, only to find that the white man had arrived in too many numbers, building villages and digging the dirt they found so precious from the hills and streams. Now, ready to leave for home, they waited while Bear Track made one last scout on the camp at the foot of the hills. "We have taken their horses," Running Fox had insisted. "They do not have any more horses. They are probably gone from that camp." Bloody Feathers had argued that Bear Track might as well make sure. So they sat by the fire and waited for his return.

"Someone comes!" one of the warriors whispered, and the others grabbed their weapons and quickly moved away from the fire. The warning was followed a few seconds later by the confirmation that it was Bear Track returning.

Running into their midst, Bear Track exclaimed excitedly, "Many ponies! The white men have brought more ponies!"

His news caused immediate reaction from his fellow warriors. "How many?" Bloody Feathers asked.

"I don't know," Bear Track replied. "I couldn't count them—maybe fifty or more. But they are grazing a long way from the camp where the white men live."

"Are there still only two white men to guard them?"

"No," Bear Track answered. "I saw four more, but two of them are only children."

While his friends rejoiced over an opportunity to steal more horses, Running Fox considered the news that Bear Track had brought. The two white men who were living in the hut had the rifles that shoot many times. Maybe their friends had the same weapons. It would be unwise to try to make a surprise raid on the herd of horses. He, Bloody Feathers, and Bear Track had single-shot rifles. The other three had only bows. When the warriors' initial excitement settled down, Running Fox counseled on the folly of matching weapons with the white men. "We will go after these horses, but we will have to wait until darkness so that we can surprise them. Their guns are too strong."

There was no disagreement with his advice, for they all knew about the repeating rifles. It did not dampen their enthusiasm for the raid, however. "Maybe we can kill some of them and take their guns that shoot many times," Bear Track said. He smiled at Bloody Feathers. "I could kill many enemies with a gun like that."

*   *   *

It was a long time coming, but night finally descended upon the mountains, and the small raiding party quietly made their way down a wooded ravine toward the valley. Much to their disappointment, the horses were no longer grazing free on the open prairie. They had been driven back to be penned in the large corrals near the hut. This called for a new plan of attack. Heading back toward the white men's camp, they trotted along in single file, hugging the base of the hills and the cover the trees afforded. When within fifty yards of the corrals, Running Fox halted the party and looked the situation over.

"There are no guards in sight," Bear Track whispered. "They all sleep in the hut."

Running Fox was not so sure. "They wouldn't leave all those horses unguarded," he said. "I think maybe there are guards hiding where we cannot see them." He studied the scene a few moments longer. "I think they would see us if we try to cross all this open space between here and the pens. I think it would be better to climb up this hill and come down near their hut. Then we can climb over the fence and take out the rails, and drive the horses out the back of the pen." He paused then and looked around him at his fellow warriors. "That is just what I think. What does someone else say?" The plan seemed good to the others, so they started up through the trees.

Young Ben Persons watched Cade Hunter's back until the rangy man from Colorado was enveloped in the darkness and had faded from sight. Then he settled himself again with his back against a sizable boulder near a rear corner of the corral. Though only ten, he was certain that he could handle himself as well as the adults, so he was a little disappointed that Cade had chosen to station him in a safe place close to the cabin. Clutching his 1864 model Spencer carbine, he felt confident and unafraid, proud that Cade had welcomed him as a partner. He had heard the men talking, so he knew they expected no trouble until the hours preceding dawn. But if the Blackfoot raiders showed up sooner than expected, he would give them something to think about. He was a good shot with the surplus army rifle, and he told himself he wouldn't hesitate to shoot the sneaky horse thieves.

The night wore on, and Ben shifted his body several times when the hard ground began to become uncomfortable. From his position, he could see the back rails of the two big corrals as well as the sides of one of them. After what seemed an eternity, he heard a soft whistle. He immediately answered it, and a few seconds later, Cade emerged from the darkness, leading his horse.

"How you doin', partner?" Cade asked.

"I'm okay," Ben answered boldly. "Is it time to get Pa and Johnny?"

"No, we've only been out here for a little over half an hour." Ben couldn't see the smile on Cade's face. "Time just passes slow when you ain't doin' nothin' but waitin'," he said.

"It don't bother me," Ben boasted. "I could stay out here all night if I had to."

"Well, I hope we don't have to," Cade replied. "I'm gonna take a little turn around the far side of the corral and look around. I just wanted to let you know where I was."

Ben watched his partner again until he disappeared around the corner of the corral; then he settled down against the boulder once more. The time began to drag as before, but a short time later he heard a bird call. He answered immediately, smiling to himself. *It didn't sound much like a whip-poor-will,* he thought, and waited for Cade to reappear. No more than a couple of seconds passed when he heard another bird call, this one like the first he had heard, but behind him. Maybe it was a real bird he had heard and not Cade. He got up and moved cautiously toward the fence corner, peering into the darkness. The actions of the next few seconds happened so fast that Ben was helpless to even struggle. The powerful arm that trapped him pinned his rifle to him, holding him captive while a hand clamped over his mouth so tightly that he couldn't make a sound.

Bear Track had been unaware of the boy's presence on the other side of the boulder until Ben unwittingly answered Bloody Feathers' signal. Surprised to find the sentinel was a mere child, Bear Track quickly sprang upon him, but found the boy to be a handful. Ben struggled to free himself, causing Bear Track to hold him even tighter. He intended to silence the boy permanently, but he found he could not free a hand to draw his knife without chancing a shout from Ben to alert those sleeping in the hut. Seeing no alternative, he carried Ben back up the hill into the firs, seeking a place where the child could not be heard.

Terrified now that he found himself helpless against the strength of the savage arms that bound him, Ben continued to struggle, but to no avail. He was transported back up into the forest as easily as if he were a sack of flour, his attempts to call for help no more than muffled murmurs.

Moving as fast as he could, for he knew the others waited for him to remove the rails in the corral, Bear Track slammed the boy down under the limbs of a fir tree. With one hand holding Ben down by his throat, he released the other hand and snatched his knife from his belt. One forceful strike through the youngster's chest should finish him quickly. He raised the knife high over his head, then thrust downward only to meet with a steel grip that caught his wrist—at the same time feeling a pistol barrel against his side, a split second before the revolver fired. Bear Track stiffened as the bullet tore into his insides, causing him to release his hold on the boy's throat. In desperation, he tried to turn to face his assailant. With one wrist still entrapped, he clawed at Cade with his other hand until the pistol fired again, ending his struggles.

Below them, at the foot of the hill, Cade could hear the sounds of alarm from the cabin as the others clamored to fend off the attack. He shoved Bear Track's body over, freeing the stunned ten-year-old. "Are you all right?" he asked, as Ben gasped for air. Still too frightened to speak, Ben nodded his head frantically. "Come on, then," Cade said, and started back down through the trees. "Stay close," he added.

By the time they reached the spot at the bottom of the hill where Cade had tied Loco, they could hear the rapid gunfire and shouts of the men now running to stop the raiders. Running Fox had managed to withdraw the top pole in the corral gate. When the pistol shots alerted the white men in the cabin, the raiders had to abandon plans to open the gate and drive all the horses out. Running Fox and Bloody Feathers, now inside the corral, made a desperate attempt to escape. They each jumped upon the back of a horse, and guiding the animal by grasping its ears, charged out of the corral, holding on with knees and hands as the horses jumped the lower rails of the gate. Running Fox hoped that other horses would follow, but Jim Big Tree and Jack Walker got to the gate quickly and drove the rest of the horses back. Right behind them, Hank turned to send a couple of rifle shots after the fleeing Indians. Seeing the raid hopeless, the remaining members of the party fled after Running Fox and Bloody Feathers.

Emerging from the trees in time to see the two Indians gallop away with two horses, Cade shouted to Ben, "Go over there with your pa and Johnny, and be careful who you aim that damn rifle at." Then he jumped up in the saddle and

urged Loco after the retreating Indians in an effort not to
lose them in the dark.

Racing across the grassy plain, he could barely make out
the two shadowy images ahead of him as they galloped toward the pass north of the camp. He urged Loco onward and
the horse responded eagerly, slowly cutting the distance between him and the Indians. Just before reaching the pass,
one of the horses veered off to his left, heading back toward
the hills behind the camp. Quickly deciding he had to follow
in case the Indian was going back to make another attempt
at the horses, Cade let the other raider go.

With the horses rapidly tiring, Cade followed the
Blackfoot up through the trees on the hillside. Once in the
midst of the firs that covered the west side of the hill, Cade
pulled up and dismounted, lest he run headlong into an ambush. The darkness was heavy and still in the forest, but he
could hear the Indian moving some forty yards ahead of
him. Looking around to orient himself, he realized the
Blackfoot warrior was making his way back toward the spot
where Cade had killed the first raider.

He could see him now, a lone Blackfoot warrior, leading
the horse back downhill, having fashioned a hasty bridle
with a rope. Cade looped Loco's reins over a fir bough and
followed. He could have shot the Indian on the spot, but he
decided that the warrior was only intent upon recovering the
body of his friend. Convinced that the raid was over, Cade
saw no reason to kill the man.

A few yards farther down through the trees and Cade's
speculation proved to be accurate. With his rifle slung on his
back, Running Fox was bending over the slain warrior. He
grasped him under the arms and started to lift him up when
he suddenly froze. Cade looked beyond him to see Ben stepping out from a low bush, his rifle pointed at the Indian.

In the darkened forest, Cade could not see Ben's eyes

wide with indecision, his hand trembling on the trigger
guard, as man and boy stood immobile in a brief vacuum of
time. The momentary image of another ten-year-old flashed
across Cade's mind, and he called out, "Ben! Don't shoot!
Let him go. Let him take his dead and go." Ben hesitated, and
Cade emerged from the brush behind Running Fox. Startled
by Cade's sudden appearance, Running Fox dropped Bear
Track's body and started to reach for his knife. Cade quickly
leveled his Winchester and aimed it at Running Fox's belly,
discouraging the Indian's desperate attempt. Moving between the raider and the boy, Cade said calmly, "Put it down,
Ben. We'll let him take his dead home. No need for any more
killin'."

Caught in total confusion now, Running Fox waited for
the rifle shot that would send him to the spirit world, knowing he could not get his own rifle off his back in time to save
his life. Cade stood squarely before him and motioned with
his rifle. "Go ahead and take your friend," he said, but
Running Fox knew no English. Finally, after Cade motioned
several times more, the Blackfoot warrior understood.
Nodding slowly, he reached down and grasped Bear Track
again. Pulling him upright, he let the body fall across his
shoulder. Cade offered no help. With the rifle still leveled at
the Indian, he watched as Running Fox struggled to heft
Bear Track's body up on the horse. Once the body was settled and secure, Running Fox turned back to look at the man
watching him. He nodded solemnly, then turned and led the
horse back the way he had come.

"Damn!" Ben exhaled after the Indian had gone, swal-
lowed up by the dark forest on the hillside. That was all he
said for a few moments, then, "I was gonna shoot him."

"I know you were, but there wasn't no use to shoot him.
He was just tryin' to carry that other feller back home. He
didn't have it in his mind to cause no more trouble." He

knew from bitter experience that ten was too tender an age to carry an image of a man dead by your hand. "Let me get Loco, and let's get back before your pa starts worrying about you." He started toward the brush where Loco was tied. "What were you doin' here, anyway? I thought I told you to go with your pa."

"You did," Ben admitted, "but I just wanted to see if that one you killed was still here."

Back by the corral, a relieved Hank Persons came forward to meet Cade and Ben when they walked across the clearing between the cabin and the trees. "Ben, where the hell did you run off to?" Hank demanded.

"He was with me, chasin' off them last two Injuns," Cade said.

"I was worried about you, boy," Hank said.

"I was with Cade," Ben assured him, as if that should tell his father that he was in no danger.

"Lost two horses," Jack Walker announced as he and Jim Big Tree joined them. "I reckon that ain't as bad as it coulda been. At least nobody got shot." Although everyone agreed that the Blackfoot raiding party would not likely try again after they found out how much firepower the camp could deliver, they didn't chance leaving the herd unguarded through the rest of the night.

Chapter 9

Cade sat on his blanket, drinking his coffee, staring thought-fully out across the prairie toward the east where the sun threatened to rise at any minute. Summer was getting thin now, and the mornings were chilly. Soon he would be awakening to find frost on the bunchgrass of the valley. He took a cautious sip of the bitter black liquid, careful that the metal cup might still be too hot to touch to his lips. The coffee was strong and good, and warmed him all the way down to his belly. Many thoughts wandered across his mind, and he figured it was time for him to move on. He had agreed to stay until Mr. Kramer and his crew arrived from Deer Lodge, and according to Jack Walker's expectations, that should be any day now. The picture of the Blackfoot warrior bending over his dead friend returned to remind him that he could have recovered one of the missing horses. All he had to do was pull the trigger, or let Ben take the burden on his young conscience. He wasn't sure why he had spared the Indian. It just seemed like there was no sense in killing him. Indians found honor in stealing horses. They'd made a try for Kramer's horses and failed. Why not let it go at that? *Besides,* he thought, thinking of Levi and Willow, *the fellow might have been Levi's brother-in-law.* The idle speculation brought a faint smile to his face. Other thoughts came to replace thoughts of Levi and Willow. The activity of the last few days had pushed Lem Snider to the back of his mind. He told himself that he could not forget his promise to Luke Tucker. It would be a sin before God to let Snider get away with Luke's murder. In spite of that, he had to admit that he was no closer to finding Lem Snider than he had been the day he left Levi's cabin on the mountain. After leaving Butte, the man seemed to have disappeared. Cade's plans to go to Helena were no better than a miner scratching around in the ground hoping gold might be under it. He had no reason to believe that Snider might be in Helena, but he didn't know of any better place to look.

In the afternoon of the second day after the Blackfoot raid, Carlton Kramer, with five men and a wagon of supplies, arrived at the Coyote Creek camp. A man of medium height, Kramer seemed to stand taller, carrying the confidence of a man accustomed to leading. With dark, wavy hair and a full beard, he presented a handsome figure of a successful man. Cade felt he was in the presence of one who could build an empire in whatever field he endeavored.

Kramer expressed his appreciation to Cade, Hank, and Hank's two sons for staying on to help guard the horses. When he learned that Cade was on his own with no ties to Hank, he conferred with his foreman, Jack Walker, about the young man and the possibility of hiring him to ride with Jack's crew.

Walker told him that Cade had been responsible for the one warrior who was killed in the raid, and that Cade had showed no lack of courage when he chased after the two stolen horses. "He helped Hank Persons bring the herd over here, and Hank said he's never seen a man better at under-standin' horses than Cade. From what I've seen, he'd be a damn good man to have on the payroll."

"That's good enough for me," Kramer said and immediately approached Cade with a job offer.

"Well, I hadn't really thought about anything but ridin' up to Helena to take care of some business for a friend of mine," Cade said in answer to Kramer's offer.

"Jack says you're a good hand with horses," Kramer replied. "I can always use a good man." He paused a moment, sensing that Cade was giving it serious thought. "I pay top wages, and you'll be working with a fine crew."

Cade had to think about it. He needed the money, and Kramer was offering him work right through the winter. But it was hard to shake the feeling that he was letting Luke down. However, with Kramer growing impatient for his decision, Cade took the offer, silently promising Luke that it would not destroy his promise, only delay it. "Good," Kramer said. "If you're as good as Hank says you are, then I'm sure Jack can put you to work right now breaking those horses."

Early the next morning, Hank and his sons prepared to start back home. Hank pulled Cade aside while Johnny and Ben were saddling the horses. He extended his hand, and Cade shook it. "Cade, I'm much obliged for your help. Them horses would have been a handful without you." The wide grin on his face faded to a more serious expression, and he lowered his voice so the boys would not hear. "I appreciate what you did with little Ben. He told me he was fixin' to shoot that Injun back up on the hill. He was scared to death, and he was some relieved when you let the Injun go." Cade didn't know what to say, so he merely shrugged. "Anyway," Hank said, his voice loud again, "we'll most likely be seein' you again since you'll be workin' with Jack. Won't we, boys?"

"Yes, sir," Johnny said and walked up to shake Cade's hand.

Ben hung back, looking undecided. Finally, he said what was on his mind. "I could stay and work with Cade. Me and Cade are partners. Ain't we, Cade?"

Cade shot a surprised look in Hank's direction, and received a weary smile and a shake of the head in return. Turning back to Ben, he said, "We're partners, sure enough. That's a fact. But your pa needs you to help him. You're too good a hand to lose." When the youngster showed disappointment, Cade strode forward and shook his hand. "Like your pa said, I'll be seein' you from time to time. We'll still be partners. You just be sure you take care of him and your brother."

Resigning himself to the inevitable, Ben smiled and said, "I will." He jumped up to get a foot in the stirrup, then pulled himself up by the saddle horn. The three members of the Persons family turned their horses back toward the mountain pass.

An amused spectator to the farewell, Jack Walker sidled up to stand beside Cade. Chuckling, he asked, "Horses and kids seem to take a likin' to you. How about women?"

"I don't know," Cade answered honestly.

The rest of the week brought long days with the horses, breaking them in to be good working stock to herd Carlton Kramer's cattle. After the first couple of days, Cade found himself in a contest of sorts with Jack Walker's top man, a man named Bucky George, not much older than Cade. The competition, unintentional on Cade's part, came about when the other men noticed the difference in the methods used to break the horses. Bucky was of the old-school method. He believed that brute force was necessary to initially show the horse that he was boss, and there would be painful conse-

quences if the animal did not submit. To Bucky, *breaking* a
horse meant breaking its spirit, a practice that was totally re-
pugnant to Cade, and one he never saw the need to employ.

Cade had learned from his father that a horse is by nature
a frightened animal. In the face of danger, his instincts tell
him to run. He feels safest when his feet are moving, or
when he's in the security of the herd, and feels that he has
the herd leader to guard his safety. A horse is perfectly
happy to be dominated by another horse, or a man, as long
as he feels he is being protected and he can trust the man.
Cade never made any comments about Bucky's methods,
but the rest of the men soon began to notice that the horses
Cade broke were willing to do anything their riders asked.
And, as was bound to happen, the day came when the two
young men had a conflict.

It was late in the afternoon, and Cade was working with
a spirited little bay mare on a lead rope in a makeshift round
pen. It was the last horse for the day. Finished with his
chores, Bucky wandered over to watch. Unable to hold his
comments for very long, he finally dispensed some unso-
licited advice. "You know, Hunter, you'd break as many
horses a day as I do if you didn't pussyfoot around with 'em
like that." Cade ignored the criticism and continued to work
the mare. "I'd have that mare ready to ride by now. The first
thing I'd do is take an ax handle and get her attention, so
she'd know who the boss was."

Bucky kept it up until several of the other men sauntered
up to the pen, sniffing a fight in the air. There was a fair
amount of curiosity about the new man who was so good
with horses. His tendency to keep to himself was cause for
speculation about a possible cautious nature, maybe even a
fear of trouble. The attention only caused Bucky to increase
his comments. "Somebody find me a limb or an ax handle

and I'll jump in there and show the poor bastard how to whip that mare into shape."

Finally Cade could no longer ignore him. "You come in here with a limb and I'll use it across your back," he said in a voice soft but clear.

This was what Bucky was waiting for. For several days, he had been building a jealous need to take some of the quiet coolness out of the new man. He climbed over the top rail and dropped down inside the pen. "I'll whip any damn horse I think needs it," he threatened, "and I'll whip your ass, too, if I think you need it—and I think you just might."

Hearing the hoots and whistles of the spectators gathered around the pen, Jack Walker strode casually over to join them. He had been aware of the gathering storm that was bound to happen between the two ever since Cade signed on. Bucky was proud of his ability to break a horse, so it was natural that he didn't take kindly to his reputation being challenged. Jack could have stopped the trouble right then and there, but he thought it best to let the young men settle it, as long as there were no guns. Besides that, he was kind of curious about the new man himself. He arrived at the rail just in time to hear Cade's reply to Bucky's threat.

Before he said anything, Cade walked the mare over to the gate and handed the lead rope to one of the men. "Turn her out with the others if you don't mind." When the man took the rope and led the mare out of the gate, Cade turned to face his adversary, who was now posturing before his audience. "Now, I reckon you're bound and determined to get yourself a lickin'. And if that's what you want, I reckon I'd be obliged to give it to you."

Bucky could not repress a hoot of joy, and he started for Cade in a run, but was stopped before he reached the center of the pen by a gunshot that brought instant silence to the noisy mob. All eyes turned to see Jack Walker with his pistol still raised overhead. "Get rid of them guns first," he ordered. Both combatants unbuckled their gun belts and hung them on the fence.

Cade turned and took a stance, leaning slightly forward from the waist, his feet planted solidly and wide apart as he waited for the man charging into him. The two were of nearly equal size. It was hard to speculate on which could take the other. Bucky may have had the weight advantage, which could prove important if the fight turned into a wrestling match. Cade, on the other hand, was quicker, with split-second reactions, a fact that was not readily apparent due to his typically reserved demeanor.

As expected, Bucky, headstrong and cocky, charged toward Cade like a runaway locomotive, intent upon running over his opponent, his head down like a battering ram. Cade remained immobile, watching his attacker until the last second when he deftly stepped aside and hammered Bucky with a right hand that, coupled with the force of Bucky's charge, sent his surprised adversary to the ground. Spitting dirt, a result of landing face-first in the corral, Bucky scrambled to his feet, sputtering furiously. Lowering his head again, he waded into Cade, swinging both fists as fast as he could. Cade stepped back, baffled for a moment. The only target presented to him was the top of Bucky's head, and he had no desire to fracture his hands hammering away at a hard skull. Bucky continued to advance, swinging wildly, his eyes on Cade's feet. Realizing he was going to have to take some of the blows in order to straighten Bucky up, Cade stopped retreating and waited. He caught a left and a right on the sides of his face, but in exchange, he flushed an uppercut that caught Bucky squarely in the mouth, causing Bucky to straighten up partway. When he did, Cade planted a right hand on the side of his jaw, putting his full shoulder behind the punch. The spectators lining the rails groaned in unison as the blow landed, causing Bucky's head to snap to the right.

Bucky went down on one knee and stayed there for a long second, trying to clear his head. Cade stood watching him. "You done?" he asked.

"Hell no," Bucky spat, his mouth bloody from the uppercut, aware that the entire crew was now watching to see what he was made of. Thinking to take advantage of his weight, he pushed up from his knee and charged again, this time with the intent to trap Cade in a bear hug and throw him to the ground. When he reached out to lock his arms around Cade, he suffered a series of rights and lefts to his stomach that caused him to double up, which gained him another devastating uppercut. Staggered, he stumbled backward, gamely swinging away as Cade pressed forward. For what seemed like minutes, the two exchanged punches until it became apparent that Bucky, though still standing, was out on his feet.

"That's enough!" Jack Walker shouted, and stepped between them. "Fight's over. Now let that be the end of it."

"I could go some more," Bucky protested lamely, fully aware that he had received the worst of it.

"Yeah, well, I don't need no more," Cade said. "Come on, let's go clean this mess up." He turned and started toward the creek. Without further protest, Bucky followed right behind him while the spectators parted to make a path for them.

Kneeling side by side on the bank of the creek, they washed the blood from their faces; the only sound heard was the wincing when an open cut was splashed with the dark creek water. When they finished the cleanup, they both sat back on their heels and studied each other silently. Finally, Bucky stuck out his hand and said, "No hard feelin's."

Cade smiled. "No hard feelin's," he responded, taking his hand. "Let's go get some supper."

*   *   *

That was the end of the conflict between the two young men. Without meaning to, the fight had served as an unofficial initiation for the new man. The rest of the crew adopted a less reserved attitude toward Cade, but the thing that amazed them most was the friendship that developed between Bucky and Cade. For Cade's part, initially, there was no desire to have any enemy on the crew, so he was not prone to carry a grudge. Bucky, on the other hand, had gained instant respect for the toughness Cade had shown. During the following weeks, when the horses were driven east of the mountains to work Carlton Kramer's major herd of cattle, the two young men seemed to have forgotten their differences. Before the end of winter, Bucky was seeking out Cade's help with hard-to-break horses, using many of Cade's gentler training methods. Jack Walker laughingly confided to Carlton Kramer that Cade Hunter had not only trained over three hundred unbroken horses, he had also trained Bucky George. The result, he said, was a more dependable remuda.

For Cade Hunter, the winter and following spring were a time of peaceful respite from the violent past that had seen his friend murdered and men killed by his own hand. He found there was something healing in the long days and endless hours in the saddle, especially in the Montana winter when cattle froze to death and horses went lame. There was no room left in a man's mind to dwell on anything beyond a cup of hot coffee and a warm place to bed down for the night.

Spring found Jack Walker and his men up on the Musselshell, helping with the spring branding of the new calves. When summer came, the cattle were moved back closer to Three Forks, and Cade had a reunion with Hank

Persons and his sons. Hank had managed to round up a new herd of horses, and he and the boys, with the help of a new hired hand, drove them down to sell to Carlton Kramer.

It was early evening when Hank arrived at Coyote Creek. He brought the horses in at a fast lope over the last mile, then cut them off and turned them in toward the corrals. Cade stood by the corral, laughing at Hank's grand entrance, and while the horses were milling about, stamping and snorting, he walked over to greet him as Hank stepped down from the saddle. "Howdy, Hank. You think you raised enough dust?"

"Howdy, Cade," Hank replied, grinning from ear to ear. "I didn't wanna bring 'em in and have nobody notice us."

Cade heard his name called and turned to see young Ben Persons riding up to meet him. "My goodness," Cade teased. "Who's this, Hank, your new hired hand?" Then he feigned a look of surprise. "Well, I'll be damned. Is that you, Ben?"

"Hey, Cade," Ben replied with an embarrassed grin.

"I swear, he's grown a foot," Cade said, turning back to Hank. "What have you been feedin' that boy, Hank?"

"He has growed some, ain't he?" Hank replied, smiling with pride. "I reckon it's his mama's cookin'." When Cade looked surprised by the remark, Hank explained. "My wife came home early spring." He paused to aim a brown stream of tobacco juice at a scurrying black beetle, missing by a generous foot. "I figured she might. Ted Randell run off and left her before the winter set in for good. She'da come with us on this drive, but she's carryin' another young'un in her belly." With Cade unable to reply with any response that seemed fitting, Hank continued. "Got me a new hired hand," he said, pointing to the Indian helping Johnny settle the herd down. "Full-blooded Shoshone." Then he spat again and winked at Cade. "My wife ain't got no use for Injuns."

They were joined in a few moments by Jack Walker who

had just taken a turn around the herd Hank had delivered, looking over the stock. "There's a few scruffy-lookin' nags in there, but most of 'em look pretty good, Hank. You sure you ain't stole some of these from somebody's ranch?"

Hank laughed. "I don't know that I care to answer that question," he joked. "But I swear, it may come to that. Damn horses are gettin' scarce in these parts."

"I saw one little mare in there that I might take for my daughter," Jack said.

"That little dun with the white stockin's?" Hank promptly replied.

"Yeah, that's the one," Jack said. "Elizabeth has been complainin' about ridin' that old bay that her mother, God rest her soul, used to ride. I told her I'd pick her out one when we got a new bunch in."

"I ain't surprised that little mare caught your eye. She looks like she's already broke, don't she? But she'll fool you. She's got spirit."

"I'll have Cade work with her," Jack said. "He'll get her broke in right."

It didn't take Cade long to polish the rough edges and have the horse as gentle as a lamb without knocking any of the spirit out of her. She took to a bridle right away and only registered minor objections to the saddle the first time. Soon she was a proper horse for a young lady. Jack wouldn't allow any of the crew to use her for work, and only rode her occasionally himself. He planned to deliver the mare to Elizabeth in two weeks' time, when he returned to escort his daughter to Deer Lodge where she had been invited to live with the Kramer family.

Carlton and his wife had always been fond of Elizabeth Walker, and she had often spent summers with them when she was a child. With Elizabeth now grown into a precocious young lady, Cornelia Kramer thought she needed the proper guidance of a woman. "Living up there in that cabin with no one to take charge of her womanhood but an old Indian woman," Cornelia railed, "it's a wonder she hasn't run off with some wild young man already." In fact, White Moon, the old Indian woman, was very protective of Jack Walker's daughter. She had been like a mother to the child when Elizabeth's real mother died in the hard winter of '71. But White Moon, who was Jim Big Tree's mother, was now getting too old to take care of the young lady. For that reason, and none other, Jack was happy to move his daughter to Carlton Kramer's headquarters in Deer Lodge. It was an opportunity for Elizabeth to become schooled in the genteel ways of the moneyed class. It was a twist of fate, however, that caused the young lady's path to cross with that of Cade Hunter.

"He's a mean one," Bucky George warned, "and if you ask me, he ain't ready to ride."

"Hell, you got a saddle on him," Jack responded.

"Yeah, but you don't see me settin' in it," Bucky replied.

Jack eyed the sleek stallion for a long moment. Dark and powerful, the blue roan leader of the herd Hank had brought in twitched his ears nervously while he eyed Jack in return. Bucky had been saving him for last. Stallions were hard to work with as a rule, and this one was more determined to resist than the younger bachelors in the herd. "He probably just needs a little more ridin' to take the rank outta him," Jack decided.

"I just don't think he's ready to buck out yet," Bucky said. "I'm still usin' a hackamore on him. He just don't wanna take a bit. I was fixin' to ask Cade to work with him some, but I believe that horse is too ornery for him to do much good."

This was surprising talk from the usually boastful Bucky George, and it caused Jack to make an unwise decision. "Hell, I ain't ever seen a horse that couldn't be broke," he said. "Hold his head. I'll see what he's got." He put his foot in the stirrup and prepared to mount.

"I wouldn't, Jack," Bucky warned as he held the bridle.

Exercising extreme caution, the foreman threw his leg over and settled his seat in the saddle. Nothing happened for a long moment, and Jack exchanged bemused smiles with Bucky, who had fully anticipated an explosion. It was coming, however, building up inside the defiant stallion like a volcano about to erupt, until it surfaced in one hellish fury. Jack's seat was thrown fully three feet from the saddle, his legs flying out to the sides like wings. He might have departed the equine tornado right there had it not been for his boots jammed firmly in the stirrups.

A considerable amount of time had passed since Jack Walker had personally saddle-broken a wild horse. It was a job that a man of his authority and age assigned to younger men. The attempted ride had begun as a show of mastery, but had rapidly transitioned into a fight for survival as Jack hung on to the saddle horn, bouncing high out of the saddle while the furious stallion bucked around the corral. Crashing against the rails of the corral, the horse tried to rake its rider off, an exercise that failed only because Jack's boot was now jammed almost through the stirrup. When that was unsuccessful, the horse suddenly quit bucking, dropped to the ground, and rolled on its side, pinning Jack's leg under it.

As soon as the horse went down, both Bucky and Cade dived on the stallion's neck, holding his head to the ground. Some of the other hands, who had come over to watch, rushed in to help. Between them, they managed to roll the horse enough to get the weight off Jack's leg while Cade calmed the angry stallion down. Jack, his face blanched

white with pain, made no sound until they were able to free
his boot. Then he spoke just two words. "It's broke," he said,
meaning the leg, not the horse.

"It's broke, all right," Jim Big Tree said when he got
Jack's boot off. "Maybe two places."

Two of the men went to cut a couple of saplings to fashion a splint while some others carried Jack to the cabin
where they laid him on his bedroll. The patient knew the
agony that awaited him, and he bit his lip while shaking his
head back and forth, silently scolding himself for trying to
show he could still ride a bronc when he should have been
at the rail watching. As was customary, someone produced a
bottle of whiskey and began pouring it down the suffering
man's throat. A willing recipient, Jack gulped it down as
best he could, knowing he was in for a lot of pain when the
bone was set. He tried desperately to get drunk, but the alcohol failed to deliver him from the reality of the moment.
That was accomplished a few minutes later, however, when
Jim Big Tree grabbed his heel and pulled the bones back in
line, the pain of which caused Jack to faint dead away.

The following days did not go well for Jack Walker. The
bone, although as nearly back to its original alignment as
Jim Big Tree could get it, showed no signs of healing. The
leg was swollen and painful, and the foreman was forced to
remain on his back for most of the time. To make matters
worse, his daughter was expecting him to come get her in
less than two weeks' time. Jack was anxious to see her safely
in Deer Lodge before an early snow fell, but as the time to
leave approached, he saw only minor improvement in his
leg. He considered making the trip in spite of his condition,
but knew he couldn't ride without severe pain. He thought
about sending Jim Big Tree to take his daughter, but laid up

as he was, Jack needed Jim there to oversee the men. Finally, after much inner debate, he sent for Cade Hunter.

At first, Cade didn't understand. "You want me to ride up to Butte to tell your daughter you ain't comin'?"

"I want you to take that little mare to Butte. Then I want you to take my daughter to Mr. Kramer's house at Deer Lodge." He paused when the expression on Cade's face told him that he wasn't sure he wanted the job. "I know it ain't what you signed on to do," Jack continued, "but you can see I can't do it myself."

In all honesty, Cade didn't know what to think. Walker was right, Cade sure as hell hadn't signed on to play nursemaid to the foreman's daughter. "Don't you reckon one of the older men might be better to do that?"

"I picked you because I figure you for a decent young man, handy with a rifle, and, as far as I've seen, trustworthy." He shrugged. "Besides, if you did anything to harm my daughter, I'd track you down and kill you. But I don't think I have to worry about that. She ain't alone. She's got old White Moon with her, and she'd put a knife in your gizzard if you laid a hand on Elizabeth."

Cade couldn't help but smile. "It's nice to know you trust me so much," he said.

Jack smiled in return. "I trust you, Cade. If I didn't, I sure as hell wouldn't have picked you. Let me put it this way: I ain't orderin' you to go; I'm askin' you. How 'bout it?"

Cade shrugged his shoulders and sighed. "I reckon."

Chapter 10

Jack Walker had built his cabin high up on the side of a mountain, five miles northwest of Butte, with the intent to isolate his wife and daughter from the rough mining town. His plan from the beginning was that it would be a temporary residence while he pushed Carlton Kramer's cattle herds across the Montana plains. As often happens, a man's plans are changed, and fate sometimes steps in to sidetrack ambitions even further. So it was with Jack. While his daughter was still a child, her mother was taken from them one long, cold winter. Faced with trying to take care of a little girl while driving a crew for Carlton Kramer, he turned to Jim Big Tree for help. With no family of her own except Jim, his mother, White Moon, was happy to take care of the child. It was an arrangement that worked out well for all parties. Elizabeth was fond of the old Shoshone woman, and Jack felt his child was reasonably safe with White Moon to protect her while he was away for months at a time. In time, however, Jack realized that his daughter had left childhood behind, and was now a young woman. He had expressed his concerns for Elizabeth to his employer, Carlton Kramer, and Kramer suggested that the young lady should come to live with them. When Kramer's wife, Cornelia, was approached with the idea of taking in Jack Walker's daughter, she enthusiastically agreed with her husband. It seemed the perfect solution to Jack. Elizabeth could enjoy the benefit of Cornelia's feminine influence before young men discovered her and started to call. As it turned out, however, it was a little too late.

Jack had built his cabin behind a large boulder that hid most of the house. A brace of fir trees stood at the back of the cabin, effectively hiding the back of the house from anyone approaching from below. A person standing at the kitchen window, however, could see someone approaching through the branches. On this day, late in the fall, White Moon stood looking out the kitchen window.

"Someone comes," White Moon stated without emotion.

Busy sewing the hem in a skirt she had made, Elizabeth let her arms drop in her lap. "Who is it?" she asked, equally emotionless. The old Indian woman seemed unfamiliar with excitement of any kind. Someone was coming, but from the dry monotone of White Moon's voice, it could be a stranger, her father, or the devil himself. So Elizabeth got up from the table to see for herself.

"John Slater," White Moon said, her face screwed up as if she had tasted something disagreeable.

Elizabeth laughed. "Well, I wonder what he wants," she replied coyly, saying it just to get White Moon's goat. It was the second time in as many weeks that the owner of the Silver King Saloon had journeyed up the mountain to call on her.

"Too old for you," White Moon stated, turning to give a stern eye to her young charge.

"He's not that old," Elizabeth replied, the impish look in her eye teasing her Indian governess. "Besides that, he's very wealthy. He owns the Silver King, and I heard Mr. Potter at the general store say that John Slater is buying up land to go into the cattle business."

White Moon looked away in disgust, making no effort to disguise her dislike for the man. "Your father whip you if he see you wriggle your tail for that man."

"We should make a fresh pot of coffee," Elizabeth suggested cheerfully. "Mr. Slater would probably appreciate a cup after his long ride up from Butte." She couldn't help but giggle in response to the sour expression on White Moon's face. "I'll go out on the porch to greet our guest."

"A good day to you, Miss Walker," John Slater called out as he walked his horse up to the porch.

"Good afternoon, Mr. Slater," Elizabeth returned politely. "What brings you up our way again?"

He reached back and untied a cotton sack from behind his saddle. Holding it out toward her, he said, "I brought you some dried apples. They got a couple of barrels of 'em at Potter's store, and I thought you might be tickled to get some, knowin' you don't get a chance to get into town that much."

"Why, that's very sweet of you," she replied, aware then that White Moon had come to stand in the doorway behind her. "But you shouldn't have gone to the trouble. Won't you step down and have a cup of coffee?" She turned and pursed her lips trying not to smile at White Moon. "We were just going to have some."

"Why, yes, ma'am, that would sure be to my likin'," he said, and dismounted at once.

In the absence of porch furniture, they sat on the edge of the porch and drank coffee reluctantly served by White Moon. After she had served it, she settled herself at the opposite end of the small platform where she could keep an eye on her charge, and sipped noisily from a large cup with a broken handle. Though he tried not to show it, the big Indian woman's presence obviously annoyed John Slater. Elizabeth was aware of it, but she appreciated the fact that the stoic woman was an effective buffer that prevented Slater from confessing his true intentions.

On other occasions, he had expressed his affections for her in his rough way, causing her some embarrassment. She was not immune to attention from an aspiring swain. It played upon her feminine instincts, but she did not truly want to encourage the man, even though it was exciting to be openly desired. In truth, she did not know many qualified bachelors, since she seldom visited the town, this in spite of the fact that the ratio of men to women in Butte and Helena made every female sought after by many. Although naturally coquettish, she realized that part of her charm could probably be attributed to the fact that Slater had few young women to choose from.

Slater's visit was not a long one, since the days were already getting shorter with the fall season. He mentioned several times that it would be getting dark before too long, hoping that he might be invited to stay the night. But Elizabeth merely responded by saying that he should not stay too long because the trail back down the mountain was treacherous in the dark. Before long, his impatience began to show through. He had made a considerable effort to appear gentlemanly, but as the hour aged, his coarse miner's edges began to show through. Elizabeth could readily see the difficulty the man was having in his attempts to hide his rough past. Finally, he gave up. "Well, I guess I'll get back to town then," he announced a bit curtly, and went to his horse.

Elizabeth thanked him again for the apples. "That man no good for you," White Moon uttered as they watched Slater disappear beyond the boulder.

Taking the sack from White Moon's hand, Elizabeth looked inside and picked out some of the dried apple slices. Handing the sack back to the Indian woman, she said, "At least we got some dried apples. Try them, they're delicious."

She grinned openly while White Moon helped herself. Watching her faithful guardian munching on the dried fruit, she felt a twinge of guilt for the concern she caused her. Elizabeth knew she should come right out and assure White Moon that she was in no way attracted to John Slater, but the somber Shoshone woman was so easily teased. And, the young woman had to admit, his attempts to woo her were extremely flattering. Still, she cautioned herself that she should probably put an end to his hopes. She could not help but be influenced by what her father had once said about John Slater. According to him, there was a lot of speculation around Butte about how Slater gained full ownership of the Silver King. Everyone knew that Slater had bought half ownership from Boyd Tyson. It was probably unfair, but to some folks around town, it seemed a mysterious circumstance that six months after Slater and Tyson went into partnership, Tyson fell victim to a road agent between Butte and Helena. True, Slater gained full ownership at that point, but to his credit, he saw to it that the widow Tyson was well taken care of. Even then, there were a few citizens of the town who thought she should have retained half ownership in the saloon. Most of the more genteel disagreed, arguing that Sally Tyson should in no way be associated with the running of a saloon. "Oh, well," Elizabeth sighed, "we'll be leaving here for Deer Lodge when Daddy gets back, so you won't have to worry about John Slater."

Maybe Jack Walker was right when he had worried about the weather. Still early fall, it was a chilly day when Cade made his way through the bustling mining town of Butte. The sky was leaden, promising a chance of snow, and giving the town a colorless look. Cade considered stopping by a couple of saloons just on the chance that someone might have seen Lem Snider. The town itself served to remind him that he had permitted the man who murdered his friend to slip quietly into the back of his mind, and he felt the burden of guilt as a result.

Passing the hotel, he saw that a couple of carpenters were in the process of adding a porch to the front, and he couldn't help but think of Luke again. His mind drifted back to the sweetgrass prairie near Big Timber when he and Luke had settled back to relax with bellies filled with freshly killed antelope. He could still picture his late friend's face when he talked about what he wanted to do with his share of the gold dust. *Maybe this might have been the hotel Luke was dreaming about,* Cade thought, *sitting on this porch with his feet propped up.* The thought caused him to shake his head sadly.

As he guided Loco up the busy street, he glanced back at the mare, and was reminded of the trust that Jack Walker had placed in him. It was enough to make him nudge Loco with his heels and lope straight through town. *I ain't forgot, Luke,* he thought. *I'll get around to it.*

Following Jack's instructions, he rode out of Butte to the northwest, passing abandoned mining claims that had once held the hopes and dreams of men desperate for the strike that would mean the difference between a life of toil and one of leisure. Looking at the rough, unhealing scars left by their picks and shovels, Cade felt a sense of sadness for the earth. Anxious to leave the mining town behind, he held Loco and the mare to a steady lope until he had left the saloons and the mines behind him.

Jack's directions were easy to follow. He rode for about five miles up the valley before he came to the stream Jack had described. Looking as if it had split a huge boulder high up on the slope, the water flowed directly out of the rock and followed a ravine of lush grass that painted a wide slash of dark green down the gray mountainside. Knowing this had to be the stream he searched for, Cade guided Loco up the

ravine. The bottom of the ravine was soft and spongy, a result of the grass-filled stream, with patches of moss here and
there—in stark contrast to the dry hillsides.

As Jack had predicted, Cade did not see the cabin beyond
the huge boulder until he was practically in the small yard
before it. Surprised, he reined Loco back and paused beside
the boulder to look the situation over. The dwelling was
small. There was a barn behind it with a small corral, and an
outhouse on the opposite side of the stream with stepping
stones leading across. There was no sign of anyone outside,
but there was smoke coming from the chimney.

"Hello the house," he called out, thinking it a good idea
to announce himself. Hearing no response, he was about to
call out again when a slight movement on his left caused
him to flinch. Startled, he turned to discover a double-
barreled shotgun looking right at his head. "Whoa!" he
blurted involuntarily, and backed Loco quickly away. The
shotgun was in the hands of the biggest Indian woman
he had ever seen, and she followed him step for step as he
backed up, the shotgun still aimed at his head. The broad
face was void of expression as she drilled him with eyes
dark and menacing, her heavy arms never wavering under
the weight of the shotgun. Remembering then, he asked,
"White Moon?"

The mention of her name caused only a slight lowering
of the weapon as she continued to stare into the stranger's
face. Finally, she spoke. "I am White Moon. What do you
want?"

Cade began a hasty explanation. The woman looked like
she *wanted* to shoot him. "My name's Cade Hunter. I work
for Mr. Walker. He sent me to take his daughter to Deer
Lodge." The explanation did not seem to satisfy the stoic
Indian woman, so Cade went on. "I've got a letter here from
Jack that says so."

"Let me see, White Moon." The voice came from the cabin door. Moments later, a slender young girl stepped out onto the small porch. She walked up beside the Indian woman and took the letter from White Moon's hand. After reading the brief message, she looked at Cade with an appraising eye. "My dad is hurt?" she asked.

"Yes, ma'am," Cade replied, "broke his leg."

She frowned as if feeling the pain herself, still eyeing Cade carefully. "Is it bad? It must have been if he couldn't come himself."

"It's a pretty bad break," Cade answered, still keeping a cautious eye on the large Indian woman, who showed no sign of lowering the shotgun. "Horse rolled on him. Jim Big Tree thinks it's broke in more'n one place. Anyway, he can't ride, so he sent me to take you to Deer Lodge." He noticed a slight rise of one eyebrow when he mentioned Jim's name, but no other change in the Indian's stone face, and he kept a firm grip on the reins to hold Loco steady. The big gray gelding was becoming impatient with the confrontation and anxious to move his feet.

"Daddy says I can trust you," Elizabeth said, gesturing toward the letter.

"Well, yes'm, I reckon you can," Cade replied. Like his horse, he was becoming impatient with the standoff.

Suddenly, she smiled. "You can get down. Don't shoot him, White Moon."

Cade threw a leg over and stood for a moment with one foot in the stirrup, watching White Moon until the somber Shoshone woman slowly lowered the barrel of the shotgun. "I'm obliged," he said as he stepped down to the ground and turned to face the young lady.

She extended her hand, smiling. "I'm Elizabeth Walker," she said. "I apologize for the rude welcome."

He took her hand, then quickly released it as if afraid he

might hurt her. "That's all right," he said, then asked, "Have you folks had some trouble up here?"

"No. That's just White Moon's usual welcome for strange men. There are a lot of aimless drifters that pass through Butte. It doesn't happen very often, but once in a while one of them finds his way up here." She looked at White Moon and smiled fondly. "She's been looking after me since I was a little girl."

"Well, looks to me like she's fit to do the job." Then, just remembering, he said, "Your daddy sent you this little mare." He untied the lead rope and led the horse up beside Loco. Her reaction was one he would have expected from a small child.

"Oh, she's beautiful!" she squealed, and immediately took the rope from him. Stroking the mare's neck, she smiled at White Moon. "Isn't she beautiful?" The Shoshone woman smiled and nodded.

Watching the girl's delighted reaction to her father's gift, Cade realized that he had expected to escort a little girl to Deer Lodge. Jack had not mentioned it, and it had never occurred to him that Elizabeth might, in fact, be a young lady. It suddenly made more sense now that Jack felt some urgency in exposing his daughter to Cornelia Kramer's influence. He was tempted to ask her age, but had enough sense to know that might be impertinent. It was impossible for him not to notice the obvious signs of womanhood, now that he had the opportunity to take a closer look. Telling himself that he'd best discourage thoughts of that nature, he brought his thoughts back to the job at hand. "When are you ladies gonna be ready to start out for Deer Lodge?"

"Oh, we've been ready for a couple of days," Elizabeth replied, still admiring her father's gift. "We expected Daddy any day, so we can be ready to leave in the morning. It's a little late to start out today, and it's a fair day's ride to Mr. Kramer's ranch."

Cade nodded. "Your dad said you knew the way to his place—said I didn't have to worry about that, so I reckon you know best. We need to rest the horses, anyway."

Cade took care of the horses, turning them out to graze in the lush grass of the ravine bottom for the rest of the afternoon while he sat down near the barn to repair a frayed strap on one of the saddlebags. After an hour or so, Elizabeth came out to join him. "You know, Mr. Hunter—" she started.

"Cade," he interrupted.

"Cade," she corrected, "you're welcome to come into the house. I hope you don't think you have to stay in the barn."

"Oh," he stammered, "well, I had a few things I needed to fix out here." In truth, he had not been sure of his place, whether he should be expected to follow them into the house or not.

She took a wooden bucket that was perched upside down on a corral post, and using it for a stool, sat down opposite him. "We're going to have some supper in a little while, as soon as the bread finishes baking. White Moon bakes the best Indian bread. If you need to wash up, I can lend you some soap, and you can wash in the stream." She paused to give him an impish grin. "You do bathe, don't you?"

Cade blushed. "Pretty regular," he said, "but I don't always have soap." At that moment, he couldn't think of the last time he had seen a bar of soap. Glancing up to meet her gaze, he realized then that the girl was teasing him.

"How long have you been working for my dad?" she asked. "You don't look like you're much older than me."

There it was again, he thought. In answer, he replied, "I'm older than I look—older than you, unless you're older than twenty-one."

She gave him a big smile, then got to her feet and re-placed the bucket. "I better go and help White Moon. I'll fetch that bar of soap if you want it."

"All right," he replied, "I reckon I could use a good scrub-bin', since I'm gonna be eatin' in the presence of ladies. I expect I'm totin' a fair amount of Montana on me." Laughing, Elizabeth turned on her heel and returned to the cabin. Cade watched her all the way back.

In a few minutes time, she returned with a big yellow bar of lye soap and offered it to him. "It's getting kinda chilly to bathe in the stream, but I can heat a bucket of water for you."

"Oh, no, ma'am," he replied. "It won't be too cold."

She shook her head and smiled. "All right, if you say so." With that, she returned to the cabin. "Don't be long."

After a swift bath in the chilly water of the stream, Cade tried his best to produce shaving lather with the lye soap, but enjoyed little success. He dragged his razor over his face anyway and managed to clear most of the brush—at least enough to leave his face feeling raw. He pulled his clean shirt out of his war bag and hurriedly dressed. Then he grate-fully sought the warmth of the cabin. Elizabeth took a step backward and made an undisguised show of appraising the obvious improvements. She made no comment. She didn't have to. Her wide grin of amusement was all that was nec-essary. Her reaction caused his face to glow not entirely from the dull razor.

Supper that night was little more than a pot of beans, boiled with some salty side meat, coffee, and White Moon's pan bread, but to Cade, it had considerably more taste than the same fare on the cattle trail. Elizabeth explained that the difference was in the herbs that White Moon collected from the stream farther up the mountain. "Well, they're the best beans I've ever had," Cade said, bringing a hint of a smile to the Indian woman's face.

While he finished his coffee, he looked around him to appraise the cabin Jack Walker had built for his wife and daughter. Small, but solidly built with well-chinked log walls and a stone fireplace, it looked capable of weathering winter's icy blasts. There were, in effect, three rooms—the largest, a kitchen—the other two were actually made from one room divided by a blanket wall to make two bedrooms. The only things that distinguished it from any miner's cabin were the woman's touches here and there in the form of curtains and knickknacks hung on the walls for decorations—and the cleanliness.

When supper was finished, Cade got up to excuse himself. "I thank you for the supper. I expect I'll get ready to turn in, and I'll see you folks in the mornin'."

"You don't have to sleep outside," Elizabeth said, looking surprised that he even considered it. "We've got plenty of room in here where it's warm."

Cade was not comfortable with that idea. It was a small cabin, and he wasn't accustomed to sharing quarters with women. He wasn't even sure what kind of noises he made when he was asleep, and he had just finished a generous bowl of beans and fat meat. "Thank you, ma'am, but I expect I'd best sleep with the horses. I'll be warm enough. That way, I can kinda keep an eye on things. I'll see you in the mornin'." He promptly took his leave.

"Suit yourself," Elizabeth said as he carefully closed the door behind him. When he had gone, she turned to White Moon. "He's about the shyest man I've ever seen, but he's rather nice-looking when he gets cleaned up," she said. The big woman fixed her with a scolding stare. "Well, he is kinda handsome," Elizabeth said with a girlish giggle.

Her remark brought forth an admonishing grunt from White Moon. "That kind nothing but trouble," she said.

"Miz Kramer teach you how to be proper lady—get you a rich husband."

"You mean like John Slater?" Elizabeth asked.

White Moon frowned. "No," she replied emphatically. Then her expression lightened. "Maybe you meet some of Mr. Kramer's friends," she said. "You never have to work then, and maybe you can take care of White Moon when she is old."

Elizabeth laughed. "You're already old," she teased. "I'll take care of you. I don't need a rich husband to do that." Her thoughts drifted to John Slater then. He was rich. There was no doubt about that. She thought about the day she first met him in the general store in Butte. Not really handsome, but tall with long, dark hair worn to his shoulders, a thin mustache as his only facial hair. He could not really be considered a dashing figure, but there was a certain wild charm about him, even with the few rough edges so many of the newly rich miners displayed. He had at once asked her permission to call upon her. She had been surprised when he was undaunted by her telling him that she would soon be leaving, saying, "Then I'll call on you in Deer Lodge. I'm fixin' to buy a piece of land up that way."

Flattered, she had not discouraged him. He appeared to be a few years older than she would have preferred, but not at all too old to consider. *He's not as handsome as Cade Hunter,* she thought, knowing that White Moon would most likely tell her that "handsome" wears off after the first winter, but money keeps you warm for the rest of your life. *Oh, well,* she thought, *I'm not about to marry either one of them.* Even so, she found that she was still thinking about the broad-shouldered young man long after he had gone outside.

* * *

Cade awoke in the gray predawn of the morning. By the time the sun made a timid appearance over the mountaintop, he had watered and saddled the horses and left them to graze while he waited for some sign of movement in the cabin. Before long, he saw a fresh plume of smoke drift up from the chimney telling him that White Moon was probably stirring up the breakfast fire. Still, he remained in the barn, not wishing to disturb the two women too early. In a few minutes, White Moon appeared around the front corner of the cabin and crossed the stream to the outhouse on the other side. On her way back, she met Elizabeth making the same trip. Satisfied that the women were dressed then, Cade proceeded to the house in hopes of getting a cup of coffee. He had almost decided to build a small fire outside the barn and get his own coffeepot from his pack.

"Good morning," Elizabeth greeted him when he walked in the door, her smile warm and genuine, as if she was really glad to see him. "We'll have some coffee ready pretty soon, and White Moon is frying bacon to eat with the rest of last night's pan bread."

Uneasy just standing there, he offered, "Want me to chop some firewood or somethin'?"

"No. We've got plenty for now and we won't need any more after breakfast." She sensed his uneasiness and decided to tease him. "You just sit yourself down at the table and wait till the coffee's ready." She winked at White Moon and said, "I don't know if we should even feed him, White Moon, somebody who prefers to sleep with the horses instead of staying in the cabin with us. Maybe he thought he wasn't safe with two spoiled doves like us two."

Fully aware he was being teased then, Cade smiled. "The horses didn't complain about my snorin'," he said. Anxious to change the subject, he asked, "What are you gonna do about all your things here? You just gonna abandon this cabin?"

"No," Elizabeth replied. "Mr. Kramer will send a couple of his men back from the Bar-K with a wagon to get the furniture and trunks. I'm just taking my clothes and a few other things." That was good news to Cade. He had been wondering if he was expected to move the whole cabin on a packhorse.

"I'll go round up the horses again," Cade said after eating, and went out the door heading for the grassy meadow behind the barn.

He had not been gone more than fifteen minutes when White Moon said, "There is a rider coming." She was standing at the back window, the same window where she had seen Cade coming up the ravine the day before. Elizabeth moved over beside her and peered out at the lone horse making its way up toward the boulder.

When the caller had almost reached the huge boulder that hid the front of the cabin, Elizabeth identified him. "John Slater," she announced, surprised, then looked at White Moon with an impish grin. She quickly brushed by the mirror, took a moment to smooth her hair, then walked out on the porch to meet her visitor.

"Good morning, Mr. Slater," she said. "What on earth brings you way up here this early in the morning?"

"I do declare, Miss Walker," he returned, "you're as pretty in the mornin' as you were the other day."

"Why, thank you, sir," Elizabeth replied sweetly. "You'll have me blushing with talk like that."

"I remember what you told me last time I was here, that you were leavin' here to go to Deer Lodge, so I rode up to tell you I'd be happy to escort you and the Shoshone woman over there. I have business with Carlton Kramer, so I'll be out to his place from time to time, anyway."

"But at this time of morning?" Elizabeth replied, finding it an odd time of day to call.

"That's just the way I am, Elizabeth—all right if I call you Elizabeth?" She nodded, smiling. He continued. "Once you get to know me a little better, you'll see I'm a man that don't waste no time, when I see what I want."

Even as precocious as she was, Elizabeth was taken aback by his bold words. "Why, Mr. Slater," she responded after a moment to think, "that's a generous offer, but I'm afraid you have wasted your morning." She nodded toward Cade still down at the barn. "You see, my father has sent one of his men to escort White Moon and me to Deer Lodge."

Slater cocked his head to look at the young man leading the horses toward the cabin. After staring for a long moment, he turned his gaze back to Elizabeth and said, "A hired hand? You can tell him you won't need him. I'll be happy to take you to Deer Lodge." White Moon came out on the porch to stand behind her charge. "Of course, I mean both of you," Slater added when he glimpsed her frown.

Doing her best to conceal the girlish excitement she felt inside over his obvious infatuation for her, Elizabeth remained calm but pleasant. "Again, my thanks for the trouble you have gone to, but I'm afraid I can't go against my father's wishes. He sent a trusted hand to escort me, and the poor man rode a long way to see us safely there." Slater made no response, turning in the saddle to stare at the man leading the horses.

Down at the barn, Cade had paused when he saw the stranger ride up to the house, his hand automatically seeking the stock of the Winchester rifle resting in his saddle scabbard. It was plain to see after a moment, however, that it was a social call upon Elizabeth. For a reason he could not explain, Cade immediately disliked the man. Walking the horses slowly toward the cabin, he looked the stranger over as closely as he could at a distance of about forty yards. Sitting tall in the saddle, Elizabeth's caller looked dressed for a social visit, wearing a black Stetson "Boss of the Plains" hat atop long, dark hair that touched the shoulders of his black morning coat. *Slick as a greased weasel,* Cade thought. He didn't like the way Elizabeth laughed and tossed her head demurely in response to conversation he was too far away to hear.

"Cade," Elizabeth said when he approached the porch, "this is John Slater. He has kindly offered to escort White Moon and me to Deer Lodge."

In that brief instant, Slater wasn't pleased to find the young man there. He continued to stare at Cade as if challenging him, his brows knotted in a heavy frown. "Yeah, boy," he finally said with an undisguised note of derision in his tone, "I can save you the ride over to Deer Lodge, and you can go on back to wherever you come from."

The remark rankled Cade, but he made no immediate response, taking his time to loop the horses' reins around a porch post. He tried to tell himself that the man's comment probably wasn't meant to sound scornful, but he couldn't deny the fact that he had taken a dislike to him the moment he first saw him talking to Elizabeth. Considering that thought, Cade had to ask himself what right he had to feel one way or another about who called on Elizabeth Walker. *It ain't none of my business,* he scolded, *but I still don't like the son of a bitch.* Turning to face Slater then, he spoke. "I expect I'll be seein' Miss Walker to Deer Lodge. I promised her pa I'd see her safely there, and that's what I aim to do." Looking eye to eye, neither man noticed the slight smile Cade's statement brought to Elizabeth's lips. However, White Moon, a silent witness to the confrontation, caught the look on the young girl's face and issued a soft grunt of disapproval, accompanied by a hard frown.

Before Slater could answer, Elizabeth said, "There, you see, John, Cade is bound to take me, but you're welcome to ride along with us if you were going up there, anyway."

Not by me, he ain't welcome, Cade thought, but he held his tongue and waited for Slater's response. Seeing that his ploy to accompany the young lady was foiled, Slater had no choice but to retreat discreetly, lest he ruin his chances with her. He had already made up his mind he was going to possess the handsome young woman, and if he had competition to eliminate, then so be it. But in the meantime, he must take care not to show his jealous intentions for Elizabeth to see.

"Thank you for the invitation," he said to Elizabeth, "but my main concern was for your safety. As it turns out, I don't need to go to Deer Lodge on business until next week, so I'll see you up there then."

"That would be nice, I'm sure," Elizabeth replied politely, gracing him with a faint smile. "I must apologize for this morning. We can't even offer you coffee or something to eat, since we were all packed up to leave."

"Think nothin' of it," Slater said. "I'll take my leave now." Giving Cade a stern parting glance, he said, "You mind you take care of them." Cade didn't bother to answer.

They stood silently watching for a few moments while John Slater rode away. Of the three, Cade was the only one focusing on Slater. Elizabeth's eyes were on Cade, while White Moon concentrated on Elizabeth. A faint smile of satisfaction played upon the young girl's lips as she detected the hostile expression on Cade's face for the departing guest. Turning then to return to the cabin, she confronted the scolding look displayed upon the broad face of White Moon, answering it with a coy smile as she breezed past the disapproving Shoshone woman.

*   *   *

Cornelia Kramer hurried out to the front porch when her maid and cook, Millie, told her that Elizabeth was here. As she passed the library, she told her husband, and he put his ledgers aside to join her in greeting their houseguest. A few moments later, he stood with his wife as they watched the three riders coming up the lane to the ranch house. Expecting Jack Walker to escort his daughter, Carlton Kramer remarked, "That's the young fellow we just hired, the one I was telling you about who's so good with horses."

When Elizabeth saw the couple waiting on the porch, now joined by their three young children, her faced blossomed out with a big smile and she waved excitedly. The children ran ahead as their mother and father walked down the steps to meet her, all with eager smiles.

Pulling up to the hitching post, Cade dismounted and took the horses while Elizabeth ran to meet her adoptive parents. After the initial excitement of the reunion, Cornelia extended an affectionate greeting to the stoic Shoshone woman standing behind Elizabeth. Watching the scene with silent amusement, Cade stood back until the women started up the steps in animated conversation. "Where do you want me to unload your things on the packhorse?" he then asked, loud enough for everyone to hear.

"Oh, we almost forgot about that," Cornelia answered. "Millie can show you where to take them." The maid, who had been standing on the porch watching, promptly descended the steps to help Cade with the baggage.

While Cade untied the packs, Carlton Kramer stepped up to extend his hand. "Well, Cade, how is it you came to escort Elizabeth? We expected Jack to bring her. Is he all right?" Cade explained that an accident with a horse had laid Jack up for a while. "Well, that's bad news, indeed. I hope he's not too long in recovering." Kramer paused for a moment, stepping back while Millie loaded her arms with a bundle of Elizabeth's clothes. When she started up the steps, he continued. "How are things going at Coyote Creek? You getting along all right with Jack and the rest of the boys?" It had already occurred to him that Jack evidently approved of the young man, since he had trusted him to escort his daughter.

"Yes, sir," Cade answered, "I got no complaints."

"As I said, I was expecting Jack, but since you're here, I might keep you for a few days. I just bought a couple dozen horses from a fellow up Clark Fork. I'd like you to take a look at them, maybe help with the breaking."

"You're the boss," Cade replied, "but I expect Jack might be expectin' me back with word that his daughter is all right."

"I'm sending a man with a wagon down to Coyote Creek tomorrow with some supplies for Jack. He can tell him that you delivered Elizabeth safe and sound," Kramer replied.

"Then I reckon I can stay and help out around here for a spell," Cade said.

"Fine," Kramer said. "You can go on down to the bunkhouse and find an empty bed. See Ralph Duncan. He should be down there now. They'll be eating pretty soon, so you're just in time for supper. Tell Ralph I said to help you get settled. He'll help you take care of those horses."

Cade turned to look in the direction Kramer pointed out, toward a long building next to one of the corrals. "All right," was all he said before starting toward the bunkhouse. As he walked away, he cast a quick glance at the three women at the top of the porch steps—Elizabeth and Cornelia Kramer chattering away like reunited schoolgirls, the solemn White Moon following silently behind. His experience with Elizabeth Walker had been a brief interval in his life, but it had somehow made a lasting impression. He could not understand why. It made little difference, he told himself, for he didn't expect to see her again.

Ralph Duncan stood by the small stoop before the bunkhouse door, leaning with one hand against the porch post, watching the arrival of the guests up at the main house. He had known Jack Walker's daughter since she was a little girl, and there was a smile on his face as he watched the young lady now ascending the steps holding Cornelia's arm. *She'll remember ol' Ralph,* he thought, knowing Beth, as she preferred to be called, would soon find time to come to see him. *Hell, I put her on her first horse,* he thought, and grinned anew. *Got her in trouble with her mama.* He almost laughed at the memory. His attention turned then to consider the young fellow approaching the bunkhouse leading four horses, three with saddles and one with empty packs. When Cade was within a dozen yards, Ralph walked out to meet him.

"You lookin' to put them in the corral, I reckon," Ralph said.

"Yes, sir," Cade replied. "Are you Ralph Duncan?"

"Yep."

"Mr. Kramer told me to see you about a bunk, and maybe some supper, if I ain't too late."

"Nah, you ain't too late," Duncan said. "Charley ain't even set the chuck on the table yet." He stepped forward. "Here, let me give you a hand with them horses." Cade handed him the reins to two of the horses. "You gonna eat with the men?" Duncan went on. "I thought you might be stayin' up at the house with the other guests."

Cade raised an eyebrow and hesitated for a moment to decide if Duncan's remark held a hint of sarcasm. Looking at the deeply lined face of the gray-bearded older man, he decided there was none intended. "Reckon not," he replied. "I ain't one of the guests. I just brought 'em over here. Mr.

Kramer told me to stick around for a few days to help you saddle-break some horses he just bought."

This was surprising news to Duncan. He wasn't aware that they were in need of more men. The headquarters ranch here in Deer Lodge was only about three hundred acres, and used mostly to train horses for the cattle herds Kramer grazed on the open range, although it was also a working cattle ranch. He figured his boss must have some reason to hire on another hand. *Could be,* he thought, *the boy just needs a job and the boss is acting out of the kindness of his heart.* "Oh," he said, "so you're a new hand. You done much work with horses?"

"Some," Cade answered as they walked toward the barn. "I ain't exactly a new hire, though. I work for Jack Walker down at the Coyote Creek camp."

"Oh, well, in that case, glad to have you help out. Come on, I'll show you where to leave them saddles." That was good news. Ralph didn't think he especially needed any help breaking in the new stock, but he was relieved to know he wasn't going to be expected to break in a new man. "We'll turn these horses out, and maybe supper will be ready by then."

"'Preciate the help," Cade said. "Just so you'll know, this little mare belongs to Elizabeth, and the trashy-lookin' gelding here is my horse. He ain't the easiest horse to get along with."

After the horses were taken care of, Duncan showed Cade to an empty bunk, then introduced him to the rest of the Deer Lodge crew. Besides Ralph, there were only six other men on the payroll at that time. All six seemed to be cordial enough when Duncan explained that Cade was going to be working with them for a few days. Soon after he had met everyone, the food arrived from the kitchen, carried by the Chinese cook, Charley Wing. All hands eagerly went to work on the victuals. Duncan grinned when he saw Cade's enthusiastic assault on the food. "It's pretty good chuck, ain't it? I'll bet it's a mite different from Coyote Creek."

"There ain't much doubt about that," Cade replied, helping himself to another biscuit. "It was worth the ride over here just for supper."

Work began in earnest the following morning. Bright and early, the crew started with the new horses. Curious as to the new man's credentials, Duncan spent a good portion of the morning watching Cade work with a wild stallion that the rest of the crew had obviously left for last. The horse was past the age when gelding would have been most effective, but he didn't appear to be overly aggressive when Cade was working with him. Just as Jack Walker had before, Duncan could not help but notice that the man seemed to have a special communication with the animal. He was beginning to understand why Carlton Kramer had asked Cade to stay on to help.

About mid-morning, Cade glanced up to see Elizabeth coming down from the house, heading for the corral. Spotting the young lady at almost the same time, Duncan climbed down from the top rail where he had been perched, watching Cade work.

Seeing the gray-haired foreman, Elizabeth's face lit up with a great big smile, and she ran to meet him. "Uncle Ralph!" she squealed and gave him an enthusiastic hug.

"Hello, Beth, girl," Duncan responded, chuckling happily. "I was wonderin' when I was gonna get to see you." The rest of the crew paused to grin their appreciation as the foreman held Elizabeth by the shoulders at arm's length to take a good look at her. "Danged if you ain't all growed up to be a regular lady," he gushed.

"How've you been, Uncle Ralph?" she asked. They chatted for a few minutes, exchanging news, while the crew went back to their chores. "What do you think of your new man?" Elizabeth asked in as casual a voice as she could manage.

"He sure seems to know his business when it comes to breakin' a horse," Duncan replied, "but he'll have to be around here a little longer before I could think much about him one way or the other."

"Did you see my horse?" she asked, excitement returning to her voice.

"Yep," Duncan replied, "right spunky little mare. She's a pretty one."

"You think I could borrow Cade to saddle my horse for me? It's such a beautiful morning I thought I'd like to take a ride."

"Why, sure, honey, you can have anythin' you want, but I can saddle your horse for you."

"Thanks, Uncle Ralph, but I need to thank Cade for bringing White Moon and me up here, anyway."

"Oh," Duncan said, a little slow on picking up on the obvious at first, then realizing. "Oh," he repeated, this time with the hint of a twinkle in his eye, "I'll call him over."

Cade led a buckskin mare over to the rail. "Mornin', Elizabeth," he said as he stood stroking the mare's neck.

"Beth would like you to saddle her horse for her. I'll take that mare off your hands. Looks like you've gentled her up some already."

"She took the bridle all right," Cade replied matter-of-factly, "but she sure ain't nowhere near saddle-broke yet." He handed the reins to Duncan and shook out a noose as he headed for the other corral to get Elizabeth's mare.

"You might oughta ride with Beth if she don't mind," Duncan called after him. "There's been some talk about cattle rustlin' goin' on near here. No tellin' what kind of drifters might be snoopin' around these hills." He caught the coy look Elizabeth sent his way, and winked in return.

Cade quickly threw a rope on the mare and led her to the barn. Needing no encouragement, Loco followed along behind. "Have you named her yet?" Cade asked as he saddled the mare.

"Yes," Elizabeth answered. "Her name is Glory. You like it?"

Cade shrugged his shoulders. "I reckon that's as good a name as any." Taking an extra tug on the cinch of the single-rigged saddle, he then handed her the reins. "Well, here's Glory, all ready to go." He walked over to the bench and paused with his hand on his saddle before turning back to face her. "Duncan said I should ride with you. Is that all right with you?"

"Sure," she said. "Come on and I'll show you some of my favorite places from when I was a little girl." Giving him a warm smile, she took hold of the saddle horn and waited for Cade to help her up. As soon as she was in the saddle, she turned Glory toward the barn door, not waiting for Cade to saddle Loco. "You'd better hurry if you're gonna ride with me," she teased.

Within a couple of minutes, Cade was in the saddle and Loco loped out of the barn after the mare. Making no attempt to move up beside her, Cade held Loco back to what he considered a respectable distance, unsure if his presence was truly welcome on Elizabeth's ride. His thinking was that he was along for protection only. They continued on that way, following a ravine that led back up in the hills until Elizabeth tired of the arrangement and pulled up to wait for him. "I'm not going to bite you," she complained when he came up even with her.

"I didn't think you would," he said. "I didn't know if you preferred ridin' alone."

"If I did, I wouldn't have asked you to come along, now, would I?" She gave him a look of exasperation before smiling broadly. "Come on, I'll show you my most favorite place." She gave the mare her heels and was off again. He followed, this time close behind her.

They followed the ravine until it began to flatten into the slope of the mountainside. Several dozen yards up the slope, they came to a game trail that led off through a forest thick with firs. Elizabeth followed the trail that sidled along the base of the mountain until finally leading down again to a clear stream and a clearing strewn with rocks. Making her way through the rocks, she guided her horse across the stream to a small grassy pasture. She dismounted and waited for Cade.

"This was my secret place," she said, laughing, when he stepped down from the saddle. "This was where I used to come to dream about when I would be a grown-up and what I would do." She laughed again at the thought. "I used to dream I would go to Omaha or Chicago and marry a rich man." She gazed around her and gestured with her hand. "Isn't this a beautiful place? I used to come here when I was feeling sad, too, like when my mother died."

Cade could only respond politely. "Yes, ma'am, it is a beautiful place, all right." He felt extremely awkward, wishing at that moment that he had some social skills. He had spent so little time in the presence of young ladies that he realized he was almost tongue-tied when it came to casual banter.

She affected a look of scolding. "Don't you 'yes, ma'am' me anymore, Cade Hunter. I'm not your mother."

Taken aback, he flushed, embarrassed. "Yes, ma'—" he started to blurt out before he caught himself. "Yes, Elizabeth," he corrected.

"You can call me Beth," she said. "After all, you did

escort me over here—saved me from road agents and wild Indians, and whatever else might have harmed me."

Although lacking in experience with the opposite sex, Cade could at least realize when he was being teased. He nodded his head slowly, a faint smirk forming on his face. "All right, *Beth*, but I was thinkin' more about callin' you Sassy. How do you know I wouldn't have just turned and run if I *had* seen wild Indians or road agents?"

She favored him with a coy smile. "Because my daddy wouldn't have sent you if you weren't the kind of man to protect a lady." She watched him closely for a few moments, amused by his reaction to her teasing. "Besides," she said, "we're friends. Come sit down, and we'll talk while the horses drink."

Cade did as he was bade, still not sure what his emotions were telling him. Beth was certainly not suffering any such restraint, chattering on about her summers here at the ranch. He listened in polite fascination, content just to hear the music of her voice. Before long, the conversation evolved into questions about him.

"There ain't much to tell you," he insisted. "I've been workin' with horses and cattle since I was fourteen, and that's about it." He shrugged apologetically. There was a lot more to tell, but nothing he felt comfortable in confiding to her, and some things he was not particularly proud of.

"What about your family?" she asked. "Where are they?"

"Dead, or same as," he replied. "My pa's dead, and my ma married again, but I haven't seen her since I was fourteen— and that's all the family I've got."

"No friends?" she persisted.

He became thoughtful for a moment. "No. I had a friend, but he got killed." He glanced up to meet her gaze, and finding it filled with sympathy, quickly flashed her a smile. "It's all the same to me. I don't really need friends."

"Well, you've got one now," she stated emphatically, and extended her hand to him. "You can't go around with no family or friends. If you're sad or in trouble, I give you permission to use my secret place."

He had to smile. Taking her hand, he exaggerated a formal handshake. "All right, friend."

"Uncle Carlton said he was keeping you around for a while," she said. "I thought that you might want to get back to Coyote Creek right away."

"No ma'—Beth," he stammered. "I'm not in any hurry to get back. I'd just as soon stay here for however long Mr. Kramer needs me."

"Any particular reason?" she asked, unable to prevent the impish gleam in her eye.

"No," he replied at first, then, answering honestly, said, "Maybe."

On a sudden impulse, she graced him with a smile, reached up and kissed him on the cheek, then quickly pulled away, leaving him wide-eyed in astonishment. "Just between friends," she said. "Come on, I've got to go back and help with dinner." Not waiting for help this time, she put a foot in the stirrup and hopped nimbly up in the saddle, then guided Glory back in the direction of the ranch.

Riding across the slope to the ravine, she preceded him down to the prairie again. This time, she waited for him to catch up, and they rode back to the corral side by side. Her conversation light and casual, she chatted away, apparently forgetful of the kiss on the cheek, as if it had never happened. Cade, whose participation in the conversation consisted of little more than a nod or occasional grunt, still felt the burn of her lips upon his cheek. Neither the man nor the woman noticed the two strange horses tied up at the hitching rail before the house, nor the men sitting on the front porch talking to Carlton Kramer.

*   *   *

John Slater paused when his eye caught sight of the two young people just approaching the far corner of the smaller corral. The sight of Cade and Elizabeth riding together served to displease him. Why, he wondered, was the man still here? He had remembered her telling him that Hunter was only there to see that she got to Deer Lodge safely. He should have been gone by now.

Slater had already made up his mind to possess Elizabeth Walker, having been obsessed with her ever since he first saw her in Butte. Willing to try wooing her with his rakish charm and obvious wealth, he didn't rule out taking her by force if it came to that. Whatever the means necessary, he intended to have her. When he learned that she was held in such high affection by Carlton Kramer, it made her all that more desirable—and the presence of Cade Hunter all the more intolerable. He could already feel the anger building inside him. The problem of the young cowhand would have to be resolved.

Realizing then that he had allowed a rather lengthy void to occur in the conversation, he brought his attention back to the question just asked him by Mr. Kramer. "You ask what my plans are for the property I just acquired next to yours," he said. "Well, I plan to raise a few cattle, some horses, pretty much the same as you. There's nothin' on the land right now but a barn and a couple of shacks. I'm fixin' to start buildin' a proper ranch house and bunkhouse." He didn't express his intentions to eventually drive Kramer out of the valley. "I just wanted to let you know that I plan to be a good neighbor. Maybe we could help each other out. With talk of the railroad comin' this way before long, there oughta be a call for a lot of beef to be shipped back east."

Carlton Kramer considered himself a fair judge of men, and this man, Slater, struck him as an opportunist that one should be cautious in dealing with. Although he came proclaiming a desire to establish a state of cooperation between the two of them, Carlton thought it best to alert Ralph Duncan to keep his eye on any stock left to graze near the south property line. As far as the man who accompanied Slater, introduced as Ned Appling, he looked the part of a common thug, and never uttered a word during the entire conversation. In spite of his impression of his visitors, however, Kramer was a polite and reasonable man, so he told himself that first impressions were not always accurate. "I appreciate your dropping by to meet me, Mr. Slater. And of course I wish you success in your cattle business."

"Before I go," Slater said, taking Kramer's outstretched hand, "it would be impolite not to say hello to your niece. Elizabeth and I are acquaintances from Butte."

"Elizabeth is not actually my niece," Kramer replied, somewhat surprised that Elizabeth had any knowledge of John Slater, "but my wife and I have been like aunt and uncle to her since she was a small child." His initial thought after Slater's remark was hope that Elizabeth was not overly fond of the man.

Slater took his leave, annoyed that he had not been invited in for dinner. *The son of a bitch thinks he's too good to break bread with me,* he thought. *Give me a year, and he'll be singing a different tune.* He and the sullen man accompanying him led their horses toward the corral to meet the young lady. Letting Cade take Glory's reins, Elizabeth started toward the house while he went to the barn to unsaddle the horses.

"Take a good look at that feller," Slater said to Ned Appling. "I wanna make damn sure you remember him, 'cause you might be payin' him a visit later on." Slater handed his reins to Appling. "Now, you go on over by the corral and wait for me."

"Well, Mr. Slater," Elizabeth called out, "you show up everywhere."

"Afternoon, Elizabeth," Slater said, removing his hat to reveal his dark hair, parted down the middle, and brushing the dust that had settled upon the shoulders of his coat. "I swear, you get prettier every time I see you."

"Why, Mr. Slater, you're gonna have me blushing again. What brings you up this way? I thought you told me you would not be in Deer Lodge until next week."

"I changed my mind. Like I told you the other day, I bought some property over on the other side of the mountain. There's only a couple of cabins on it now, but I'm gonna start a cattle ranch, and I'm gonna build the finest house in Montana, a house fit for a queen. The woman that lives in that house will live like a queen, too. Not like a woman who marries a down-on-his-luck cowhand." He glanced toward the barn after the comment.

"My," Elizabeth responded, "that sounds romantic. I didn't know you were married."

"I ain't. But I aim to be, and I'm a man who gets what he aims at." His dark, brooding eyes locked on hers, leaving no question as to who that person might be. He nodded toward the barn. "How long is your pa's hired hand gonna hang around?"

"Uncle Carlton asked him to stay and help break some horses," she replied. Lowering her gaze from that of the outspoken man, Elizabeth preferred to remain coy, pretending not to recognize his obvious attempts to charm her. "Well, you sound very confident. I wish you luck in finding a wife."

"Oh, I already found her. She just don't know it yet."

"My, you *are* confident," Elizabeth said, mildly shocked by the man's brazen persistence. Headstrong in her own fashion, she was not prone to be picked off the shelf like a can of peaches. Deciding it best to cut the meeting short, she said, "Well, Aunt Cornelia is waiting for me to help with dinner, and you're probably anxious to get back. It was nice to see you again." With that, she turned and left him standing there to look after her as she walked away.

You little bitch, he thought, his eyes focused on her slender body. *You might think you're too good for John Slater, but we'll see about that.* Turning to look at Ned Appling slouching by the corral, he ordered, "Come on, let's get the hell offa this place."

At that moment, Cade walked out of the barn, on his way back to the horses in the other corral. His appearance in the barn door caused both men to stop, clearly measuring each other. A smug grin crossed Ned's face as he openly stared at Cade, sending a silent promise that there would be more between them. Although taking the measure of the man, Cade had no idea why he was being challenged, but the feeling in his gut told him that he definitely was. *Maybe he just doesn't like my looks,* he thought. Then, glancing from Appling to Slater, he thought, *Or maybe there's another reason.* Whatever, he had a feeling that he hadn't seen the last of Appling.

Oblivious to the sinister standoff behind her, Elizabeth ascended the porch steps to find a disapproving White Moon waiting for her at the top. "You play with fire," the Indian woman scolded. "That man, Slater, has evil in his eye."

Elizabeth laughed at her stern guardian. "He is kinda interesting in a rakish way," she said, just to inflame White Moon. It served its purpose.

"That man is no good for you," White Moon retorted sternly. She had not been really concerned about John Slater before, because she believed that Elizabeth was just being her impish self, and not really interested in the man. She had even teased her about the rich miner. Now she wanted to make sure that her young charge had her head on straight.

"You'll get yourself in trouble if you keep wagging your tail in front of him." Warmed up to the subject, she launched an attack on a second front. "Where did you go with Cade Hunter? You were gone a long time."

Elizabeth grinned mischievously. "I took him to my secret place," she answered coyly. "It was a beautiful morning for a ride."

Exasperated, White Moon followed the precocious young lady into the house. "I'm going to tie you up and take you to your father," she mumbled, causing Elizabeth to laugh. "Too much trouble for me," White Moon said.

Chapter II

His stay of a couple of days stretched into one of several weeks, as Cade continued to work with the horses, and eventually take over most of the responsibility for breaking difficult animals. It suited Cade fine because it kept his day occupied with the horses, a task he always enjoyed. It also exempted him from performing the other chores delegated to a cowhand at the home ranch. Unlike herding cattle on the open range, there were many chores done while not in the saddle—mending fences, milking, tending chickens, repairing buildings, working the garden, and so on—chores that most cowhands didn't care for. There were some advantages, however—sleeping in a warm bunkhouse with a kitchen, and the town of Deer Lodge, with its saloons and bawdy houses within walking distance.

The Deer Lodge Valley was a land of lush grass and plenty of water, which made it suitable for raising cattle. Surrounded by mountains that protected the valley from much of the harsh weather, Cade could appreciate why Carlton Kramer had settled here. Life was peaceful for him again. He was seeing Beth at least once every day, and while he took this as happenstance, Ralph Duncan was astute enough to notice the various excuses the young lady found to warrant her presence at the horse ring. He made no comment, finding it amusing and harmless that the two young folks seemed to enjoy each other's company.

The Bar-K crew was a laid-back group of men, the best that Cade had ever worked with, no bullies and no malcontents. He had made one good friend that he would occasionally go into town with to have a glass of beer. Red Reynolds was close to Cade's age. A red-haired man from Nebraska, he earned the nickname Skunk when a wayward skunk wandered into the outhouse while Red was performing his morning ritual. The uninvited guest prompted Red to evacuate the outhouse while still in the process of evacuating his bowels, much to the entertainment of the rest of the crew. Ralph Duncan, in a fit of laughter, suggested that since the outhouse was a "two-holer," they could have easily shared the toilet. An easygoing, good-natured man, Red took the japing without complaint, insisting the only reason he fled was because he thought it was a female skunk. Cade enjoyed the man's sense of humor, and the two young men became friends almost from the first day. It was a natural friendship, since they were the only really young men in Duncan's crew.

For the first time in a while, Cade felt that he had found a home base. Working in a well-operated organization, he was content to do his job every day without complications, save that of the unexplained feeling of uncertainty caused by his encounters with Beth Walker. The young lady was troubling to the extent that he wasn't really sure what their relationship was. She often called upon him to ride with her in the evenings, giving as excuse White Moon's concern for her safety. She never gave any sign of affection for him beyond that of a friend, and there was never a repeat of the kiss she had given him on their first ride to her "secret place." Red rode him unmercifully about the evening rides, convinced that there was a reason she never went with anyone else. "You better watch your step, boy," Red teased. "That gal might be shakin' out a noose for your neck."

Cade, in his quiet, imperturbable way, ignored the teasing, which usually frustrated Red. He spent considerable time, however, trying to make sense of Elizabeth Walker, but in the end, he always had to conclude that she was just being her lighthearted self, and that she felt safe with him. Content for the time being, he nevertheless thought about his dream of someday raising horses on his own. Those thoughts always brought back the image of the green, grassy prairie between the Yellowstone and the Crazy Mountains. That, in turn, revived more serious memories and his unfulfilled vow to Luke Tucker. He issued a silent apology to his old friend for the contentment he now felt. He could not avoid a feeling of guilt for this peaceful time of his life. It would not last.

"Is he dead?" was the simple question John Slater asked when he stepped off the porch to meet the rider walking his horse slowly up to the house.

"Hell, he don't never leave the place," Ned Appling complained, "except when he's ridin' with that girl. And you told me not to shoot him if she was around."

"Dammit," Slater cursed, "you oughta be able to get a shot at him when he's workin' the herd."

Ned shrugged. "He don't never drive cattle. He don't do nothin' but break horses. I could get a shot at him, but I'd have to be too damn close to the ranch to do it."

Slater was not happy with the lack of results. "Dammit, Ned, you're supposed to be the best gun hand I've got. Am I gonna have to send one of the other boys to do this one damn simple job?"

"That's up to you, I reckon," Ned replied evenly. He thought about the problem for a minute while they glowered at each other, then said, "Since bushwhackin' don't seem to be workin', maybe I can just call him out—you know, in a fair fight. The way he wears that Colt, it don't look like he uses it for anythin' but killin' snakes."

"That might be the best way to do it at that," Slater said, nodding slowly as he thought about it. He had never seen anyone faster with a gun than Ned Appling. "You can't go to the ranch to do it, though. That would be too obvious. He's bound to go into town sometime. You go on back to Deer Lodge and wait for him, but dammit, I ain't payin' for you to get drunk every night in the saloon."

"Don't worry. I aim to be sober when I'm workin'." He stepped up in the saddle again, and turned his horse toward the barn. "I'll start back first thing in the mornin'." He could not understand Slater's obsession with the Walker girl, but it was immaterial to him. He had killed men over smaller prizes, and it was the killing he enjoyed. There didn't have to be a reason.

"Come on, Cade," Red sang out when Cade walked in the bunkhouse door. "Let's go to Sullivan's and get us a drink of whiskey. It's payday, and I don't want no glass of beer—at least until after I've had my drink of whiskey."

"Sounds like a good idea," Cade replied. It had been a while since he had had a drink. "Let me clean up a little bit."

Several of the Bar-K hands were already at the rail in Sullivan's Saloon when Cade and Red walked in. Seeing their friends at the end of the bar, the two made their way through the crowded room to join them. "Hey, Skunk," one of the men called out, "what took you so long?"

"Some of us are civilized enough to wash a little of the cow shit offa us before we come to a fine establishment like Mr. Sullivan's," Red shot back, getting a wide grin from Dick Sullivan behind the bar.

"I see you brought Cade with you to carry you home," another hand commented.

"That'll likely be after we carry you home, Harvey," Red returned, laughing good-naturedly.

"Well, hurry up and get drunk," Harvey said. "We're gonna have a card game in a little while."

The playful banter went back and forth for a few minutes more between the cowhands from the Bar-K. Sipping his whiskey slowly, Cade remained an amused spectator while Red tossed his first shot back and tapped the bar with the empty glass to get Sullivan's attention. The thought crossed his mind that Harvey might be right. At the rate Red was starting the evening, he might have to carry him home. The thought caused a fleeting memory of the times he had been called upon to carry Luke Tucker home after a night of drinking. He didn't permit the thought to linger, however. He was not in a mood for guilty melancholy tonight.

In the back corner of the small barroom, another spectator watched the lighthearted kidding with more than casual interest. Unnoticed at a small table, Ned Appling sat, his fingers playing idly with his empty glass, his unblinking gaze focused on the quiet cowboy beside the redhead they called Skunk. *He ain't japing with the other men,* he thought. *Maybe he's a little bit shy.* The thought brought a baleful grin to his face. *I'll let him get a little more whiskey in him—slow him down a little.* Taking a harder look at the Colt Peacemaker Cade wore, he could see that it was riding in the holster that evidently came with the weapon, nothing special about it. Ned decided the extra whiskey might not be necessary. *He ain't ever pulled that iron in a gunfight,* he thought, and almost chuckled.

At Red's insistence, Cade let Sullivan pour him another drink. Taking the glass in hand, he turned to watch Harvey and a couple of the boys pulling chairs up to a table to start the card game. "How 'bout you, Cade?" one of them asked.

"No thanks, Nate," he replied, "I'll just watch a while." He was about to explain that he didn't have much luck when it came to poker when his arm was suddenly jolted from behind, causing him to spill half of his drink. He turned to look into the smirking face of Ned Appling.

"You're blockin' the damn bar," Ned growled. "How's a man supposed to get a drink with you standin' in the way?"

"Sorry," Cade said, and moved farther down the bar. He recalled having seen the man before, but at the moment his thoughts were distracted by the card game just getting started, and he couldn't place him.

Not to be denied a confrontation, Ned moved down the bar after Cade, and roughly shouldered him again. "By God, you just ain't gonna get outta the way, are you?"

Cade turned to face Ned again, puzzled by the man's behavior. He glanced at the open expanse of bar behind the menacing face. "Mister, nobody's keepin' you from orderin' a drink that I can see. Why don't you just go on about your business and leave me alone?"

"Who the hell do you think you are, you son of a bitch, tellin' me where I can stand?" He stuck his face up close to Cade's, taunting, his hand resting on the handle of his pistol.

Suddenly a wave of silence swept over the crowded room as the noisy patrons became aware of the incident unfolding at the bar. It came to him then. Cade remembered the man as the one who accompanied John Slater at the ranch. He had only seen him from a distance, but he was sure now that he was the same man.

Realizing what was taking place, Red stood up from the table. "Hold on there, Mister, you got no call to hassle Cade."

Ned shot a quick glance in Red's direction. "Set down,

Skunk. This ain't no affair of yours. This is between me and this son of a bitch tryin' to hog the whole damn bar."

His fuse lit, Red started forward, but Cade held out his hand to stop him, his whiskey glass still in the other hand. "Take it easy, Red. Sit back down and let me take care of it. I'll talk to him."

"Talk, hell!" Ned blurted. "I'm done talkin'. You're wearin' a gun. Now you'd best get ready to use it, or you're gonna crawl outta here like the low-down coward you smell like."

"Mister, for some reason, you think you've got a problem with me. S'pose you tell me what's eatin' at you. What is your real problem with me?" Cade asked, his voice calm and steady. "I'm thinkin' John Slater has somethin' to do with this."

"I don't give a damn what you're thinkin'," Appling bellowed. "If you don't step back and draw that damn gun, I'll shoot you down where you stand." With his hand hovering over the handle of his pistol, he stepped back to give himself room.

Still somewhat amazed to find himself in this standoff, Cade quickly assessed the situation. A quick glance told him that he might be in real trouble—the way the man's gun holster was slung to provide quick access, tied down to his leg, the holster itself, heavily oiled with a piece in the front cut away for minimum interference. Cade realized that this was his profession. Knowing he had no chance in a gunfight with Appling, he stepped after him as Ned backed away, crowding him. Pushing his face up close, Cade whispered loudly, "If you don't turn around and get outta here, I'm gonna kick your ass."

"What?" Ned blurted, hardly believing what he had just heard. "Why you son of a—" he started, reaching for his pistol.

Before he could draw the weapon, Cade's free hand clamped down hard on Ned's gun hand, holding the pistol firmly in the holster. With his other hand, he splashed the remainder of his whiskey into the surprised man's eyes. Appling jerked his head back from the stinging alcohol, and before he could open his eyes again, Cade planted a hard right hand that landed beside the point of his chin. Ned's knees buckled, and he grabbed the bar with his free hand to keep from falling, giving Cade time to pull his own weapon. A sharp rap across the bridge of Ned's nose was enough to send him on down to the floor, too groggy to know what had happened. Cade reached down and took Ned's pistol from him, then grabbed him by his heels and dragged the half-conscious man out of the saloon.

While this was taking place, the entire saloon had remained caught in stunned silence. As Cade came back inside, the room filled with noise again as Bar-K hands and everyone else suddenly recovered their voices. "Goddamn," was all a shocked Red Reynolds could utter.

"He don't say a helluva lot," Harvey exclaimed, "but it don't do to rile him, does it?"

Cade stood there, holding both guns for a long moment. Of all the patrons in the saloon, he, more than anyone, knew that it wasn't over. It wasn't a coincidence that Ned Appling was in that saloon tonight. He was sent there to call Cade out, and he would be back. Dick Sullivan moved up beside Cade then and cautioned in a low voice, "I think maybe it would be best if you called it a night, and maybe you'd better use the back door."

"Yes, sir," Cade replied. "I expect you're right." He could appreciate the fear the saloon owner had of the beaten man coming back to look for Cade and shooting up his saloon. He turned to find Red standing behind him. "It's all right, Red, I was thinkin' about going back to the bunkhouse, anyway. I'll see you later." He laid Ned Appling's pistol on the bar and left.

Outside, Cade stood at the back door of the saloon for a few minutes, allowing his eyes to adjust to the dark. The rowdy din of the patrons in the saloon provided a steady hum through the rough plank door behind him as he listened for any unusual sound in the dark. Looking left and right in the narrow alley that ran between the buildings and the creek behind them, he could see no sign of anyone lying in wait. Sensing no immediate danger, he stepped out of the shadow of the door and started walking back to the ranch.

Glancing briefly down the side alley between the saloon and the dry goods store and seeing no one, he passed behind the store, and walked out to the street on the other side. Pausing again to scan the main thoroughfare, he saw nothing but a few horses tied out front of the saloon. The street was empty all the way down to the south end where the Montana Territorial Prison stood. It occurred to him then the irony of a planned assassination in the very shadow of the prison. He wondered if the man who had come to kill him had ever been a guest at the notorious institution.

It could be, he told himself as he walked along the dark road, that he had jumped to the wrong conclusion regarding the incident in the bar. Why would a man of John Slater's obvious wealth and apparent standing hire a common gunman to eliminate a rival suitor? It didn't make sense, especially in light of the fact that Cade was no suitor at all. Maybe, he thought, Appling just had a burr under his saddle and felt like a fight. He remembered then the challenging stare from Appling the first time he had seen him. Thinking about it now, he was surprised he didn't recognize the man right away in the saloon tonight. Still, Appling was Slater's hired hand. Cade could not discard the possibility the fight was at Slater's bidding. Jealousy was a disease shared by rich men as well as saddle tramps.

He was almost back to the bunkhouse when he heard the sound of hooves on the road behind him, pounding hard in a full gallop. He turned just in time to hear the snap of a bullet as it passed beside his head a split second before the crack of the rifle. Instinct saved him from the second shot as he dived into the bushes by the side of the road, rolling over and over when he hit the ground, desperately searching for some form of cover. A low mound was the only reasonable protection he could find at the moment. He crawled behind it, pulled his Colt from the holster, and prepared to return fire.

Suddenly taking form in the darkness, horse and rider appeared, bearing down on him with rifle blazing shot after shot that ripped the grass on the mound, pinning him down on his belly. The horse was almost upon him when he heard the click of Appling's firing pin on an empty chamber. With angry determination, Appling drove the horse on, attempting to trample Cade, who rolled away, out from under the pounding hooves. As soon as he was free of the danger of being trampled, Cade raised his pistol and fired at his assailant who was galloping away in the darkness to reload his rifle. Given the opportunity, Cade scrambled to his feet and ran for the bunkhouse.

Too far committed at this point to worry about the close proximity to the ranch, and enraged beyond caution, Ned jammed more cartridges into his rifle, wheeled his horse and galloped back toward the mound. Catching a glimpse of the fleeing man in the darkness, he turned the horse sharply and chased after him.

Running for all he was worth, Cade rounded the corner of the bunkhouse and made for the shed built on the back. Spotting the barrel standing in the corner between the bunkhouse and the shed, he headed straight for it. In almost one continuous motion, he leaped up on the barrel and pulled himself up on the shed roof. There he crouched, his heart pumping in a desperate effort to supply the oxygen his lungs screamed for. In a few seconds' time, the dark horseman rounded the corner of the building. Kneeling on the short roof of the shed, Cade was face-to-face with the man in the saddle for a brief instant before he pulled the trigger. The bullet slammed into Ned's chest at point-blank range, knocking him over to one side as his horse galloped on. Cade leaped to the ground and ran after him. Slumped in the saddle, Ned's body sagged from side to side as his horse gradually slowed, finally coming to a stop. Cade approached cautiously, his pistol aimed at Ned's back, but the wounded man never looked back. After what seemed a long time, the rifle dropped from Ned's hand and he slid off to the side, landing dead on the ground, a bullet through his heart.

Within seconds, Cade was joined by a couple of men from the bunkhouse; one of them was Ralph Duncan. Up at the main house, a lantern appeared on the porch, the family having been awakened by the shots. In a few minutes, Carlton Kramer came down to the bunkhouse to investigate. He got there just as Cade finished telling Duncan what had happened, and why there was a dead man lying between his bunkhouse and barn. "Are you sure that's the same man?" Kramer asked, then held his lantern close over the body while Duncan rolled it over. "That's the same man who was with Slater, all right," he said, answering his question himself. Then he turned to Cade. "Why would he come gunning for you? Have you had a run-in with him before?"

"Well, not since about a half hour ago in the saloon," Cade answered. "He tried to start somethin' with me then. Before that, I haven't had any dealin's with the man. Some of the men were there. They can tell you the straight of it."

"Hell, man, I believe what you say," Kramer quickly replied. "I'm just wondering if we ought to even bother Bob Soseby about it."

"I don't see why," Duncan said. "Seems to me like Cade, here, has already handled it." Bob Soseby was a guard at the prison who worked part time as a deputy sheriff for the little town.

"Since the man was one of John Slater's crew," Kramer said, "we ought to at least send word to him."

"I expect so," Duncan agreed.

"I'm thinkin' it's up to me to carry his body over to Slater's place—since I'm the one that shot him." In truth, Cade would just as soon drag the body down to the pig lot and let the hogs enjoy him. There was no doubt that Appling had specifically targeted Cade. He had never seen Ned before that first day when he had accompanied John Slater to the Bar-K. He had to be sent by Slater, so Cade wanted to dump the body at Slater's front door and face the man. "I'll tote him over there in the mornin'," he said.

Kramer looked at Duncan and shrugged. Then looking back at Cade, he said, "I suppose that's the thing to do. Turn his horse in the corral and put his body in the barn overnight so the dogs or a stray coyote don't find it."

Returning to the house, Kramer was met at the door by his wife and Elizabeth. "What is it, Carlton?" Cornelia Kramer asked. "What was the shooting?"

"Is Cade in trouble?" Elizabeth asked before he could answer his wife, even before there was any mention of Cade.

"Nothing for you women to worry about," Kramer assured them. "Evidently a man who works for John Slater made an attempt on Cade's life, and Cade shot him. I'm fairly satisfied it was a case of self-defense. I'll know for sure in the morning when I talk to some of the boys who witnessed the trouble."

"Cade wouldn't shoot anybody in cold blood," Elizabeth insisted, her face captured by a frown.

Kramer paused for a moment while he studied the young woman's face. "You know that for a fact, do you?" he asked. When she hesitated to answer right away, he continued. "There is very little anybody knows about that young man except he has a knack for handling horses. He just showed up one day, from nowhere, heading nowhere. He seems nice enough. I like him, too. But it's about time somebody warned you to be a little more cautious in your choice of friends."

Taken aback, because she never expected a lecture from Carlton Kramer, Elizabeth was speechless for a moment. She looked at Cornelia for support and received nothing more than raised eyebrows telling her that she agreed with her husband. "Well, I know he wouldn't hurt anybody unless he had a very good reason," she said, then excused herself for bed.

Back in her bed, under a heavy quilt, she did not fall asleep right away. Her thoughts were of the quiet, sometimes brooding, young man who had so recently ridden into her life, and she questioned the suddenness of her interest in him. She could not rationally explain her attraction to him, and, too, she could not deny it. At times it came to her, to lie heavily upon her mind, and she would try for a while to make sense of it. Then, like this night, she would eventually give up trying to solve her weakness for Cade Hunter. *He just needs someone to take care of him,* she told herself as she finally drifted off to sleep.

The solid cloud cover that had moved over the valley and darkened the nights for the past week suddenly became restless. A cold wind swept down from the northwest, stirring the clouds into an unsettled state of agitation, bringing early snow flurries skipping across the Flint Creek Mountains to lightly blanket the prairie grass with silver. Cade saw it as a warning from Old Man Winter that he would be visiting the valley in earnest before long.

With Red's help, Cade lifted Ned Appling's body up across the saddle of his horse and tied his hands and feet beneath the horse's belly. "He's already a little stiff," Red commented, "I thought we were gonna have to crease him across his behind to bend him, but he ain't board-stiff yet." He finished tying off the body, then walked around the horse to stand by Cade while he secured a lead rope to his saddle. "Maybe I oughta ride over there with you, you know, just to keep you company. We don't know nothin' about that crew of Slater's. I ain't ever run into any of 'em, to tell you the truth. Folks say he's runnin' cattle into that stretch of land on the other side of Clark Fork, so I expect he's got a crew."

Cade paused to give Red a patronizing look. "You mean you wanna make sure I don't get into any more trouble. Right?"

"Well . . ." Red sputtered, "you ain't had much luck in gettin' along with any of his men so far."

"I expect Duncan would appreciate you helpin' move those cows in closer to the lower range," Cade said. "I can take care of myself." Red shook his head, concerned. Cade could readily see the reluctance in his friend's face. "I'll be careful," he said, trying to reassure him, then climbed into the saddle.

Chapter 12

"Well, lookee comin' here," Joe Stover remarked to the other three men lolling around a fire in front of a battered old barn. As one, they turned to stare in the direction he indicated.

"Ain't that Ned's horse that feller's leadin'?" Bonner asked. A big man, he got to his feet, trying to get a better look at the stranger slow-walking a mottled gray horse toward them.

"Looks like," Joe replied, "and I reckon that'd be Ned ridin' belly down across the saddle."

"You'd best go get Mr. Slater," Bonner said. "Looks like ol' Ned got hisself in a little trouble last night."

Unaware of the special mission Slater had sent Ned Appling on, the rest of his men had assumed that Ned must have slipped off to go to town the night before. The only speculation among them had been whether or not Ned had quit, or had just decided to have a night out for himself. Slater had issued strict orders for none of the crew to visit the town except on the occasion when it was necessary to drive a wagon in for supplies. Joe maintained that the reason was because Slater was new in the valley and he didn't want the good citizens of Deer Lodge to see the rough-looking band of cowhands he had hired. In truth, there was more experience in rustling cattle in Slater's crew of misfits. Like any saddle tramps, they favored the pleasures afforded by the saloons and bawdy houses, but Slater saw to it that there was plenty of whiskey kept at the ranch. Considering the fact that there were no more than a few head of cattle to take care of, there was little reason to complain.

While Joe went to the cabin to alert Slater of the visitor, the others continued to sit and stare at the rider now crossing the tiny stream that trickled down from the hills north of the ranch. "Wonder who's gonna move up to take Ned's place?" one of them speculated aloud. They all looked toward Bonner then, thinking there was little doubt who it would be if it came to a contest of strength. Ned had been the one who seemed to have Slater's confidence, and he was sure as hell the quickest with a gun. He had been the one who hired the rest of them, and even they found it strange that they had been recruited to drive cattle for a wealthy man like John Slater. In fact, it was a common joke among them, until Ned explained that Slater was a man who wouldn't hesitate to use any means to build his cattle empire, and he needed men who were not troubled by conscience and didn't ask questions.

With light flurries of snow swirling around him, Cade guided Loco slowly toward the cluster of rough buildings gathered at the foot of a long, rocky ridge. No more than shacks, abandoned by the previous owner, they stood in sharp contrast to the sturdy structures of the Bar-K. Cade looked the spread over as he rode toward the fire by the barn. Evidently, Slater was slow getting started on building his ranch, he thought. There were only a few odd cattle to be seen on the place, and from the looks of the group warming by the fire, it appeared no one was working.

When still fifty yards or so from the men watching him

approach, he reached down and pulled his rifle from the scabbard and rested it across his arms, just in case there were others here who, like the late Ned Appling, fancied themselves handy with a gun. No one by the fire moved to meet him as he rode up to about a dozen yards, and no one spoke, as they stoically watched him pull Loco to a stop. He scanned the impassive faces for a long moment, wondering if Slater had found the lot of them in the prison at the south end of Deer Lodge's main street.

Distracted then by the sight of John Slater emerging from the door of the cabin followed by another man, Cady reined Loco back to hold him steady while he untied the lead rope. Wearing a heavy fur coat, Slater stalked angrily across the yard toward Cade. The silent snowflakes seemed to eddy behind him as he strode forth, his long, dark hair swaying to and fro under his hat. Cade remained silent until Slater marched up to stand defiantly before Loco. Dropping the lead rope to the ground, Cade said, "I believe this belongs to you."

His eyes blazing with anger, Slater locked his gaze on Cade. Without breaking his relentless eye contact, he ordered, "Get him down from there!" Joe and Bonner immediately stepped forward to lift the corpse from the horse and lay it on the ground.

Looking at the crusted blood on Ned's vest, Joe said, "Shot through the chest."

Still with his eyes never leaving Cade's, Slater demanded, "Who shot him?"

"I shot him," Cade replied evenly.

"You got your damn nerve ridin' in here with his body," Slater growled, "after murderin' him."

"Poor ol' Ned," Joe lamented. "I know damn well it warn't a fair fight."

Cade gave the man a scathing glance. "Poor ol' Ned," he

repeated sarcastically, "got a bullet in his chest, not his back. He came lookin' for trouble and he found it." Loco stamped nervously when a gust of wind blew sparks from the campfire. Cade held the big horse steady while he locked his eyes on Slater again.

"That's your story, Hunter," Slater growled, "but I say the day ain't come when you could take Ned Appling in a fair fight. By God, I oughta shoot you down right now."

"You could try," Cade replied calmly.

"Look around you," Slater shot back. "You're a damn fool for ridin' in here like this." His angry frown faded slowly to a wicked grin. "I make it five to one—pretty good odds that you won't make it outta here alive."

The remark caused a perceptible change in the passive stance of Slater's men as they at once realized what their boss was threatening. A couple of them moved in a little closer, their hands dropping to rest on their gun butts. "Maybe," Cade replied, casually swinging the muzzle of his Winchester around to level at Slater, "but I make it dead certain that you're goin' with me if the first shot is fired."

At a standoff then, Slater held his hand up to keep his men in check, realizing that what Cade promised was very much possible. "Get off my land while you've still got the chance, Hunter," he spat. "You're askin' for trouble comin' here in the first place. Ned Appling had a lot of friends. They ain't gonna be too happy when they find out Ned was murdered. If I was you, I'd get the hell outta this territory before one of 'em catches up with you."

"Yeah," Cade replied, "ol' Ned's got a lotta friends now that he's dead. How many did the back-shootin' son of a bitch have while he was still alive?" He and Slater glowered at each other for a long moment before Cade asked what he came to find out. "I had no quarrel with the man. You sent a paid gunman to call me out. Now, suppose you tell me why you sent him after me. There ain't no reason for you to be gunnin' after me, but if it's got anythin' to do with the fact that I'm a friend of Elizabeth Walker's, then you're a bigger fool than I thought—and a miserable excuse for a man."

"Goddamn you!" Slater roared. "If you didn't have that rifle on me . . ." Enraged that Cade would bring up the girl's name to make him look foolish in front of his men, he pushed his heavy coat back to free his holster, provoked to the point of almost drawing the weapon. Thinking better of it when Cade raised the rifle, preparing to fire, he dropped his hand to his side again, his dark eyes burning with the fury surging through his body. Clenching his teeth, he growled, "Get off my land." Another gust of wind swirled the snowflakes around the fire, and swept Slater's long, black hair from his shoulders, for a moment revealing an ear with the very tip of it missing.

The shock slammed Cade's entire system like chain lightning. Stunned almost to paralysis for a second, he could only blurt the words, "Lem Snider!" In the span of that one jarring instant, it suddenly hit him why something about Slater's looks had troubled him from the beginning. The man's appearance had fooled him—the long hair and the absence of the bushy beard, but the clipped ear was no coincidence. The look on Snider's face when his name was called verified it. He was the man who had murdered Luke Tucker, and that explained why he wanted Cade dead. Snider must have recognized him as the man he had left in the river for dead.

Though only a few seconds passed while Cade was rendered incapacitated by the face-to-face encounter with the man he had vowed to kill, it was enough time to encourage Joe Stover to act. Seeing Cade's rifle waver slightly, Stover reached for his revolver. Catching the movement out of the corner of his eye, Cade's reflexes came to his aid. He whipped the Winchester around and cut Stover down before his pistol cleared the holster. The action that followed that shot happened so fast that Cade would have difficulty remembering afterward exactly how he had escaped with his life.

When Cade had been forced to turn and deal with Stover, Snider dived inside the barn door behind him while everyone else scattered for what cover they could find, scrambling to draw their guns in the process. Bonner was able to get to his pistol and get off one shot that passed under Loco's neck, causing the horse to bolt and Cade to hang on. Another shot from the barn barely missed Cade's head as his horse took off in a gallop. Realizing the horse had more sense than he did at that explosive moment, Cade laid low on Loco's neck and retreated under a hail of gunfire.

As he bolted across the tiny stream and raced across the prairie grass, now white with a frosting of snow, he looked behind him to see one of the men jump on Ned Appling's horse—it being the only one saddled—and give chase. Looking for the right spot to wait for him, Cade picked a low swale in the prairie. Though it offered little cover, he nevertheless pulled Loco to a sliding stop and leaped from the saddle. Cocking the Winchester, he knelt on one knee, aimed at the pursuing rider, and waited for the shot. Ignoring the wild pistol shots that creased the snow on either side of him, he continued to wait until the rider was within a hundred yards. Then, without haste, he slowly pulled the trigger, knocking the man from the saddle.

Safe for the moment, he had time to think about what to do. His brain was still reeling with the shock of finding Lem Snider right under his nose, and he had not been prepared for the confrontation. Had he known, he would have, without hesitation, shot the murdering thief as soon as he stomped out of the cabin. Like flashes of lightning, past images raced through his mind. He thought about the morning when Snider arrived suddenly with an offer to escort Elizabeth to Deer Lodge. There was something about the man that triggered a sour feeling in his gut right from the start. He should have paid more attention to what his instinct was telling him. And later, he should have known that jealousy was not the sole motive for sending a killer to challenge him.

The more he thought about it, the more obvious John Slater was. According to what he had been told when he came to work at the Bar-K, no one really knew much about Slater. Newly rich, it was said he had acquired a fortune as a miner. No one had the means to thoroughly check his story out, even if anyone had cared enough to do so. Cade thought about Luke Tucker's blood-encrusted body, pumped full of holes, the source of Slater's wealth, and he felt the fire burning in his veins anew. The sensation was followed at once by the sickening thought of Lem Snider calling on Elizabeth Walker. One thing he knew to be a fact, if nothing else, was that Lem Snider was a dead man.

It was time to slow down his racing brain and think coolly about his course of action to rid the world of the evil presence of this wanton killer. He thought about the location of Snider's ranch buildings underneath the brow of the rocky ridge. That would be the best approach, from the ridge above the ranch. There was no more time for planning the assassination, however, for some motion on the prairie caught his attention at that point. He looked out beyond the horse with the empty saddle, now standing motionless about fifty yards away from the body lying in the light covering of snow. Three riders were bearing down on him, and not sparing the horses. Snider had not waited for him to call.

*   *   *

"Kill the son of a bitch!" Lem Snider had roared as he ran from the barn and emptied his revolver after the galloping horse. Bonner and Bob Plummer were already emptying their weapons at Cade, but not one shot counted. Knowing he could not afford to let Cade escape to reveal his identity, he yelled, "Saddle the horses! We've got to stop him before he gets back to the Bar-K." When Plummer stopped to help Joe Stover, Slater roared, "Leave him, dammit!" and shoved Plummer ahead of him as he ran to the corral to saddle his horse. His face twisted with rage, he charged out of the corral, hoping Pete, ahead of them on Ned's horse, would catch up to Cade before he was able to find a place to hide. In a matter of minutes, the horses were saddled, and they took off across the white prairie after Pete.

After a short ride, they came upon Ned Appling's horse standing idly near a clump of sage. "Yonder!" Jim Bonner yelled, pointing to a body lying in the snow-covered grass.

The sight of Pete Johnson's corpse only served to further infuriate Lem Snider, and he whipped his horse unmercifully. "Get after the son of a bitch!" he roared. "I want him dead!" Galloping past the body, they suddenly were forced to pull up short when a series of rifle shots singed the air around them. No one was hit, but it was enough to cause them to draw back out of range until they spotted Cade at the foot of a narrow ravine that led back up the mountain behind him.

Satisfied that they had at least caught him before he could get back to the Bar-K, Snider calmed his rage enough to think about the situation. "All right," he said, "it's gonna be hard to get a shot at him where he's holed up." He thought about the man he'd already left for dead once. *This time,* he told himself, *I'll make damn sure. I'll cut his damn head off and see if he comes back from that.* At that moment, he couldn't remember hating a man more—not for Cade's ability to come back from the dead, but because the irritating young man threatened to explode his new image as a successful rancher. The jealousy over Elizabeth's apparent interest in the younger man was just a minor reason to rid himself of this nuisance.

His rage under control at last, Snider looked at the two men awaiting his orders. It was a manhunt now, and the odds were in his favor. Looking over the terrain that separated the three of them from their lone adversary, he concluded that to charge the ravine where Cade was holed up would amount to nothing less than suicide. "He thinks he's in a good spot to sit tight and pick us off if we try to rush him," he said. "But he ain't got no way outta that hole if we keep him pinned down. Bob, you're a better shot with a rifle than either one of us, so you see if you can't get up a little closer— maybe there." He pointed to a rise in the prairie about one hundred yards ahead. "You make sure he stays in that ravine. Me and Bonner will work up behind him on that mountain and flush him outta his hole. One of us is bound to get a shot at him."

Bob hesitated for a moment, looking out across the open expanse of grass between where they now stood and the slight rise in the prairie floor. "That ain't much cover, even if I do get across that open space," he complained. He glanced up to meet Snider's smoldering gaze and quickly added, "I reckon I can make it, though."

Snider nodded his head slowly, eyeballing Bob intently before he spoke. "You can make it. Hell, you'll still be just barely in range of that Winchester he's usin'." He paused a moment, waiting for Plummer to move. "Get goin', dammit! I ain't got all day."

They waited until Plummer had safely reached the designated spot behind the rise before pulling back and circling around to pick a place to start up the mountain behind Cade.

The mountains west of Deer Lodge were a rugged range
with the lower slopes dense with fir and pine. Snider was
confident that he and Bonner could work their way down
upon their target and surprise him. As they climbed on their
horses and rode off toward the mountain, they heard the
crack of Bob Plummer's rifle behind them.

Cade heard the bullet thud into the ground a few feet
short of the edge of the ravine, but chose not to return fire.
He had seen one of Snider's men driving his horse hard to
reach a low rise in the prairie, dismount, and scramble for
cover. Cade had not bothered to shoot at him, knowing the
range was too great to expect any success, and he was mind-
ful of the number of cartridges he had left. He couldn't afford to be wasteful. A long-range shoot-out would soon
deplete his ammunition.

Seeing that only one of the three had advanced to the position behind the rise, it was not difficult for him determine
the strategy they had decided upon. He turned to look at the
steep mountainside behind him, a thick maze of trees and
rocks. He decided right away that if the roles were reversed,
he would definitely pick the high ground. The thought
caused him to question his initial wisdom in picking the spot
in which he found himself. He squinted out along the base
of the ridge, trying to see if he could spot the other two riders, but they had evidently disappeared behind the point of
the ridge directly behind him.

It was a question now as to how long it would take them
to get to a killing position above him. He decided that his
best chance was to find another spot to take on the three of
them. Crawling back from the rim, he got to his feet and
went to the bottom of the ravine to get his horse. Stepping
up in the saddle, he gave Loco his heels, and the big horse
sprang into action. Up over the edge of the ravine he bolted,

hooves pounding the ground beneath the light covering of snow. Cade heard the shots ring out, both slugs impacting with a hard thump, one in the gray's neck, the other just behind the girth cinch in the horse's belly.

Loco's scream of pain was unlike that he had ever heard from a horse before. In the panic of the moment, Cade did not have the time to think about it, but it would return to haunt him later on. The horse tried to run, but staggered for a few steps before crashing to the ground and sliding several feet in the snow. Cade came out of the saddle and tumbled over and over before coming to rest a few feet from his horse. His first reflexive action was to recover his rifle. Then, although Bob Plummer was firing shot after shot at him, he tried to help his wounded horse. It took but one quick look to realize that Loco was finished. To spare the suffering horse further agony, Cade put a bullet into his head. It was the second time he'd had no choice but to put down a horse. This time, it seemed more difficult than it had with Billy.

With the sobering sound of stinging lead still flying around him, there was no time to mourn the faithful horse. With no other options from which to choose, he hastily grabbed the few extra cartridges from his saddlebag, crawled back to the ravine, and rolled over the edge. As soon as he disappeared from sight, the rifle fire stopped. Sitting there, listening, he suddenly realized his throat was dry, and he wished he had taken his canteen from the saddle horn. He thought about going back for it, but as soon as his head appeared above the edge of the ravine, Plummer opened up with the rifle again. *He's moved a lot closer,* Cade thought. He was forced to duck down again. No more time to sit around.

Knowing that Snider and the big fellow that Cade had seen back at Snider's ranch were most likely already working their way along the slope above him, he knew he had to get out of this hole. His decision made, he hesitated no longer. Running at a trot, he followed the ravine up through rocks and fir trees, intent upon positioning himself higher than the two who were coming to surprise him. As the slope steepened, he pushed on, laboring under the effort, until the forest of firs began to thin out, giving way to solid rock outcroppings and a small mountain meadow. Satisfied that he was surely above Snider and Bonner, he dropped down behind a rock to catch his breath. As his breathing became more regular, he waited and listened.

It was not long before he heard the sound of two horses plodding softly along the ground under the trees below him. Although he could hear them, he could not see them through the dense branches. Heading for the sound, he cautiously made his way back down the mountainside, being careful to expose his body as little as possible, gambling on the idea that their attention would be focused below them.

Again entering the band of trees that ringed the mountain, he stopped frequently to listen. Continuing on down through the dense growth, he stopped again when he came upon the signs of scuffed-up needles where the two had led their horses. Now with a trail to follow, he moved more quickly, but the steepness of the slope caused him to exercise caution lest he stumble and go sprawling down the mountain. Making his way around a sizable boulder, he suddenly caught sight of them. Raising his rifle to fire, he was a split second too late, for they took a turn straight down the slope. Since they were leading their horses, this put the horses between them and Cade and effectively shielded them from his line of sight. Every shot had to count, since he only had the cartridges in the magazine plus a handful of extras, so he lowered his rifle, and continued his careful pursuit.

Guessing that Snider and Bonner had most likely reached the top of the ravine where he had been holed up, he tried to hurry to catch them before they realized he had deserted the spot. He was a few moments too late, for he heard a shout from the bottom of the ravine. "He's lit out!" Bob Plummer yelled. "I got his horse! He's on foot and back up behind you somewhere!"

The warning was enough to cause both men to quickly react and take cover behind their horses. Straining to search the forest above him, Lem Snider peered out from under his horse's neck. Seeing nothing, he ordered, "Get up here, Bob." He and Bonner continued to scan the trees and rocks higher up the slope while they waited for Plummer to catch up to them. "Spread out," Snider ordered when Plummer climbed up beside them. "We'll move up this slope. He can't have got far. We'll flush him out."

Some seventy-five feet above them, Cade waited, his rifle resting in a crevice between two rocks. For several long minutes, there was no sign of the three men stalking him, then suddenly the branches parted below him to his right. He only got a glimpse of a shirt as the man cautiously pushed the branches aside, but it was all he needed. The Winchester bucked, and the cry of pain that immediately followed told him he had hit his target. He ejected the spent cartridge and swung his rifle around, ready to shoot again.

Knocked to the ground by the rifle slug in his chest, Bob Plummer rolled partway down the slope before being stopped against a tree trunk. "I'm shot!" he wailed in agony. Snider moved quickly over toward him, darting carefully from tree to tree. "I'm shot," Bob moaned again, holding his hands over the hole in his chest. "I think I'm dyin'."

Snider gave him no more than a casual glance. "Where is he?" he asked, more concerned with getting a shot at Hunter than worrying about the wounded man. When Plummer did not answer right away, Snider called out to Bonner, "Jim! You see where that shot came from?"

"No, but I think he might be up behind that big split rock straight up from where you're standin'," Bonner called back. Then he asked, "How bad is Bob hurt?"

Snider took another quick look at the suffering man. "Hell, he's a goner. See if you can climb up to them trees just below that rock, and I'll cover you." He pulled Plummer's rifle from the dying man's hand, ignoring the pleading eyes that stared up at him.

Jim Bonner was far from being an intelligent man, but he didn't have to think that one over before replying. "It'd be a whole lot easier for you to climb up there. You're right below him. He'd have an angle on me, and I'm a helluva lot bigger target than you are."

"Dammit! I said I'd cover you. You ain't yeller, are you?"

"I ain't yeller," Bonner came back. "I ain't stupid, neither."

Snider fumed over the situation for a few moments, trying to decide what to do. Hunter had the upper hand at this point. Snider had planned to use Bonner to draw Cade's fire, possibly giving him a clear shot at Cade. Thanks to the big man's reluctance to sacrifice himself, Snider was going to be forced to take a bigger risk. He didn't like taking risks unless he knew he had no choice. Hunter had to die. Snider had too much to lose if people knew the truth about John Slater, a man he had invented. "All right," he called over to Bonner, "we'll go up together." When Bonner didn't reply, he called out again. "All right?"

"All right," Bonner responded. He wasn't sure it was a wise move to leave the thick cover of the firs in an attempt to trap Hunter between them. In his mind, Snider wasn't paying him enough to take a fifty-fifty chance that Hunter would shoot at Snider, giving Bonner the shot at Hunter. He decided to make a show of following Snider's orders while not really sticking his neck out too far, until he saw some sign that Snider was not trying to use him as bait.

"Pepper that rock good so he has to keep his head down," Snider instructed. "That'll give us a chance to get up in them rocks below him." He immediately began to lay down a barrage of fire, cocking and shooting as fast as he could. Bonner followed his lead.

For Cade, pressed tightly against the boulder, it was like being trapped in a deadly hailstorm with bullets bouncing off the rock, ricocheting in every direction. Although there was a chill wind sweeping the rocky mountainside, he could feel the dampness of perspiration under his arms while he hugged his stone fortress, waiting for the pause in the barrage. He knew he was going to have to act quickly, anticipating his assailants' plan, for he knew they were probably on the move while they kept him pinned down. Suspecting they may have pinpointed the crevice he was using as a prop for his rifle, he rolled over to the edge of the boulder and waited. The moment he detected a pause in the firing of at least a couple of seconds, he came up on one knee, his rifle ready. He was in time to get a glimpse of one man, but that was all the time he needed to send a rifle slug slamming into Bonner's shoulder. He dropped down immediately after pulling the trigger and heard Snider's bullet ricochet sharply off the rock above his head. As quickly as he could pull the trigger and chamber another round, he sprayed the rocks from where he guessed Snider's shot had been fired.

Bonner yelped in pain and fell backward. Sliding back down the slope until he felt he was safe, he stared at the hole in his coat. "Slater," he yelled, calling his boss the only name he knew him by. "I'm hit! The son of a bitch shot me!" He hastily pulled his coat open to discover blood already seeping into his shirtsleeve. "I'm bleedin' like hell," he yelled out.

"Get back up here, dammit!" Snider roared. "We've got him cornered now. I see where he's hidin'."

Bonner had never been wounded before. The sight of his own blood draining down his sleeve and shirtfront was enough to make him panicky. "I'm bleedin' bad," he called out. "I need a doctor."

Lying up the slope from him, taking cover behind a large rock, Snider could only guess how bad Bonner was hurt. "It don't sound like you're hurt that bad. Where'd he get you?"

"In my shoulder, but it's still bleedin' like hell, and it feels like there's a bullet in there the size of my fist."

"Shoulder?" Snider responded, while trying to keep an eye on the split boulder above him. "Hell, that ain't nothin'. Get your ass back up here. We'll fix up your shoulder after we're done with Hunter." It was enough that Plummer had gotten himself killed, without Bonner crying over a shoulder wound. The big son of a bitch had left him to shift for himself, and Snider didn't like the situation. Hunter had only had two clear shots, and he struck meat both times. The thought crossed Snider's mind that he needed Curly Jenkins. He could have told Curly to go up that slope and kill the man behind the boulder. Curly was too dumb to question the advisability of it. Snider could still see the stupid expression on Curly's face on the day he shot him.

He waited a few more minutes, but he saw no sign of Bonner. "Dammit, Jim, hurry up!" he called. His call was met by silence that lasted for several minutes, and then he heard the sound of Bonner's horse as its hooves clattered on the rocks at the mouth of the ravine below him. *You yellow dog!* he thought, for he realized then that Bonner had turned tail. In a fit of anger, he rose up in an effort to spot the retreating man, and was immediately startled by a bullet that tore a hole in his coat sleeve. Diving for the cover of the rock, he fumbled to return fire, but was foiled by the lack of a target. Gripped by frustration and anger, he realized that without Bonner, he was at a distinct disadvantage. Hunter held the high ground, and as deadly as he had proven to be with that Winchester, he could sit up there behind that boulder and take potshots at him every time he made a move. The very thought of it caused his blood to boil, knowing that all he had gained with Luke Tucker's gold could be lost if Cade Hunter was allowed to escape. Yet he couldn't make a move toward him without risking his neck. He decided to try a different approach.

"Hunter!" he yelled. "Hunter! Can you hear me?"

"Yeah, I hear you," Cade called back.

"Hunter, listen, we don't have to settle this thing with guns. I know you're sore for what I done to you and Luke, but, hell, you mighta done the same thing if you'da been me. That dust was as much mine as it was Luke's." He paused again. "I might be willin' to cut you in for a share of that gold, and nobody gets shot. Whaddaya say? Let's talk about it."

"I don't wanna talk about the gold dust," Cade answered. "I wanna talk about Luke Tucker and his body shot full of holes. Tell you what, you come on out in the open and we'll talk about that."

"Nah, I don't think I'll do that. Why don't you come out from behind that rock, then I'll come out." He pulled his revolver from his holster and laid it on the ground beside him. "Listen, I didn't wanna have to shoot Luke Tucker. Hell, I always liked Luke. It was them two fellers with me that done it. That's the reason I shot them. They were about to shoot me, too, if I hadn't been quicker'n they were. I was plannin' to ask you and Luke for a share. That's all I was after, but

them two boys were wild. They shot you before I could stop
'em."

"I'm willin' to do this peaceable. Now, to show you I
mean what I say, I'm throwin' my guns out so you can see
'em. You throw yours out, and we'll talk about a partnership.
There's still plenty of that dust to split." He tossed Bob
Plummer's rifle out a few yards from the rock. "Here's my
handgun," he yelled, and threw the pistol out next to the
rifle. "Now you throw yours out, so I know I can trust you."

If there was one truth in the world that Cade was sure of,
it was the knowledge that Lem Snider would lie to Saint
Peter if he thought he could get away with it. What Snider
could not know was that Cade's last extra cartridge was
chambered in the Winchester. He had been in the process of
taking the .44 cartridges from the cylinder of his pistol and
loading them in his rifle when Snider threw his weapons out.
He quickly replaced the bullets in his pistol. "All right,
Snider," he yelled, "we'll talk. Here comes my rifle." He
pitched it carefully a few feet from the boulder so that the
barrel was pointing downhill. "I don't have a handgun." He
hoped Snider wouldn't remember that he was wearing a
Colt. It mattered little, for he was certain Snider was not
without a weapon. He knew it was risky, but he was determined to avenge Luke's death, even if it meant a contest to
see which liar was quicker. He was down to six cartridges,
and one of those was in his rifle lying out on the open
ground. He couldn't afford to continue a long standoff. "All
right," he shouted, "I'm comin' out!"

Peering through the crevice in the boulder, he saw Snider
stick out his arm and signal. Cade quickly moved to the
other side of the rock, knowing Snider's eyes would be focused on the near side. Suddenly lunging from cover, he
dived on the ground, his pistol ready, but the steepness of the
slope caused him to slide several yards farther than he had

planned. Snider, anticipating Cade's appearance around the near side of the boulder, stepped clear of the rocks just far enough to bring his rifle to bear. The unexpected appearance of Cade at the far side of the boulder forced him to whirl and fire quickly, his shot wide by a foot. With no time to take dead aim, Cade returned fire, also missing, with two shots that ricocheted off the rocks Snider had been hiding behind.

Caught in the open, Cade scrambled back up the slope in an effort to get behind the boulder again. Snider had already jumped back out of sight. Both men had gambled on getting that one clean shot, and neither had been successful. Snider, however, realized that Cade did not have time to get back out of sight. He quickly stepped out in the open again, just in time to see Cade reach the side of the boulder on his hands and knees. There was time for one shot, and he made it count. His bullet caught Cade in the side, causing him to collapse on the ground.

Clawing for a handhold, Cade managed to pull himself behind the huge rock that had been his protection. With a malicious grin of triumph, Snider cocked his rifle and moved up the slope to finish the wounded man.

Wincing from the fiery pain in his side, Cade dragged himself away from the edge of the rock, his shirt already soaking with blood. He struggled to slide his back up against a tree trunk behind the boulder. Knowing Snider would be coming to finish him off, he was suddenly emotionally drained with a feeling of failure, for he felt he had let Luke down. Aware of his life's blood draining from his side, he cocked his pistol, determined to take Snider with him.

Never anxious to charge after a wounded animal, Snider stepped up to the side of the boulder, taking great care. With his rifle trained on the edge of the rock, he gradually eased himself along the cold surface of stone until he was almost to the edge. Then he suddenly stepped clear of it, prepared to shoot, hastily searching for the wounded man. In the time it took for Snider to spot him propped up against the tree trunk, Cade got off two shots. One glanced harmlessly off the side of the rock, the other struck Snider just below the collarbone, spinning him around, causing him to stumble and fall backward.

In a panic to recover, Snider scrambled to his hands and knees, clutching his rifle desperately. He was out in the open, and expected Cade to appear over him at any moment, but Cade did not come. Snider tried to reconstruct the picture he had only seen for a split second. Hunter was propped up against a tree with a bloody stain over half his shirt. In spite of the pain in his shoulder, Snider almost laughed aloud. *He ain't coming after me because he can't,* he thought. *He's gut-shot.* Since he felt sure he had the time, he took a moment to judge the seriousness of his own wound. Deciding that it was not life-threatening, he pulled a bandanna from his coat pocket and stuffed it inside his shirt. *That'll hold till I can get into town to see the doctor,* he thought.

Keeping a watchful eye on the huge boulder a few yards up the slope from where he knelt, Snider considered his next move. Hunter was no doubt waiting for him to show his head around that rock again in hopes of a lucky shot. Snider weighed the probability that Hunter would bleed out and die, like Plummer. He could just leave him to die, and not risk taking another bullet. But, he argued, maybe he wasn't hurt as bad as he looked. *I've already killed the son of a bitch once, and he came back. I'd better make damn sure this time.*

Cade knew he was hurt bad. Every time he tried to move, his body confirmed it. There was nothing he could do but wait and do the best he could with the ammunition left in his Colt. He knew he had hit Snider, but he wasn't sure how bad the wound was. It had been several long moments since Snider spun away from the edge of the rock. Maybe he, too, was badly hurt. *And maybe he ain't,* Cade thought, and decided he was going to have to move from the spot he was in the first time Snider peeked around the rock.

The tree trunk he was resting against was not very big, but he pulled himself around behind it, figuring it was better than nothing. He tried to get to his feet, but the pain felt as if he was ripping his insides apart. So he dropped to the ground again and waited, pressing his free hand against the wound to try to stop the bleeding.

Come on, you son of a bitch, Cade thought as the seconds ticked away, and there were no further attempts by Snider. Suddenly a sound on top of the boulder caused him to react, ready to shoot, but he held his fire when he saw a fist-sized rock bounce to the ground. Instinct told him to redirect his aim to the left of the boulder, knowing that the rock had been thrown by Snider in hopes of distracting him. As he figured, Snider stepped halfway out, firing his rifle as he did. The rifle slug buried in the tree trunk, and before Snider could cock and shoot again, Cade fired. His shot was rushed and missed Snider's chest, ripping into his arm instead. He had time to shoot again, but the second time, there was nothing but the sharp click of the hammer striking an empty cylinder.

Crying out in pain, Snider quickly pulled back to safety. "Damn you!" he roared in pained anger as he took stock of his wounds that now soaked both sleeves with blood. His overpowering rage caused him to ignore the excruciating throbbing near his collarbone. Determined to kill the man who had brought this trouble down upon him, he picked up his rifle again, and started to edge up to the side of the rock. Then a thought struck him, and he paused to consider. In the heat of the exchange of gunfire, something had slipped by him, and it came to him now. After he was shot, there was the sound of a hammer falling on an empty chamber. *Hunter's gun is empty.*

With a new sense of urgency, he forgot his wounds, and rushed back to the edge of the boulder, in an effort to get to Cade before he could reload. Not willing to throw all caution to the wind, however, he eased his head around just far enough to see with one eye. What he saw surprised him. Instead of frantically jamming cartridges in his pistol, Cade sat calmly, leaning against the tree trunk, his pistol aimed at Snider. But he did not shoot. Stunned for a moment, Snider realized that he had been staring at the gun for several seconds, and Hunter had failed to shoot.

Gradually, he eased himself away from the rock until he was standing fully exposed to the man holding a gun on him. "You're out of bullets," he said, hardly believing it himself. Holding his rifle at his hip and aimed directly at Cade, he moved a step closer, still halfway suspecting a trap, but getting bolder with each step. Finally, he stopped, now no more than a couple of feet from the wounded man. "Ain't that a shame," he taunted, "you run plumb outta bullets."

"Maybe," Cade answered and pointed his pistol at Snider's head, causing him to jerk back abruptly and raise his rifle to shoot. But he didn't pull the trigger when Cade's gun failed to fire. "Bang," Cade said softly before tossing the pistol aside.

Standing there with both sleeves of his shirt bloody, a triumphant smile slowly spread across Snider's face as he fully realized the irony of the moment. "Out of cartridges," he repeated as if enjoying a great joke. "I bet you've been lookin' for me ever since I shot you and run off with your gold." He shook his head, mocking the helpless man at his feet. "Well, you found me. A lotta good it did you. You wound up just like ol' Luke." He raised his rifle and aimed it at Cade's face.

"Maybe I oughtn't to finish you off too easy. You caused me a helluva lot of trouble. Maybe I'll just pump a few more holes in you, so you can die real slow. Only this time, I'm gonna wait you out to make damn sure you don't turn up again like last time."

"Kiss my ass, Snider," Cade replied. "I'll wait for you in hell."

Snider chuckled, pleased by Cade's defiance. He lowered the rifle's front sight a little. "The first one's goin' in your gut."

Cade heard the rifle fire, but he did not feel the bullet tearing into his abdomen. Stunned, he looked into Snider's face, astonished by the stark expression of surprise that suddenly replaced the mocking sneer. Another shot rang out, and Snider dropped to his knees for a few seconds before falling facedown on the rocky ground.

Scarcely able to comprehend what had just taken place, Cade was not sure if his life had been saved or not. The big man he had wounded in the shoulder was out there somewhere. There was no time to do anything about it, however, for in the next second, he heard the sound of a horse's hooves on the gravel by the boulder. A moment later, leading the horse, Red Reynolds appeared at the edge, a dread look of anticipation etched across his face. "Cade?" he said. "Are you still alive?"

"I think so," Cade answered, "but I got a hole in me that ain't supposed to be there." The intense strain that had captured his entire body suddenly left him, and realizing that he was in fact alive, he at last relaxed.

The sudden release of tension caused Red to think Cade was dead. In a panic then, he rushed to his side. "Cade!" he blurted, grabbing his friend by the shoulders. "Don't die! Dammit, Elizabeth will kill me."

"Dammit, Red," he exclaimed, "I won't unless you're

gonna shake the life outta me." The pain in his side from Red's sudden assault was evidence enough that he was still alive.

Red released him at once, then sat back on his heels and grinned. "Well, for a minute there, you looked like you was checkin' out. How bad are you hurt? You don't look too good."

"I don't know," Cade answered. "I took a bullet in my side. I ain't sure how bad it is. All I know for sure is that I can't move without feelin' like I'm tearin' out my whole insides."

Red grimaced as he considered their predicament. "Well," he concluded, "I'm gonna have to carry you down offa this mountain. I sure can't do nothin' for you up here." He knew it was going to be painful as hell, but there was no choice in the matter. Cade needed a doctor. "If I can get you up on my horse, you think you can stay on till I get you down to the bottom?"

"I reckon I'll have to," Cade replied, though he was not looking forward to it.

"All right, then, let's get to it. You already look like you lost all the blood in you." He went back to lead his horse in closer. Passing Snider's body, he paused to roll him over with the toe of his boot. "Looks like I came along at a pretty good time, don't it? This son of a bitch was fixin' to shoot you." He shook his head as if trying to make sense of it. "Why was he fixin' to shoot you, anyway?"

"It's a long story," Cade replied. "I'll tell you about it later."

Red paused to chew his lower lip as he considered that. Looking back at Cade, he asked, "I came across another dead feller down the hill a piece. You do that, too?"

"Yeah," Cade answered, grimacing with pain as he tried to shift his body to a better position to try to get up. "How the hell did you happen to come up here?" Then before Red could answer, another thought occurred to him. "What did you mean back there when you said Elizabeth would kill you?"

"Well, see, that's just it," Red replied as he dropped the reins and prepared to help Cade up. "Elizabeth came down to the corral lookin' for me. She said she'd heard about you takin' that jasper you shot back to John Slater's ranch. For a while there, she went on about how bad you was probably feelin' about killin' a man, even if it was self-defense. She lit into me like it was my fault for lettin' you go over there by yourself. She said if all Slater's men were like the one you shot, she was afraid you'd get in more trouble." He looked at Cade with an apologetic expression. "I told her I offered to go with you, but you said no. That didn't really satisfy her none. She told me to climb on my horse and not to come back without you." He cocked up one side of his mouth in a little half smile. "I was damn near too late, wasn't I?"

"You might be yet," Cade said. "Let's see if we can get me on that horse."

It was a painful task, but they managed to get Cade in the saddle, although not without starting the bleeding again. It was all he could do to remain upright, and before they had descended halfway down the mountain, he had to fall over on the horse's neck. Trying to pick the easiest way down the slope, Red led the horse across and back to avoid the steeper parts. At the top of the ravine in which Cade had first taken refuge, they found Snider's horse standing waiting. Red took the reins and led both horses down into the ravine. Looking back at his obviously suffering friend, he said, "Maybe I can make one of them things the Injuns use to tote things when we get down to level ground. Might make it easier to haul you to the doctor."

Cade didn't answer. He was concentrating on trying to

hang on to the horse. He knew his friend pretty well, and he figured Red didn't have an ax to cut poles, or enough rope to fashion a travois. He also knew he wasn't going to be able to stay on that horse all the way back to Deer Lodge. He was already feeling light in his head and weaker by the moment. In an attempt to get his mind off the pain in his side, he tried to think about what Red had told him about Elizabeth. Why, he wondered, had she sought out Red to come after him? Was she really that worried about him? He tried to imagine her youthful, smiling face when she teased him. And he felt a warm tingle on his cheek where she had lightly kissed him on the first day they rode to her "secret place." These were the thoughts that were drifting through his mind when they reached the bottom of the slope, where Red caught him just as he was about to slide to the ground unconscious.

"This ain't gonna work," Red said. "It's too far back to Deer Lodge. You're gonna bleed to death bouncing around on that horse. I'm gonna have to go get the doctor and bring him to you." It was a painful truth, and the evidence was written on Red's face. He didn't want to leave Cade while he made the ride all the way back to town, but he was afraid the ride might be enough to finish him. "Tell me what to do, Cade," he pleaded softly.

Recovering his senses somewhat after his near fall from the horse, Cade told Red to leave him there in the ravine, but Red protested that there was no shelter there from the cold night. Then Cade thought about Snider's ranch. There was no one there now. All of his men were gone. "His ranch is only about a mile or so back that way," he said. "You can leave me there. I'll be all right. You can build up the fire, and I'll be warm and dry while you go get the doctor."

Cade could see the relief sweep over Red's face, but his friend questioned his suggestion. "You sure you wanna go to Slater's ranch? Ain't he got more men there?"

"He didn't have but four left," Cade explained. "You'll find one of 'em dead between here and the ranch, one of 'em dead at the ranch—you saw one of 'em back up the hill. The other one's shot and he took off. There ain't nobody left."

After a ride that seemed a lot longer than the actual distance, Red slow-walked the horses into the tiny cluster of shacks that had served as John Slater's ranch. While Cade waited, slumped over in the saddle, Red took a quick check of the buildings and decided right away that the cabin Snider had used for his ranch house was the better of the two dwellings. With Red's support, Cade was painfully helped into the cabin.

With no other options, Cade was reluctantly settled on a homemade bedstead that, unbeknownst to him, had been used by Snider. Too weak and sick to protest, Cade lay exhausted while Red built a fire in the fireplace. Once there was a healthy flame going, he took a look at Cade's wound to see if he could do anything to help, and decided he could not. "At least you ain't bleedin' no more," he said. "You think you can hang on till I get to town and back with the doctor?"

Cade nodded, then said, "If you leave me some water."

Red took a look at the water bucket in the corner by the table, thought better of it, and fetched his canteen from his saddle. "Here, you better take this," he said, placing the pistol he had found on Plummer's body next to the bed. Then he stood back and took a long look at his friend. "Don't shoot yourself with it," he said as he turned to leave. "I'll be back as soon as I can." Cade nodded and tried to smile. Before the sound of Red's horse's hooves had faded away, Cade sank into a sound sleep—the last thought on his mind was that Luke could now rest in peace.

Chapter 13

Kneeling by the clear stream that bubbled down from the rocky ridge above him, Bonner soaked his bandanna in the chilly water, carefully cleaning the blood away from the wound. Though painful, it did not appear as serious as he had at first thought. The fact that he had run made no impact upon his conscience. He had no conscience to speak of. Jim Bonner was no fool as far as Jim Bonner was concerned. First Ned Appling, then Stover, then Johnson, then Plummer—the man that Slater wanted dead had taken them out one by one. And when he himself was shot, Bonner decided it was time to remove himself from the list of Hunter's kills. *Slater be damned!* If he wanted the man so badly, he could do the job himself.

The thing that Bonner wondered about now was what the final result had been. He had heard a lot of shooting after he fled the mountainside. He had to wonder who walked down off that slope when the shooting was done. Looking closely at the hole in his shoulder, showing only a small amount of blood now, there were other thoughts that overcame his concern for the bullet lodged in his shoulder. Slater was a wealthy man. He owned a saloon in Butte, but he had spent a great deal of time on the ranch recently purchased here in the valley. According to what Ned Appling had told Bonner, Slater had bought the ranch with gold dust. The more Bonner thought about it, the more it made sense to him that Slater would keep his gold or cash close to him—maybe hidden somewhere at the ranch. *By God, it's worth a little look-see around that ranch,* he decided. Thinking it best to wait until dark, he stuffed a dry piece of shirt over his wound and sat down against a tree to bide his time until sundown.

Walking his horse slowly across the open space between the old barn and the cabins, Bonner stopped to consider the horse in the corral. It was Slater's horse. *So Slater was the survivor of the shoot-out on the mountain,* he thought. This put a different shine on the situation, and he had to take a moment to decide if he wanted to face Slater or not. He thought of the shouted curses that Slater had hurled after him when he was retreating from the gunfight. What would Slater think now if he came back after running out on him? He might be inclined to shoot him on sight. Bonner could not decide—surprise him, kill him, and search for the gold, or try to talk his way back, using his wound as excuse for deserting, then kill him when the opportunity presented itself? It would take some serious thought. Slater was a dangerous man.

Inside the cabin, Cade lay in fitful slumber, a chill having descended upon him. The fire in the fireplace had died down to a few rosy cinders that cast a dull glow in the darkened room. He had thought about dragging himself from the bed to put more wood on the fire, but he was reluctant to revive the pain that such movements were certain to cause. Although it disgusted him to do so, he had pulled Snider's blanket over him instead, and dropped back into his uneasy sleep. He was not aware that he had company until the cabin door creaked ajar and Bonner cautiously peeked into the room.

"Slater," Bonner whispered, "you all right?"

Blinking sleep from his eyes, Cade looked up to see the huge man now filling the low doorway as he stepped inside. "Yeah," he whispered in response.

"I weren't shot as bad as I thought, so I went back up that mountain to help you, but you was already gone by then," Bonner lied. Getting no reply, he reached slowly down and rested his hand on his pistol. "Are you shot or somethin'?" When there was still no reply, he knew something was wrong—maybe Slater had caught a bullet. The possibility of that was enough encouragement for Bonner to make up his mind. Expecting to see evidence of a gunshot, he suddenly reached down to grab a handful of the blanket, and snatched it off the wounded man. Even in the soft firelight, he could plainly see the muzzle of the Colt .45 staring up at him, but for only a split second before it exploded in his face. With eyes wide in shocked surprise, Bonner sank to the floor beside the bed and lay still. Though it took little effort on Cade's part, it was enough to tire him out. He dropped his arm back beside him on the bed and lay there without moving. In a few minutes' time, he was asleep again.

"Where you go?" White Moon demanded, standing in the doorway of her room. "It's the middle of the night."

"Shhh . . ." Elizabeth replied as she tiptoed down the front hallway. "You'll wake everybody."

"Where you go?" White Moon repeated sternly.

Elizabeth explained that Red Reynolds had tapped upon her window to tell her that Cade had been seriously wounded, that he was on his way to fetch Dr. Bates.

"Why he wake you up to tell you that?" the Shoshone woman asked.

Elizabeth shook her head, exasperated that White Moon had to ask. "To give me time to get dressed and get my horse saddled," she answered. White Moon seemed astonished. "Because Red knows I care about Cade," Elizabeth explained. She didn't bother to tell White Moon that she had persuaded Red to ride after Cade. When White Moon still seemed puzzled about where Elizabeth was going in the middle of the night, Elizabeth told her that she was going to meet Red and the doctor on their way out to John Slater's ranch and join them. White Moon was totally confused at that, until Elizabeth relayed Red's accounting of the shootout on the mountain. "John Slater shot him, so I'm going to help him if I can," she concluded.

"Not without me," the somber Indian woman stated emphatically, finally understanding. She turned immediately to fetch her clothes.

"Well, hurry up," Elizabeth said, "and don't wake Aunt Cornelia."

"What the . . ." was as far as Red got when he saw the cabin door standing open. Already feeling a need for caution when they had found another horse, saddled and tied to the porch post, he motioned for the others to stay back until he checked the cabin. Pulling his revolver, he dismounted, stepped quietly on the porch, and edged slowly toward the door. Inside, he found Cade just as he had left him, with the exception of one oversized corpse lying on the floor beside him. "Well, I'll be gone to hell," he muttered under his breath. He holstered his weapon and signaled the doctor. "You ladies better wait a little while," he said, then went to Cade's side.

Cade opened his eyes to find Red's face inches from his, Red's eyes wide and staring. When Cade's eyelids flickered open, Red recoiled a few inches, startled. "I thought you were dead," he said.

"I thought I was, too . . . a couple of times," Cade said. "When I woke up just now and saw that ugly face of yours, I was sure I was in hell." He formed a weak smile for him.

"I see you had company while I was gone," Red said. "I'd best drag him outta here." He took another look at the body and added, "That is, if I can. He's a big'un." He shook his head in wonder. "You sure picked a helluva bunkmate."

Cade smiled. "Well, at least he don't snore."

Dr. Judson Bates entered the cabin as Red was in the process of pulling Bonner's body away from the bed. Still grousing about being routed out in the wee hours of the morning, he paused to register a look of disgust for the scene. "Merciful heavens," he snorted, "this place looks like a pigsty."

Red returned his look with a wide grin, and nodded toward Cade. "He don't live here, he's just visitin'."

Bates turned to watch Red pull Bonner's body out the door. "Damn fools," he muttered. "I don't know why I bother. Patch 'em up and they go out and get themselves shot again." He glanced back at the patient, then called after Red, "Tell the women to come on in here. I need somebody to build that fire up again and heat up some water."

Elizabeth was already on her way in, having waited as long as her patience would permit. White Moon was right on her heels. "Oh, Cade," Elizabeth sighed in distress upon seeing the strong young man in such pale condition. Charging past the doctor, she ordered, "White Moon, build up that fire and heat up some water. We've got to get him out of those clothes and clean him up."

White Moon nodded and quickly responded. Dr. Bates stepped aside to avoid being run over by the big woman. He gave Elizabeth a look of mock alarm, astonished by the young woman's taking charge of the situation. "Well," he said somewhat chagrined, "I don't know why you bothered to get me out of bed."

Realizing then how assumptive her actions may have seemed, Elizabeth smiled at the doctor apologetically. "I just thought you might want him out of that bloody shirt."

Bates laughed. "I do. Let's get him cleaned up a little so I can see what we've got."

Even with the flurry of activity that had suddenly filled the tiny cabin, Cade was only halfway conscious of what was going on. Afterward, he remembered talking to Red and feeling the doctor's probing, but he also was aware that Elizabeth was in the room—even though he thought that unlikely. It was a little before midday when he woke up with a sense of where he was, and discovered that Elizabeth was there indeed. "Beth? What are you doin' here?"

"Somebody has to make sure you take care of yourself," she said, pleased that he had awakened. Guessing that he was well enough now to scold, she continued. "Were you out of your mind, coming out here by yourself? Red told me about John Slater. I couldn't believe it! He was going to kill you!"

Although still very weak, he tried to smile. "Yeah, Red saved my bacon, but I reckon he mighta spoiled your weddin' plans."

She favored him with a deep frown. "Bite your tongue," she scolded. "I never had any such feelings for John Slater." Smiling again, she said, "Dr. Bates said it's a good thing you stayed put here last night instead of trying to ride back to town." She sent a gracious smile toward the doctor then. "He's got you all patched up, and you'll be on your feet in no time."

"I reckon I can stay on a horse long enough to get back to the Bar-K now."

Bates cocked his head toward his patient when he heard Cade's remark. "You don't need to ride anywhere for a day or two. You were mighty lucky, young man. That bullet didn't damage any major organs, but it only missed by a hair. You're gonna have to be laid up for a spell until some healing starts."

That caused a look of concern to fall upon Cade's face. "I can't stay here," he protested.

"Yes you can," Elizabeth interrupted. "We're gonna stay with you, White Moon and me. We're going to clean this place up, and Red's going to butcher a cow. Dr. Bates says you need fresh meat to build your blood back up."

A silent observer to that point, Red piped up then. "Yeah, I'm gonna go cut out one of Slater's herd and butcher it." He laughed. "I ain't seen more'n half a dozen cows around here. Ain't much of a cattle empire." He took a few steps toward the door, then stopped and turned to face Cade again. "I still can't figure why that man wanted you dead so bad. You sure you ain't stepped on his toes somewhere before, and you just forgot about it?"

"I've seen him before, and I sure as hell never forgot about it," Cade answered. He then went on to tell them about Luke's gold, and how Lem Snider had murdered Luke Tucker. "I guess he recognized me all along. He looked at me kinda funny on the mornin' we left Butte for Deer Lodge, like he'd seen a ghost. I just didn't recognize him."

Listening with eyes open wide, Elizabeth was horrified to learn of John Slater's murderous past. She could not help but quiver suddenly when she thought about his quest for her affections. Glancing at White Moon, she was met with a smug expression and the words, "I told you—no good."

Cade couldn't really say he liked the idea of remaining in Lem Snider's cabin at first. There was still a loathing for spending any length of time in any dwelling that Lem Snider had called home. But he soon softened his feelings of resentment after White Moon and Elizabeth burned Snider's personal items and scoured the cabin. Red killed one of Snider's cows, but left the butchering to White Moon, while he escorted the doctor back to Deer Lodge. He promised Elizabeth that he would also reassure the Kramers that she was all right. She had left them a note the night before, but she was afraid they would be worried until they heard more from her.

When Dr. Bates and Red had departed for town, White Moon put some beef over the fire to roast. The aroma wafting from the roasting meat reminded Cade that he had not eaten for some time, and he was thankful that Snider's bullet had not pierced any internal organs. The day passed peacefully enough with only one minor confrontation between patient and nurse—an argument over whether Cade was going to struggle to get out of bed to answer nature's calls, or use the bucket White Moon found in the barn. "Don't be silly," Elizabeth scolded. "Dr. Bates said you were to stay in bed for at least a couple of days. Besides, you act like you've got something nobody's ever seen before."

"Maybe so," Cade replied, "but I ain't ready for you to see it."

A compromise was reached with the two women agreeing to leave the cabin while Cade used the bucket. "It's not fair," Elizabeth complained, joking. "The ladies have to go outside and freeze our behinds when we get nature's call, while you get to go inside where it's warm."

By nightfall, Cade was tired and more than ready to sleep. Elizabeth checked the bandage around his torso as Dr. Bates had instructed, then tenderly tucked the blanket around him. Feeling his eyes searching her face as she tended him, she met his gaze and smiled.

"I don't know how your daddy would feel about this," he

said softly. "I reckon maybe with White Moon here to look after you, he wouldn't get too upset."

She didn't answer at once, continuing to smile down at him. Then she glanced over to see that White Moon was tending something on the fire, and leaning close, kissed him lightly on the lips. "It wouldn't matter if he did, would it?" she whispered. "You're going to see a lot more of me, Cade Hunter. Now close your eyes and go to sleep."

She left him then to lie awake wondering what her remark really meant. Was there a promise implied? Or was it just wishful thinking on his part? When he finally drifted off, his dreams were filled with visions of Elizabeth and the grassy plains between Big Timber and the Crazy Mountains; Luke Tucker, and Levi Crabtree and Willow.

He awoke the next morning feeling stronger and hungry. From the kitchen section of the cabin, he could hear White Moon complaining that the spit she had tried to fashion had loosened two of the fireplace stones, causing the spit to collapse and spill water from the pot suspended from it, almost putting her fire out. Elizabeth went to help her, but discovered the stones would not stay firmly in place, so she removed them and was surprised to discover a hole in the stone hearth. Puzzled to find what appeared to be dirty canvas rags stuffed in the bottom of the hole, she then realized that what she had uncovered were leather pouches, eight in all, each one filled with gold dust. Speechless, she turned to Cade and held up one of the pouches for him to see.

It was surprising to Cade that Snider still had eight of the original pouches. "Luke's gold," he murmured softly as Elizabeth brought it to him. "So that's what's left—there were sixteen to start with."

"Maybe half of it's gone," she said with a mischievous smile, "but it still looks like enough for a man to plan his life and maybe start a family."

Uncertain as usual when around her, he replied cautiously, "I reckon, if a man could find a woman who would have him."

Elizabeth shook her head and struck a pose of exasperation. "I swear, Cade Hunter, you might be the dumbest man I've ever met."

"I reckon," he said.

"You hurry up and get yourself well," she said, taking charge as usual. "I can see you've got a lot to learn about calling on a lady."

"Yes, ma'am," he replied, happily, "but I can learn pretty fast when I set my mind to it."

Standing by the fireplace, listening to the conversation between the two young people, White Moon rolled her eyes heavenward, sighed, and shook her head.

Charles G. West

**"RARELY HAS AN AUTHOR PAINTED THE
GREAT AMERICAN WEST IN STROKES SO
BOLD, VIVID AND TRUE."
—RALPH COMPTON**

TANNER'S LAW

Tanner Bland returns home from the Civil War to
find that everyone thought him dead, and that his
younger brother married Tanner's fiancée. So Tanner
heads west to join an old army buddy, Jeb Hawkins,
and hit the gold mines of Montana.

But the wagon train they join is not what they hoped
for. Because in the train with them are the four
good-for-nothing Leach brothers—and before they
hit Montana, there'll be more than enough blood
for all...

Also Available

Range War at Whiskey Hill
Duel at Low Hawk

Available wherever books are sold or at
penguin.com